Wendy Hayden Sadler met her husband in Hong Kong, married him in a whirlwind romance eighteen days later, and stayed in the then colony long enough to raise three children. She has also written two plays for theatre, and is currently working on her third novel and a third theatre script.

BRINGER OF CLOUDS AND RAIN

Bringer of Clouds and Rain is a Chinese euphemism for 'Lady of the Night'. But why has the man she loves branded Maxine in this way? Having been betrayed by her fiancé, Jonathan, Maxine is whisked off to a holiday in Hong Kong with the mysterious Adam Warwick. Together, they discover Hong Kong . . . and each other. But Maxine becomes jealous as the secretive Adam spends time with the beautiful Eleanor. When Jonathan reappears, in an attempt to win back Maxine's affections, there follows a maelstrom of misunderstandings, culminating in the ultimate insult — Bringer of Clouds and Rain.

WENDY HAYDEN SADLER

BRINGER OF CLOUDS AND RAIN

Complete and Unabridged

ULVERSCROFT
Leicester

First published in Great Britain in 2005

First Large Print Edition
published 2006

The moral right of the author has been asserted

This book is a work of fiction. The characters and situations in this story are imaginary. No resemblance is intended between these characters and any real persons, either living or dead.

British Library CIP Data

20170608

Sadler, Wendy Hayden
Bringer of clouds and rain.—Large print ed.—
Ulverscroft large print series: romance
1. Hong Kong (China)—Fiction 2. Love stories
3. Large type books
I. Title
823.9′2 [F]

ISBN 1–84617–482–1

Published by
F. A. Thorpe (Publishing)
Anstey, Leicestershire

Set by Words & Graphics Ltd.
Anstey, Leicestershire
Printed and bound in Great Britain by
T. J. International Ltd., Padstow, Cornwall

This book is printed on acid-free paper

Dedicated to
Kenneth
my husband and editor
whom I met and married in
Hong Kong

1

From the moment Maxine entered her apartment, she knew that all was not as it should be. There were shoes carelessly abandoned in the hall and an untidy trail of discarded clothes leading to the bedroom she shared with Jonathan. The shoes, the garments, the perfume that hung in the air, all were instantly recognisable . . . but they were not hers.

Silently, Maxine crossed the hall and pushed open the door. She didn't see Annie immediately; she was under Jonathan and they were under the duvet. From the pitching of the bedclothes and the sounds of heavy breathing, it was obvious that they were not playing Scrabble.

For a moment, Maxine actually felt guilty, as if she were the one caught in a compromising situation. She almost said 'excuse me', then realised how inappropriate those words would be. After all, the man was her fiancé, the woman her best friend and they were making love in her bed.

The blood drained from her face, her legs turned to jelly and the room began to spin.

Maxine reached out a steadying hand to the doorframe. Her lips parted in denial and yet not a sound escaped them.

Slowly and as silently as the thick carpet would allow, Maxine backed out of the room and came to a standstill in the centre of the untidy and cluttered lounge. She felt sick and began to tremble. Shock, she supposed. It is not every day one discovers that two of the most important people in your life are betraying you in the most humiliating way.

The rhythmic creaking of the bedsprings grew ever more urgent turning her shock to anger and anger to rage. It boiled to the surface and with it came an almost overpowering urge to scream abuse at the traitors, to drag them apart, and from her bed. Maxine turned towards the bedroom and even took a step in that direction before she got a grip of herself. No, she would not, could not demean herself in that way.

How long has this been going on? she wanted to know, and why had she taken so long to recognise the many telltale signs for what they were? Too vividly, she recalled the muffled *sorry wrong number* telephone calls; Jonathan's suspiciously late hours at the office and the assignments that had taken him with ever more frequency away from home. She remembered too, the presents and messages of love that invariably followed those absences and supposed nights out with the boys.

Balm to a troubled conscience, she now realised. How could I have been so blind?

The lovemaking in the bedroom reached a noisy conclusion, prompting Maxine into action. Not wanting an emotional scene where she would be outnumbered two to one, she took the judicious way out and quit the apartment. Besides, there was something she wanted to do that no longer required Jonathan's approval.

★ ★ ★

Maxine focussed her thoughts on a certain long, slinky gown. It had been love at first sight and she had dearly wanted to wear it to her company's annual ball. She had checked on its availability several times, and twice gone so far as to try it on. The soft fabric of the gown had skimmed over her slender form as if it had been made especially for her. The claret red looked sensational with the golden highlights in her long blonde hair, or so the boutique assistants had enthused. But then, each time she had been tempted to pay the outrageous price, her thoughts had turned to Jonathan: always encouraging her to save towards the mortgage on their first house

3

while never actually managing to save a penny himself.

She knew that, if asked, he would say exactly what she wanted to hear. 'It looks wonderful, darling. Of course you must have the gown.' But there would be a hint of reproach in his eyes; just enough to suggest it was an extravagance they could do without.

To hell with extravagance, Maxine now raged to herself. If it's still available I'll have it, and a pair of the highest heeled, most expensive evening sandals I can find. From this moment on, I'll have whatever I want. What's more, although he doesn't yet know it, that two-timing bastard is going to pay for it all, right down to the nail varnish on my toes.

With only an hour to shop-closing time, Maxine reversed her little car into a parking lot as near to Staines town centre as she could possibly get and hurried through the late afternoon shoppers towards the more exclusive part of town. She had one other call to make, and that was on the way.

★   ★   ★

Maxine had never been into a pawnshop before and for a moment she hesitated in the grubby, down-at-heel entrance. She focussed

4

on the balding, middle-aged man behind the glass-topped counter, who, under a bright lamp, was repairing the intricate mechanisms of a gold fob watch.

Becoming aware of a potential customer, he glanced over the top of his wire-framed spectacles and smiled encouragingly. 'Can I help you?' he invited.

Quickly, Maxine slipped the engagement ring off her finger. It was the only thing of real value Jonathan had ever given her. Nostalgic memories flashed through her mind to be quickly eclipsed by more recent and thoroughly humiliating ones. Feeling no pangs of conscience over what she was about to do, Maxine stepped forward. 'I'd like to pawn this,' she said with a breathless rush, placing the ring firmly on the counter.

In no hurry, the pawnbroker picked it up and held it to the light. Slowly, he revolved it, examining closely the sapphire and diamond setting.

Nice, very nice, he told himself. He continued to take his time. Delaying tactics suggested a lack of interest, which gave him a bargaining edge. It also gave him an opportunity to sum up the customer and her expectations.

Harold Morgan had been in this business most of his adult life. He thought he was immune to the endless stream of losers who passed through his door and to their hard-luck stories. Yet there was something about this girl: a vulnerability that appealed to him. And if he was not mistaken, she'd been crying.

'Are you sure you want to part with this?' he asked, surprising himself with the question. Business was business and he was not usually so considerate. But then, he teased himself, neither was he usually a sucker for a pretty face.

'Quite sure,' Maxine confirmed, in a quiet voice that shook only a little.

He saw a tear escape and slide down her cheek and then the angry impatience as she dashed it away with the back of a hand.

Again, he hesitated. 'Want to talk it over with your fiancé first?' he asked kindly.

Her eyes focussed on his wedding band. 'Would you want to talk it over with your wife if you found her in bed with your best friend?' she asked.

Bloody hell, Morgan found himself thinking, poor kid.

Without pause, he replied, 'No, m'dear. You're better off without him.'

Ten minutes later, emotions once again tightly under control, Maxine walked out of the pawnshop minus the engagement ring.

There was a determined set to her classical features, a forced spring in her step and money in her purse. She was well aware that she had received only a fraction of the value of the ring, but was satisfied that Jonathan would be paying to the last penny for her gown, accessories and hairdressing bill.

With a bitter little smile, she patted the pocket that held the pawn ticket. If Jonathan wanted the ring back, then he would have to pay the pawnbroker himself.

★ ★ ★

By the time Maxine, loaded with purchases, returned to her apartment, Jonathan had gone out. The bed was neatly made and not a clue remained to suggest he had been *entertaining*. On the hall table, propped against the lamp, she found a note telling her not to wait up, he would be late, and that he loved her. He had surrounded her name with kisses and drawn a heart under his own.

She took an educated guess. He's probably gone clubbing with his boozy airline friends. If so, he would return in the small hours, thoroughly inebriated and very amorous. His lovemaking would be totally ineffectual.

Maxine screwed the paper into a ball and tossed it across the room where it hit the wall and fell neatly into a bin. 'Good riddance,' she muttered contemptuously.

With purpose, she moved from room to room. Everywhere, she saw evidence of Jonathan's untidiness. In the living room, near the armchair he had made his own, old newspapers and a couple of empty beer cans lay discarded on the floor. The ashtray, balanced precariously on the arm, was full almost to overflowing. The contents of the bookcase, along with its generous assortment of videos, cassettes and CDs were, as always, in total disarray. In the bathroom, towels and dirty laundry lay where Jonathan had dropped them, waiting for her attention. She knew what she would find in the kitchen even before she looked. Jonathan never cleaned up behind himself.

As her discontented gaze swept around the apartment, Maxine noticed, and not for the first time, that Jonathan's personality and poor taste had crept in to dominate every room. She was aware that the items that took pride of place were all his, brought into her apartment when giving up his own. His rugs, his pictures, his ornaments . . . her apartment had become a storage depot for his possessions while her own had, in the course of time, been pushed to the back of cupboards.

Maxine tried to remember the last time their conversation had progressed beyond the mundane to the meeting of minds and the sharing of interests and hobbies. Surely, this void had not always stretched between them?

She sighed, and in a moment of weakness allowed her mind to travel back in time to candle-lit suppers and intimate conversation, when love was new and life full of passion and promise. Up until their engagement there had been not a doubt in her mind about her future with Jonathan. And then, soon after, he had taken her North to meet his mother and two elder sisters. They had smothered him with affection and waited on him hand and foot, not allowing him to do a thing for himself. Even much of his talking had been done for him, she noticed, and Jonathan had positively revelled in the attention.

Much about Jonathan had become clear. That he never expected to lift a finger around the apartment continued to irritate Maxine, but it no longer surprised her. Such a doting background also explained his easy confidence around women and his total conviction that he could charm his way out of any situation, no matter how awkward.

Jonathan, she realised, was hardly likely to fulfil her expectations of a sharing partnership unless she did something about it. And she would do something about it, she had promised herself, because for sure, she was never going to be his doormat. Yet, somehow, she had become just that. Gradually, without noticing, she had begun to take a backseat to his more dominant, extrovert personality. She was required to be an enthusiastic spectator at his hockey matches and a willing partner at his social events, yet he showed little interest in her friends and activities. Her friends had been neglected and allowed to fade away. The nights out at theatres, cinemas and restaurants had become few and far between as had her twice-weekly visits to the gym, the impromptu visits to her friends' flats, the long girlie telephone calls and the shared confidences. She had fallen into the same mould as all those other women who had passed through Jonathan's life. She too had loved him too much . . . and it had stripped her of her individuality and her independence.

Well, not any more, she promised herself. She would turn back the clock, bring fun and laughter back into her life and she would start by ridding herself of Jonathan.

It took Maxine about an hour to throw all his belongings, together with the linen off her bed, into black bin liners. These she heaved onto the landing. Taped to the most prominent bag were the red pawn ticket and a note that said: 'Push the key under the door, you won't be needing it any more.'

★ ★ ★

There was something distinctly disturbing about the voice recorded on the house phone. Carrie tossed her jacket onto the sofa and then glanced at her watch. It was late . . . very late. Should she return Maxine's call and risk waking Jonathan, or wait until morning? She played the message over again. It sounded urgent.

Carrie dialled Maxine's number, a number she knew by heart, and waited. The telephone rang seven times then switched to record.

'Hi Maxine,' she said anxiously down the line in her distinctive cockney accent, 'if you're there . . . pick up. It's me, Carrie . . . returning your call.'

Instantly, as if Maxine's hand had been hovering over the telephone, there was a click, followed by her voice.

'Carrie. Hi.' She responded with an anxious rush. 'I'm here.'

'You're vetting your calls,' Carrie accused. 'What's up? Who're you avoiding?'

'Jonathan,' Maxine replied in a small, watery voice. 'I've kicked him out.'

There was a moment's pause before Carrie

asked, 'For good?'

'Yes for good,' Maxine replied.

Carrie heard the sniff at the other end of the line. She frowned, glanced again at the clock on the mantelpiece in her thoroughly modern, minimalist lounge. She didn't relish the idea of yet another late night. Even so, she asked with hardly a hesitation, 'Want me to come over, luv?'

'No,' replied Maxine, taking into consideration the distance between her apartment and the semi-detached Carrie shared with her current boyfriend. 'It's late Carrie and you don't live that close. I just need an agony aunt to talk to.'

Maxine had tried to put a smile in her voice, but it hadn't come off too well. She'd been curled up on the sofa for hours hugging her pain to herself, waiting for her friend to come home and answer her recorded messages. While she waited in the lonely darkness of her sitting room, she had remembered a time before Jonathan, when she could have called on any one of a dozen sympathetic confidantes. But now, her only friends were her work colleagues, and Carrie was the colleague she most wanted to talk to. Maybe tomorrow, she would confide in Janet also, but not tonight . . . her wounds were too raw.

Carrie could hear Danny upstairs, moving from bathroom to bedroom. Without her to keep him awake, he'd be unconscious before he could count from one to ten backwards.

'OK,' Carrie responded gently. With a lingering look at the stairs and an inner sigh for the physical pleasures she would be missing, Carrie folded her long legs under her and lowered her yoga-toned curves into the nearest armchair. 'I'm listening. Take your time . . .'

Maxine relived all the horrors of the day, and when she'd finished, there followed a short, stunned silence that was eventually broken by Carrie, with just one word.

'Bastards!' she said, with feeling.

★   ★   ★

Jonathan's persistent banging on the bolted door eventually brought Maxine into the hall. Since she could not yet bear to face the scene of the crime, she had not been to bed but had remained on the sofa. She hadn't slept, but then, she hadn't expected too, hadn't even tried; she was far too wound up for that. Instead, her over-active brain had conjured up every possible scenario to Jonathan's homecoming. Now that the moment had arrived, she deliberately moved slowly, and despite the jittery nerves and erratic beating of her heart, took a certain vindictive pleasure in the annoyance she knew her delaying tactics were causing.

With the chain in place, Maxine cracked open the door and was instantly greeted with an overpowering smell of cigarette smoke and alcohol. She grimaced, drew back, and for a moment was tempted to close the door on him.

As if reading her mind, Jonathan stuck a foot in the crack. Not waiting for her to speak, he asked aggressively, 'What the hell's this all about?'

He pushed at the offending door. The chain rattled violently, but held fast.

Keeping his belligerent eyes on her, he waved an arm at the half dozen black bags littering the landing. 'And what's all my stuff doing out here?' he demanded.

Maxine took a deep steadying breath, and making a huge effort to keep her voice on an even keel, replied, 'You've been evicted.'

'Evicted,' Jonathan thundered. 'What the hell are you talking about?'

Her chin went up. She forced herself to look him in the eye. 'I came home early this afternoon . . . ' She did not finish the sentence; she saw no need to.

There followed a stupefied silence while

Jonathan took in the full implications of her words. A wary look came into his grey eyes as he remembered Annie's long limbs, smooth and white . . . naked and horizontal. Just how early was early? Early enough to catch him at it with Annie? No, surely not. He would have heard her . . . wouldn't he? Probably saw Annie leaving the apartment and jumped to conclusions.

'So?' he challenged, going for bluff.

'So what do you think I saw?' she asked.

'You saw Annie on her way out,' he laughed, dismissively. 'She called to put a message under the door. Of course, I invited her in for coffee.' He congratulated himself on his fast thinking.

'Of course you did . . . and what else did you invite her in for?' Maxine asked. Though her stomach was doing cartwheels, her voice was still deceptively calm.

Jonathan continued to brazen it out. 'Not jumping to conclusions, are you, sweetheart? Working yourself up over nothing?' He didn't wait for a reply, but went on to remind, 'It's not me she came to see, you know. She's your friend, not mine.'

'A pity you didn't leave it that way,' Maxine replied with bitter sarcasm.

Jonathan didn't like the way the conversation was going. 'What are you accusing me of?' he asked, feigning hurt innocence.

'Oh, no you don't Jonathan!' Maxine snapped, her voice beginning to rise in anger. 'You can't bluff your way out of this one. I know what I saw . . . and I saw the two of you . . . in bed.'

Jonathan broke out in a cold sweat. There was a long, tense pause. He changed tack and began, 'Christ, Maxine, I'm sorry. Look, we need to talk this through . . . I can explain . . . '

The chain stayed where it was.

'I can't stay out here all night,' he whined, running a frustrated hand through his ruffled brown hair. 'And what am I supposed to do with all these bags?'

'You've got your mobile . . . call a cab. I'm sure one of your girlfriends will take you in.' she said, nastily.

'Maxine, be reasonable,' he pleaded, growing desperate. 'Do you know what time it is?'

'Of course I know what time it is. It's you who seems to have a problem with time, not me,' she accused. 'It's you who comes and goes at all hours of the night and day.'

Jonathan was getting nowhere. This was not the trusting, malleable Maxine who was usually so easy to manipulate. He began to lose patience. His wheedling grew louder, and then turned into aggressive demands.

Along the dim lit landing, doors were opening.

'Are you two going to keep this up all night?' asked a surly voice from several doors along.

'If you don't stop all this noise,' grumbled an elderly lady in a pink candlewick dressing gown and a tight cap of curlers, 'I'll call the police.'

The burly Australian who shared the flat opposite with two other equally hefty men, summed up the situation at a glance. He had seen Maxine many times and he fancied her for himself. 'She doesn't seem to want you any more, mate,' he grinned happily. 'Better bugger off, before she asks me to throw you out.' He winked conspiratorially at Maxine.

Maxine flashed him a weak smile of appreciation.

Jonathan lowered his voice and made one last appeal. 'Be reasonable, Maxine . . . take the bloody chain off the door,' he hissed.

'Go to hell!' was her parting shot as she closed the door firmly in his handsome face.

★   ★   ★

Maxine lay awake till dawn, her mind stuck on replay. It seemed she had only just fallen

17

asleep when the telephone rang. It was Jonathan.

'Hi Sweetheart . . . ' he began, as if nothing had happened.

She hung up on him and disconnected the phone.

He left messages on her mobile. She erased them and left the phone switched off.

Undeterred, Jonathan called her at the office. Not wanting to draw attention to her problems, Maxine accepted the calls. His attempts at explanation and his impassioned entreaties for forgiveness succeeded in reducing Agnes, the soft-hearted eavesdropping switchboard operator to tears. Maxine, however, managed to put on a convincing show of being totally unmoved.

What really wrung his heart, she suspected, was not the loss of the woman he claimed to love, but the loss of the free accommodation that came with her.

When Jonathan moved into her flat, it was agreed that both the lease and standing order to the landlord would remain in her name, while Jonathan's contribution would go into a high interest savings account. With her additional savings, they hoped to have the down-payment on a mortgage within a couple of years.

Last night, when clearing his things from

her apartment, Maxine had come across several bank statements, all of which clearly showed that not a penny of his sizeable salary had gone into a savings account.

The revelation had both hurt and infuriated her. But now, in the light of day, she could take a more philosophical view. Jonathan was out on the street, while she still had a roof over her head. Further more, months of penny pinching had given her a very healthy bank balance. And on that cheering note, Maxine turned again to the work on her desk.

It was a hectic morning and nearly lunchtime before Carrie's sleek Titian bob appeared around Maxine's partitioned office space. Her warm amber gaze swept over Maxine's untidy hair, the make-up applied with less than usual care and the uncoordinated clothes. This was definitely not Maxine's usual style.

'You okay?' she asked.

'I'll survive,' Maxine responded with forced bravado.

'Good . . . that's fighting talk.' She grinned, encouragingly. After a moment's hesitation, she asked about the rival she knew only by name. 'Annie been in touch by any chance?'

It crossed both their minds that Annie would by now know she'd been found out.

'No,' Maxine replied, and then added with a shrug, 'and she's not likely to get in touch, is she? What would be the point?'

'An apology?' Carrie suggested, darkly.

Annie had been Maxine's last remaining friend from the old set. They had been together at Birmingham University and had shared a flat until Jonathan came into her life. Now, thanks to Jonathan, even Annie was lost to her. Maxine's long, slender fingers fidgeted nervously with a paperweight. 'It's a bit late for apologies, don't you think?' Maxine said.

She was right, of course. Irreversible damage had been done and Annie would know that. The friendship was over, unsalvageable. Carrie let the subject drop.

Remembering several pages of photocopying still to be done, Carrie glanced at her watch and grimaced. 'Got to go,' she announced. 'Lunch is on me. Okay?' She didn't wait for an answer, but was off, sashaying across the open plan office, her high heels clicking into the distance.

Janet was the next to appear.

'Why is Carrie buying lunch?' she asked, suspiciously. 'She celebrating something I don't know about?' Despite the pure Home Counties accent, there was a hint of Caribbean in the vibrancy of voice, the colour of skin, the dark eyes with their curling lashes and the fullness of figure.

Janet then noticed the absence of Maxine's engagement ring and the sleepless eyes. 'Right,' she said after a moment's thought. 'See you later, sweetie.'

*   *   *

'The man's a rat! You're better off without him,' was Janet's instant verdict over lunch. She'd been dying to say as much for weeks . . . ever since overhearing Jonathan's chat-up line to one of her friends at a party.

She had wanted to believe she'd misheard his steamy suggestions, but Carrie had put her right the next day. Jonathan, it would seem, had tried it on with others. They had decided not to tell Maxine. Not yet anyway. Neither wanted the responsibility of shattering her elusions.

Maxine toyed with her pub lunch, and then surprised them by saying, 'I know what you're thinking. He's always been a bit of a lad . . . ' She saw the uneasy look that passed between her friends, ' . . . but whenever I complained,' she went on, 'he'd make out I was imagining things.' She pushed an olive aimlessly around the plate. '*Look but don't touch* was his favourite saying.'

'Obviously the *look but don't touch* only

applied to you,' Carrie observed.

'Typical male double standards,' chipped in Janet.

Maxine laid down her knife and fork, her food still hardly touched. 'All those flowers and chocolates,' she said, in dreamy reminiscence, 'and those sentimental notes of apology for working late . . . ' She paused. 'And the poetry . . . '

All three recalled the loving verse that appeared to have been scrawled in drunken haste on a scrap of paper.

'Crap!' had been Carrie's instant, silent verdict. Now she took pleasure in voicing her opinion aloud.

Maxine glanced up, but refrained from comment. A wry smile spread slowly across her face. Truly, the verse had been sadly lacking in talent.

'Gifts are only for special occasions, otherwise they're definitely suspect,' Carrie announced with an air of great experience.

Janet was less cynical, but being in a co-operative mood, she nodded her agreement. 'A cover-up for a guilty conscience,' she added, unnecessarily.

'Well now I know,' Maxine agreed with a weak attempt at a smile. For a moment, lost in private thought, she stared with unseeing eyes at the busy bar where some of their colleagues jostled for service. 'I had my suspicions,' she eventually murmured as if to herself.

Yes, of course she had. But there had been no proof of Jonathan's guilt . . . and how do you accuse the man you love and want to trust when there is no proof? Suspicion had brought out all the very worst traits in her character, along with a festering discontent and a mass of insecurities. Now, at last, she had her proof, and despite the shock and the pain of knowing the worst, the knowing was in some ways a blessed relief.

'I thought of ending our engagement . . . a few times, actually,' Maxine confided.

Janet looked up sharply. 'You never mentioned it,' she said. 'Well not to me, anyway.'

Her brown eyes shifted to Carrie. But Carrie was staring at Maxine and she also seemed surprised by the revelation.

'Well no, I didn't mention it to anyone,' said Maxine, sheepishly. 'It was only ever a *nearly*. I could never quite bring myself to take that final step. I kept telling myself things would improve. But they never did. I guess I needed this final push to bring me to my senses.' After a moment, Maxine continued, 'When I think of all the times I lay awake wondering where he was . . . all the times he came stumbling in at three . . . four in the morning, blind drunk . . . '

'Where had he been?' Carrie asked, intrigued.

'I don't know. He never said,' Maxine gave a bitter laugh, 'and I used to wonder if the drink brought on loss of memory.'

'Selective memory, more like,' Carrie volunteered, remembering a past flame of her own who had suffered from the same affliction.

'In the morning,' went on Maxine, 'he'd be all lovey-dovey smiles, and he'd behave as if explanations were beneath him and unnecessary.' She fell into a thoughtful silence, recalling the carefree days before Jonathan when she had been her own person. And she remembered how slowly, over the months, her confidence had ebbed away leaving her feeling dull and inadequate; good for housekeeping, cooking, the occasional lay . . . and not much else. And then she dwelt on the time she refused an evening out with Annie, and been accused of being stuck in a rut. 'You used to be game for anything,' Annie had said peevishly. 'You used to be fun.'

Was Annie already betraying her with Jonathan, even then? she wondered.

'God, I've been such a fool!' Maxine said with renewed heat. A few inquisitive faces turned in her direction. She ignored the attention, but lowered her voice. 'And to think all the time I've been faithful to him, he's been playing around behind my back . . . and with my best friend of all people.'

'Your best friend may not have been the only one he's been playing around with. Have you considered that?' Carrie asked, in her direct way. Who knows what a good-looking egocentric like Jonathan gets up to?

'The thought has crossed my mind,' Maxine grudgingly admitted. 'Last night, I asked Jonathan if there had been others, and if so, how many. He didn't reply. He just looked reproachful as if to say, 'How can you ask me such a thing?' As if he hadn't just given me very good reason for asking.'

'Actually, I think Carrie meant . . . ' Janet chipped in, reclaiming Maxine's attention.

'Yes, I know what she meant,' interrupted Maxine. Each time she thought of the health hazards he might have exposed her to, she felt sick with apprehension.

'Better get yourself checked out,' suggested Carrie, forthright and practical as ever.

★　★　★

Although Agnes would never admit to anything so base, she was, in fact, one of those who enjoy a really good scandal and the juicier, the better. She loved her job as switchboard operator at Comp-Dynamics. The switchboard was so informative. The eavesdropping added spice to her otherwise dull little life. Yet, Agnes herself didn't gossip. Anyone could tell you, where her job was concerned, she was the soul of discretion.

However, Agnes's closest friend, Dora Thompson, who worked in the typing pool, was a totally different proposition. She could be relied upon to tell her colleagues anything that came hot from the switchboard without ever disclosing her source of information.

It therefore came as no surprise to Agnes, when, at midday, the news of Maxine's broken engagement and her fiancé's outrageous indiscretions had travelled full circle of three floors of the office grapevine and come back to her ... with a few added embellishments acquired along the way.

The missing engagement ring was conspicuous by its absence and went a long way to confirming the rumour. In no time at all, bets were being taken on whether or not the break-up was permanent.

There were those among the men who thought that Jonathan's main sin was getting caught with his nib in the inkpot. Jonathan's would-be successors applauded the sin and hoped he would continue to blot his copybook. With the exception of Agnes, it was female opinion that any man capable of sleeping with his fiancée's best friend should be castrated.

'Ouch,' said one of the men. 'That's a bit stiff.'

'Not for long!' quipped Mrs Melrose, the tea lady.

*   ⋆   ⋆   ⋆

Maxine had not long returned to her desk when Jonathan chose to make his fourth telephone call of the day.

Agnes came on line. 'Your persistent lover . . . ' she said to Maxine, sighing audibly. Agnes had glimpsed Maxine's attractive fiancé only once; on one of the rare occasions he had driven up to the entrance of Comp-Dynamics to collect Maxine from work. The black Porsche, the designer clothes and the casual confidence had all combined to make a lasting impression.

'Put him through,' Maxine snapped. Her conversation with Carrie and Janet on the subject of health was still fresh in her mind so that now, she was feeling positively malevolent.

Without a qualm, she clicked the telephone loudspeaker to the 'on' position. Perching on the corner of her desk, arms folded, she listened, along with everyone else in the department, to Jonathan's amplified voice.

'Maxine . . . sweetheart?' Afraid that she would hang up on him again, he hurried on, 'I love you. Give me a chance to explain . . . please.' There was a moment's pause. The line stayed open. Reassured, his discarnate voice continued to wheedle, loud and clear. 'I know how you must feel . . . walking in on Annie and me like that . . . but . . . honestly darling, it's nothing to get all steamed up about.'

'As I remember it . . . you and Annie were the ones getting all steamed up,' corrected Maxine.

With satisfaction, Maxine watched the hustle and bustle of a busy department grind slowly to an attentive halt. Conversation petered out as, one by one, heads turned in the direction of her office space.

'You're making too much out of it, darling . . . it was nothing, honestly . . . just a moment's weakness. She doesn't mean anything to me . . . I swear it. You're the only one I've ever wanted.' He paused; Maxine did not respond. Emboldened, he went on. 'It wasn't really my fault. I mean, I didn't invite her over. She just turned up . . . said you were expecting her and then homed in on me

. . . and things somehow progressed from there. God, I was such a fool to invite her in. But how was I to know she was going to come on to me like that?'

With growing comprehension came knowing smiles, the digging of ribs, and whispered witticisms. A few came grinning to listen in the cubicle doorway.

'What kind of person goes behind her best friend's back like that?' Jonathan asked indignantly, happy to become the injured party. 'Really, Maxine. You want to choose your friends more carefully. I don't go much on the company you keep.'

'You're right. I *do* keep rotten company,' Maxine agreed. 'It's time to jettison the unworthy . . . and the hangers-on.'

Jonathan didn't like the sound of that. 'No need to go to such extremes, not before we've had time to talk this through properly . . . ' he paused, then added belligerently, 'these things are never one-sided you know.'

Someone was heard to whisper. 'This guy's full of crap.'

Maxine was silent. She was deriving a certain vengeful pleasure from hearing Jonathan bare his soul to the world.

'Maxine . . . you still there?' Jonathan asked, panicked.

'Yes. I'm still here,' she replied coolly.

'Meet me for supper,' he begged. 'Give me a chance to explain.'

'Even you can't explain your way out of this one,' she said.

'Give me a chance . . . please,' he pleaded.

Twenty pairs of eyes were riveted on Maxine. You could hear a pin drop in the silence as the department held its collective breath.

A hint of a smile played at the corners of her lips.

'No, I don't think so, Jonathan. I'm just not interested enough,' she purred. 'I'm going to find myself a real man; one who knows how to please a woman.'

'Maxine . . . ' she heard him splutter. 'You going to bring that up again? It only happened a few times . . . I told you, I was stressed. Too much going on at work.'

'Too much going on alright, but not at work!' Before he could get another word in, she added sweetly, 'You may give the crown jewels to Annie, with my blessing. She might find them satisfactory, but then, her expectations were never quite . . . ' she looked for the right words, ' . . . up to standard.'

With a click of a button, Maxine terminated the call.

The spell held intact for just a second, and

then was broken by motherly Mrs Melrose. 'Good for you sweetheart,' she called from the full length of the department.

The department exploded into enthusiastic applause.

2

Maxine leaned towards the gilded full-length mirror and applied the finishing artistic touches to her makeup. Then she took a couple of steps back, and turning this way and that, appraised with a critical eye, her reflection from top to toe.

Her long hair had been expertly swept up high to the back of her head where it was held in place by a single ornamental clasp from which golden curls cascaded to the nape of her neck. Her lipstick and nail varnish were exactly the same shade of red as the long elegant gown that fitted her to perfection. But for the narrow diamante straps, the creation was simplicity itself. With movement, side slits in the soft fabric of the skirt revealed her long shapely legs and red satin evening sandals. Exquisite diamante teardrops were at her throat and ears.

Remembering that all were by courtesy of Jonathan, a satisfied smile spread slowly across her face.

It was the evening of the Comp-Dynamics annual ball and Maxine had that afternoon booked into the luxury Georgian Castle Hotel in Windsor.

It seemed an age since she had gone unaccompanied to an important social event. She would probably be the only one without a partner, she realised, and from that point of view, Jonathan's infidelity could not have come to light at a worse possible time.

Involuntarily, her gaze went to the romantic four-poster bed she was to have shared with him and again she felt the pain of loss — but only for a moment. Tonight, she reminded herself, she would have to share neither bed, bathroom, nor wardrobe with a man who thought only of his own needs. She missed the companionship but she refused to miss the man.

Maxine glanced at the bedside clock. Preparations had gone so smoothly that she was now ready too soon. Time on her hands meant time to think. The smile faded as she found herself wondering for the hundredth time why Annie had betrayed her. Annie was envious; always wanting whatever gave others pleasure. It was as if she saw all women as competition and all men as fair game, but she had never crossed Maxine ... not that she knew about, and never given her cause for grief, until now. Surely Jonathan didn't mean anything to Annie? She had said, more than once, that she didn't like him. When had she changed her mind?

Her stomach churned. Anger and resentment were never far from the surface.

To distract her thoughts and ease her loneliness, Maxine turned on the radio and tuned into some cheerful music. A stiff drink to get her into the party mood was what she needed, Maxine told herself, turning to the mini bar.

The sudden shrill ringing of the telephone brought her to a halt. Contact with the outside world could mean company. She reached for the phone, and then hesitated. It could be Jonathan. Having included him in her original plans, he would, of course, know where to find her. Maxine didn't want to speak to him, especially not now. Given the chance, he would ruin her evening.

On instruction, no more of his calls to her desk had got past the switchboard. There still remained, however, the constant fear that she might find him waiting on her doorstep. Today, playing safe, she had returned home from work early, hurriedly packed all her requirements into an overnight case and driven up the motorway to the hotel in Windsor.

Now, as she hovered over the ringing phone, she worried that Jonathan was about to commence his pestering all over again.

Irritably, Maxine snatched up the receiver.

'Hello,' she snapped.

'Maxine?' said a cheerful cockney voice. 'It's me, Carrie.' The broad accent was music to the ears. 'If you're looking for a safe house, I'm in room 315 with Danny. Tequila Slammers in five minutes,' she announced.

★ ★ ★

It was company policy that managers and directors put in an appearance at important staff functions. Adam Warwick was neither a Manager nor a Director of Comp-Dynamics . . . as yet. He was a guest — the honoured guest of the Chief Executive, Neil Hamilton.

Adam's own IT Company founded by his late father was based in East Asia. As Chairman of Warwick International, travel, and lots of it, was very much a part of Adam's life style. In only one week, business had taken him to Singapore and Tokyo and on a gruelling round of meetings and conferences, official receptions and early morning power breakfasts. Only that afternoon he had flown in from Japan: a fourteen-hour journey door-to-door, with a time difference of nine hours. He had not slept during the flight, but had worked almost the entire journey on an important report, stopping only for meals.

From Heathrow Airport he had been

chauffeur-driven directly to the elegant Castle Hotel where he'd checked into a suite. With just enough time to spare, he showered and changed into formal eveningwear before joining Neil Hamilton and his wife at the cocktail reception. Together with the rest of Comp-Dynamics' senior management, he had soon moved into the ballroom. Severely jet-lagged as he was, it was hardly surprising that he was looking forward to a speedy end to an evening that had, as yet, scarcely begun.

From his previous visits to Comp-Dynamics, Adam knew a few of the people around the elaborately set table. None were close friends of his, nor were they likely to become so, under the circumstances, but after several long meetings in the company boardroom, a rapport had developed putting them comfortably on first name terms.

Adam toyed with the stem of his wineglass. His weary gaze went to the wad of raffle tickets, the proceeds of which were destined for worthy charities. He had only to wait until the entertainment and the draw were over, he told himself, and then he could discreetly slip away. His sympathetic host would understand. Hamilton had already suggested he might like to give the ball a miss. Although tempted, Adam had declined to do so. He knew an occasion like this would speak volumes about the company and staff morale.

Neil Hamilton was somewhere in his late sixties, Adam guessed, and ripe for retirement. But for his age, he doubted the man would have given the proposed merger of his company even a moment's thought, despite the company's current difficulties.

Adam had done his homework well. He knew Comp-Dynamics was steadily growing and had sound potential for success, and he knew about its under-funding and cash flow needs. He also knew that several rival companies, aware of its present vulnerability, were sniffing around with a view to a hostile take-over.

With an infusion of capital and new ideas, Adam had no doubt that the company could be made to prosper. Besides, he wanted Comp-Dynamics. It was a producer and supplier of an innovative new component required by, and vital to, one of Adam's other companies. It was this same component that made it so attractive to his rivals.

After weeks of negotiating, a fair deal had been struck. Now it was up to company solicitors to tie-up loose ends. With luck, he told himself, all should be signed and sealed by the end of the month.

Whilst the attention of Neil Hamilton was temporarily distracted by his wife, Adam let his gaze roam at will around the elegant room with its high-vaulted ceiling and crystal chandeliers. At a guess, there were approximately three hundred people present, dressed to impress and bent on having a thoroughly good time. One day, if all went according to plan, he would be able to put names and personalities to some of these animated faces and would learn their value to Comp-Dynamics and therefore, ultimately, to Warwick International. For now, he could only go on first impressions, and they were good.

He became aware that he in turn was attracting covert attention from several quarters. But then, that was hardly surprising. He was, after all, an unknown seated with the company's hierarchy. The curious would be wondering who he was and where he fitted into the scheme of things.

He was about to return his attention to the chatter of the middle-aged and rather over-flowing woman on his left, when suddenly a splash of red caught his eye. The girl in the slinky red gown had skin the colour of honey and an abundance of golden hair. She was one of a trio and among the last to find their way from the cocktail reception to the ballroom. He surreptitiously watched her search for familiar faces as she and her friends slowly meandered through the crowd towards their allocated table.

★ ★ ★

Tequila on an empty stomach and a glass of wine in the reception room were a heady boost to Maxine's confidence, as was her awareness of the interest from several quarters that marked her progress across the room. The engagement ring had been a successful deterrent to unwanted attention. But the engagement ring was now in a dingy back-street shop and attention was no longer unwanted.

A quick glance at the place cards was enough to inform Maxine that no irresistible talent had found its way onto her table. Silently, she cursed the staff in Human Resources responsible for the seating plan, and at the same time thanked God for the company of Carrie and Danny.

'Hmmm. This is going to be fun,' she whispered, drolly, to Carrie.

Carrie's focus shifted from the place cards across to Janet's table. 'No wonder she's got a silly grin on her face . . . ' she lowered her voice so that Danny couldn't hear, ' . . . she's sat with the best-looking blokes in the room, the lucky cow.' Her eyes narrowed

— Janet was in Human Resources. 'I bet she had something to do with the table plan,' she said, suspiciously.

Just then, Janet glanced across at them, combed her fingers up through her dark uncontrollable curls, fluttered her curly eyelashes and gave her sweetest smile.

'Of course she did,' Maxine grinned. 'It's her idea of a very good joke.'

'I hope she still sees the funny side of her *very good joke* when we muscle in on her territory after dinner,' Carrie said, flashing her sweetest smile back.

Several lavish courses came and went; wine was plentiful. With the serving of liqueurs, the bright lights were dimmed. On cue, the band upped its volume, inviting a mass migration to the dance floor. Those who preferred to circulate soon occupied their vacated chairs and it was not long before Janet sauntered over with a couple of desirables in tow.

Maxine by now was the life and soul of the party and well on the way to being in love with everyone. Gone was her earlier fear of being an unwanted wallflower. Slipping back into her old carefree ways was not going to be so difficult after all, she happily concluded.

★　★　★

In all her life Maxine had never won so much as a tube of Smarties. Even so, she watched with eager anticipation every raffle ticket taken out of the drum, listened with mounting excitement for every number announced and gave just as much raucous encouragement to the lucky winners as everyone else did.

By the time they arrived at the mystery star prize the atmosphere was positively electric with excitement.

'Red, 888,' boomed the Master of Ceremonies over the microphone. There was a loud roll of drums from the band. It seemed that the whole room held its breath.

Although the winning ticket lay bold as brass in front of Maxine, she was convinced there had been a mistake. She drew in a deep, steadying breath. 'Oh my God,' she muttered.

Janet was by now very tipsy and seeing double. She leaned across to look at Maxine's tickets, her voluptuous breasts almost spilling out of her low cut gown. 'Can't be any of yours,' she giggled. 'They've all got six digits.'

'Red, 888,' boomed the voice again. 'Anyone . . . ?'

Carrie leaned across and blinked her eyes into focus. 'Bloooody 'ell, Maxine,' she shrieked, 'You've got the winning number.'

With that, she and Janet unceremoniously

heaved their friend out of her chair and shoved her in the general direction of the dais.

Almost immediately, the spotlight picked Maxine out from the gloom: a splash of brilliant colour against a backdrop of white table clothes and predominantly dark eveningwear. The band quickly struck up with *Lady in Red*.

To loud applause, trying to give the appearance of being perfectly steady on her feet, Maxine floated between the tables.

High-spirited friends called out encouragement as they pushed her forward towards the waiting Master of Ceremonies: a professional who Maxine did not know.

Still not fully trusting to luck and with an uncertain smile, she raised the ticket for his inspection. Only when he answered her with a broad smile of his own, asked for her name and invited her up onto the dais, did she fully accept there had been no mistake. She, Maxine Lowry, was the winner of the mystery star prize.

He manoeuvred her to face the audience and the full glare of the spotlight. Then raising the microphone to his lips, to another dramatic roll of drums, he said for all to hear, 'Congratulations Maxine Lowry. You have won tonight's mystery star prize! One weeks holiday for two in . . . '

He paused for affect. The audience held their breath.

With wry humour the word *Blackpool* popped into Maxine's head.

' . . . Hong Kong,' he announced, loud and clear. 'With flights, hotel and all expenses paid.'

An instant rowdy response came from all four corners of the ballroom. But, for Maxine, it took a moment for the message to penetrate. Then, her hand flew to her mouth while her stomach did several cartwheels.

'Hong Kong!' she gasped. 'Oh my God . . . Hong Kong!' She had never been outside Europe, and now, if this man was to be believed, she was about to embark on a journey to the other side of the world.

Only recently, involvement in an unfinished project had prevented her from accompanying Jonathan and his colleagues on a weeklong travel industry familiarisation trip to Hong Kong. She had not particularly wanted to be a camp follower to Jonathan and his colleagues, but Hong Kong of all places . . . Jonathan had returned with glowing reports and little sympathy for her disappointment.

The Master of Ceremonies was holding out the much-coveted prize, which came in the shape of twin envelopes. A photographer was poised to capture the momentous occasion for the company's monthly staff magazine.

Maxine's manicured fingertips moved towards the offerings. Then they paused. He had said a holiday for two. Warily, she eyed the envelopes.

But for the effects of a few too many, she might have had her wits about her and simply accepted the prize. Instead, for a moment, she allowed resentment to get the upper hand, and with that resentment came the thought, I'll be damned if I'm going to take that rat Jonathan on holiday with me!

With agile fingers, she extricated a single envelope. Then, with uncharacteristic impetuosity and only a hint of a slur, she said to the Master of Ceremonies, 'I'll take this one . . . you can re-raffle the other.'

As she later told a disappointed Carrie, Jonathan had occupied centre stage in her life for so long that it did not, at that moment, occur to her that she didn't have to take him . . . that she could, in fact, take anyone she chose to take.

'Are you sure?' beamed the MC. Not waiting for an answer, he turned to the sea of eager upturned faces. 'Did you hear that ladies and gentlemen? Maxine has generously offered to re-raffle one of the tickets.'

'Maxine, don't do it . . . ' called out an intoxicated channel account manager she knew as Andy. Putting his hands together in mock supplication, he inveigled, 'Take me . . . I'm ready, willing . . . and very able.'

'Not so able,' said the pert, attractive girl at his side in an audible whisper.

There was raucous laughter from those near enough to hear.

'You'd have a better time with me,' offered another hopeful, pulling an affronted Andy back into his seat.

Maxine giggled; her blue eyes sparkled with good-natured humour.

From the other corner of the dais another inebriate called, 'I'm all yours darling — you won't regret it.' He stood up and gave a pelvic thrust while his friends egged him on.

'He's all talk . . . ' warned his girlfriend. 'Believe me . . . I should know.'

Another round of laughter swept the room. Maxine was clearly revelling in the unaccustomed attention.

'Too late gentlemen,' the MC cut in. On a dramatic note, he announced, 'Maxine has decided to go on a *blind date*. A show of appreciation for Maxine, please.'

The smile left Maxine's face. In all her life, she had only ever gone on one blind date. She'd been set up with a human picture gallery of tattoos and the evening had been a disaster from beginning to end. 'I'm not going on a blind date!' she objected in a panic. 'I never said . . .'

But her objections were drowned out by hoots of approval and enthusiastic clapping.

* * *

The amused smile was wiped clean off Adam Warwick's handsome face. If he had realised he held a winning ticket for a holiday in Hong Kong, he would have left before the end of the draw and taken the ticket with him. But for his neighbour, he might even have done the next best thing: turned it facedown on the table and ignored its existence. However, before he could act, the woman had pinned it to the table cloth with one of her long, fuchsia-pink talons. 'Adam, that's it, isn't it? That's the number,' she boomed excitedly.

From her other side, someone leaned in for a closer look. 'She's right,' he confirmed in a loud, jovial voice. 'Looks like you're going on a blind date with the lovely Maxine from Sales,' he grinned.

'Lucky dog,' a man at a nearby table was heard to mutter, enviously.

Adam did not feel like a *lucky dog*. Hong Kong was no novelty for him, he lived there.

Besides, he of all people could hardly go on holiday with a member of Neil Hamilton's staff, as those in the know were aware.

He recognised the lucky winner of course as the woman who had earlier caught his eye and had these past few minutes held his full attention. He knew a lot of beautiful women, not all of them interesting, but this one had the power to draw him like a moth to a candle.

Yes, he was tempted . . . what man wouldn't be. His thoughts turned fleetingly to his full work schedule and he questioned the amount of work outstanding and how long it would take him to tie up loose ends. A sense of disappointment followed when he thought of his crammed appointment book. Even if the holiday could be pushed back a month, he'd still have to re-schedule a vast number of appointments and work night and day in order to fulfil all his commitments. And, even if he could find the time, he warned himself, it would be unethical to get involved with a woman who would soon be one of his own employees.

Hamilton, he saw, was regarding him with interest. He seemed mildly amused, but made no comment. He was either wishing himself in Adam's shoes or washing his hands of company policy that would soon cease to concern him.

To loud applause and lots of good-natured encouragement, Adam came reluctantly to his feet and began to thread his way towards the dais. He would, of course, do the right thing: decline the prize and suggest it be drawn again. However, before he reached the dais, Adam underwent a change of mind. It was not her obvious physical appeal that over-turned his decision. Rather, it was the anxiety he saw in the sapphire blue eyes that picked him out of the crowd and locked with his own, and that glimpse of vulnerability there just before the hesitant smile.

To many, the girl had become the coveted prize and Hong Kong merely a bonus. To turn down such a prize could be construed as rejection and he felt he could not do that to her . . . not in front of so many.

He made a snap decision. For now, he would accept what was on offer, and later, when they were alone, he would return the ticket she had so foolishly donated for another draw. Unfortunately, he would not be able to explain his reason for doing so. The merger was a well-kept secret and must remain so until legally finalised. He'd just tell her he was too busy to take the necessary time off and advise her to take a friend.

If she was after romantic involvement,

there was no doubt she could have her pick of just about any available man in the room — any man but this one.

★ ★ ★

Straining to see beyond the glare of the lights, Maxine made out the moving silhouette of a tall, athletically built man. Then, the spotlight found him and brought him into sharp focus, revealing dark penetrating eyes, hair almost black, and strong handsome features.

Regretting her impetuous relinquishment of the second ticket, Maxine had been praying the winner would be a woman. Instead, coming towards her was a living copy of an Armani advertisement.

Her heart missed a beat; her stomach did a funny little flip. Anxieties of a moment before miraculously melted away. The gods were smiling on her at last. She thought of all the envious teasing and the inevitable speculation ahead of her, and she smiled.

Her candid gaze followed his progress to the foot of the dais. There was, she noticed, something coolly appraising about the way those dark eyes moved over her. Somehow, she sensed rather than saw his reluctance to accept the envelope from the master of ceremonies, and for an anxious moment thought he was actually going to turn it down. Her smile dissolved and she felt herself bristle under the imagined slight.

And then their eyes met, and as if coming to a decision, he exchanged the winning raffle ticket for the prize and introduced himself as Adam Warwick.

Maxine turned the name over in her mind but could not recall having heard it before. As for the man himself, she was quite sure that if they had ever met, she would have remembered the occasion in detail, along with the time and place of their meeting. Adam Warwick was a man not easily forgotten.

She watched him move with easy confidence to stand beside her on the dais. She felt her flesh tingle to the touch of his dinner jacket as the fine black wool brushed against her arm, and to the scent of his expensive after-shave. So aware of him was she, that his presence inhibited her to the point of shyness.

There followed more congratulations and shaking of hands until finally, after the lucky couple had been photographed together with their prizes, they were allowed to leave the platform.

'Come back after the holiday,' was the MC's parting shot in a fair imitation of a Cilla Black accent, 'and tell us how you got on Chuck!' Then, he added with an even broader grin, 'And tell me if I need to buy a new hat.'

The audience responded with laughter, and another round of applause followed.

Maxine had no intention of rebounding from Jonathan into a new emotional entanglement, but a little light romance, could surely do no harm . . . would be good for her in fact.

She wondered what this man at her side was thinking . . . more specifically, what he was thinking of her? Not a lot, she decided. For, although he smiled, he did not seem overjoyed at the prospect of a week with her in Hong Kong. She wondered if she could do anything to change his mind. A whole week in each other's company would not be much fun if he was with her under sufferance.

Preceding her off the dais, Adam Warwick turned to help her down the steps. The drink that had made Maxine bold still retained some of its potent effect. Taking the outstretched hand, she deliberately held it just a fraction too long. He did not respond with the enraptured enthusiasm she hoped for. Instead, taking her lightly by the arm, he led her out of the spotlight to a quieter part of the room.

Undeterred, she smiled provocatively up into his dark eyes and with the hotel cocktail bar in mind, suggested, 'Why don't we go somewhere quiet and celebrate our good luck with a bottle of champagne and then we can get to know each other better.' Realising how brazen that must sound, she gave an embarrassed giggle. God, whatever had prompted her to say such a thing?

Her thoughts had indeed progressed from cocktail bar to bedroom but it was, after all, only a thought and not one she was likely to put into action. He was not to know what had crossed her mind so why then was he regarding her with that quizzical smile?

'I mean . . . ' she tried to amend.

'I'm afraid not,' he cut in, gently. 'Any other night, I might be tempted by the offer, but tonight . . . ' he continued, 'I plan to catch up on sleep.' A feeble excuse for putting a stop to what could become an awkward situation, he told himself, but for now, it will have to do. Later, when the merger is no longer a secret, she'll understand.

Maxine blushed. He had misconstrued her meaning and in the most embarrassing way. Not only that, but he had said he needed to catch up on sleep. The night was still young, and that he preferred sleep to an evening with her sounded like a deliberate put-down.

Adam saw the radiance go out of her smile. Silently, he cursed himself for not choosing his words with more care. For a moment he considered explaining the long flight and the resultant jetlag. But then again he decided against explanations that would invite the kind of questions he was not yet free to answer.

Instead, with reluctance, he offered her the envelope and said, 'You might like this back . . . so that you can take a friend.' In an attempt to soften what he knew sounded very much like a rejection, he added, 'I'd like to go with you to Hong Kong, but right now I just don't have the time. I have commitments I can't turn my back on.'

Having already inspected the long artistic fingers and noted the absence of a wedding band, Maxine had been happy to assume him single. Now she wondered what kind of *commitments* he alluded to; a girlfriend, a fiancée? Not having the time was, without a doubt, a very lame excuse. In her experience one could always find the time to do the things one wanted to do . . . if one wanted to do them badly enough. Obviously, she and Hong Kong didn't interest him. After such a blatant put-down, Maxine could not, would not admit, even to herself, to feelings of disappointment.

Well, now I know exactly where I stand, she told herself, feeling thoroughly deflated and very foolish.

She looked haughtily at the envelope he offered, but made no move to take it from him. Instead, in acid tones, she pointed out, 'If I had wanted to take a friend, you would not now be holding that envelope.' Becoming vaguely aware of curious onlookers, she lowered her voice almost to a whisper and smiling sweetly for the sake of appearances, told him, 'I don't approve of blind dates. And despite what that fool said,' she looked meaningfully back towards the dais, 'I've no intentions of going on a blind date with you, nor with anybody else, not now, not ever.' She paused for affect, then added, 'You've won a solo holiday . . . if you can find the time and can stay awake long enough to enjoy it.' In case there remained any doubt in his mind about her meaning, she emphasised, 'I don't come with the ticket, I don't want it back and I don't care what you do with it.'

Her forthright words seemed to take him by surprise. She saw the slight rise of dark brows, the faint smile that came to hover on a well-shaped mouth and the look in his eyes that seemed to say, 'Now is that so?'

3

Eleanor stared down at the notepad on the carved rosewood table. There was a turbulent expression on her flawless Eurasian features. With an irritable flick of the head, she tossed her shiny black mane off her shoulders and shifted the cordless phone back into her right hand.

'But why must you stay at the Mandarin, Adam? Why can't you come here like you usually do?' She asked petulantly in beautiful English that held only a trace of an accent. 'Staying in a hotel doesn't make sense.' The dark almond-shaped eyes turned to focus on the spacious drawing room, a room that clearly spoke of wealth and good taste. Here were oriental treasures collected over a lifetime — a lifetime that went back far beyond Eleanor's twenty-three years.

'Don't you see enough of me?' teased the resonant, much-loved voice on the other end of the phone. 'I've only been away a week.'

'I never see enough of you,' she replied. 'And I hate your job for taking you away so much. You always have to go somewhere,' she complained. 'And why do you have to go so often to England?'

He did not reply. He had answered that question many times before.

'I'll be in Hong Kong for two whole weeks before I have to make another trip, and as always, I'll spend as much time with you as possible, I promise.' His voice was gently reassuring. He was well aware of Eleanor's insecurities. 'Now, sweetheart, don't forget to pass my flight details on to Ah Fong,' he reminded, patiently.

She glanced again at the note she had hastily scribbled for the chauffeur.

'Are you sure you don't want me to collect you from the airport?'

'Not likely! I've had experience of your driving . . . remember?' he chuckled.

She remembered. She had been showing-off her skill behind the wheel of her new sports car, and had taken the narrow, twisting road to Deepwater Bay too fast for safety. His experienced hand on the steering wheel had saved them from certain disaster.

'In that case, I'll come with Ah Fong in the limo,' she replied with cheerful resignation.

★　★　★

The vast international departure hall at Heathrow airport positively hummed with noise and activity. Everyone was going somewhere and the holiday spirit seemed to crackle in the air like live electricity. Pulling her heavy case through the milling crowd, Maxine followed the signs for the British Airways check-in counter where she joined the shortest queue.

While she waited, Maxine searched for the tall, athletic build, the dark hair and attractive features that had occupied much of her thoughts since the night of the ball. Adam Warwick did not appear to be in any of the queues, nor did he arrive by the time her passport and ticket had been processed and returned by the counter staff.

'Can you tell me if a Mr Adam Warwick has checked in yet?' she asked as she watched her case go from weigh-in to conveyer belt, and on out of sight.

'Adam Warwick,' the woman repeated, 'let me see.' She turned back to her computer and scrolled through the passenger manifest. 'He doesn't seem to be on the passenger list . . . ' She paused, and then corrected, 'Oh yes, here he is. He cancelled.' She glanced up as if to inquire if there was anything further.

Maxine thanked her and, gathering up her belongings, moved away from the desk.

Irritably, she wondered why she should be feeling so let down. If the man chose not to use his ticket, that was his loss, not hers. Why should she care?

⋆ ⋆ ⋆

The pawn ticket, money and ring changed hands.

After no more than a cursory glance at the ring, Jonathan moodily dropped it into his jacket pocket and turned to go.

'Your receipt . . . ' the pawnbroker called after him.

Impatiently, Jonathan turned back to the counter.

'An absolute bloody beauty, if you don't mind my saying so,' rhapsodised Harold Morgan. 'A gem among gems,' he baited his customer. He was remembering the girl with the large tear-bright eyes and the heart-rending story of betrayal.

'Pleased to know you noticed,' growled Jonathan sarcastically, thinking the man was referring to the ring. 'It's valuable . . . worth a hell of a lot more than you paid my fiancée. Daylight fucking robbery!' he accused nastily.

'Wasn't referring to the ring,' the broker corrected, unruffled by the surly tone and bad language. 'I was referring to your fiancée . . . ' He gave a knowing smile. '*Ex* fiancée,' he corrected, taking pleasure in emphasising his customer's loss. 'A ray of golden sunshine, she was when she came in here. Full of the joys of spring. Looked ready to take the world by storm,' he lied, mixing his metaphors. 'A beautiful girl like that . . . no knowing what she might get up to now she's on the loose.' Harold was enjoying himself . . . it had been a boring day . . . until now.

Jonathan snatched the receipt, and looking like thunder, slammed out of the shop and into the early autumn drizzle. He was in a foul mood. No one had ever ended a relationship with him before.

'We'll see about that!' he muttered through clenched teeth.

For days Maxine had refused to take his calls. Finally, returning from a marketing meeting in Brussels, he had tried her work number again. Some dozy switchboard operator had volunteered information that Maxine had won a couple of tickets and flown off to Hong Kong with some guy called Adam Warwick. No, the woman knew nothing about the man . . . and neither, it would seem, did Maxine. The information had cost him a drink in the Cock and Pheasant, but only one. The mousy looking woman had bored him to tears with her lovelorn sighs.

His eyes narrowed. What did his fiancée

think she was doing going off with someone other than himself? And to Hong Kong of all places . . . the destination she had suggested for their honeymoon. Although he had carefully avoided committing himself to a date, marriage was, nevertheless, out there on the distant horizon. Of all his girlfriends, she was the only one he had ever considered marrying.

God! What bloody awful timing . . . her walking in on him and Annie like that? It was not as if the girl meant anything to him — just an ego boost, nothing more . . . and Maxine had blown it out of all proportion. Given a chance, he could have got her to see reason. But no, she had to go off leaving their differences unresolved. It would be two weeks before he could patch things up between them — two weeks before he could move back into the apartment . . . *her* apartment.

Yes, it was hers, and had been long before he came on the scene. The tenancy agreement, even when renewed, had stayed in her name, and although they shared all other bills, she had, without complaint, continued to pay the rent. This had suited him at the time . . . but now, he had regrets. He should have had the tenancy agreement made over to his name and then she would not have been able to throw him out. Nor, with her precious belongings still in the flat, would she have run off with another man.

His thoughts came back to the woman for whom he had risked everything. Annie had not been worth it. He knew that now. He should not have played around so close to home.

The cause of his present dilemma had called him at work. Accommodation was his for the asking and a lot more beside, Annie had offered with not a hint of remorse over the loss of her best friend. He had not been remotely tempted by the offer. If he wanted Maxine back, now was not a good time to take chances, and especially not with Annie.

Pretending regret, for Jonathan did not believe in burning his bridges, he had declined Annie's invitation. Instead, he had temporarily moved in with a couple of drinking buddies who could only offer him a sofa bed . . . and for that they expected him to pay rent.

He put his hand in his pocket and felt the hard, cold metal against his fingertips. Pawning his ring was going too far. It had the smack of finality about it. Well, he'd see about that. She was not going to make a fool out of him. No woman dumped Jonathan West and got away with it and certainly not the woman he loved and intended to marry.

4

Without difficulty, Maxine found her way through the official channels of Chek Lap Kok Airport and rescued her case from the carousel.

Now, confronted by the gleaming interior of a vast, ultramodern airport, she hesitated and wondered how best to proceed. Moving with the flow of arriving passengers, she searched for directions that would mean something to her.

With her ticket, there had been no mention of being met. Maxine therefore assumed she would have to find her own way onto Hong Kong Island. She had memorised the name and address of her hotel and was debating whether to take a taxi, the rail link or the airport bus, when suddenly she was surprised to see her name in bold letters. Holding a card in front of him was a young Chinese man in uniform.

Seeing that her eyes were drawn to the name, the man called out in a discordant Cantonese accent, 'Miss Lowry?'

'Yes,' she acknowledged. 'I'm Maxine Lowry.'

He glanced at the passport still in her hand. Satisfied that he had the right person, he informed her, 'Hotel limousine waiting.' With a flash of white teeth meant to reassure, he promptly took the case from her hand, and leading the way, headed off through the crowd.

Exhausted after a long cramped journey, disorientated by her surroundings, Maxine was only too happy to follow without question someone who appeared to have her welfare at heart.

The next half-hour passed in a blur of lush green hills and modern highways, then a long bridge, a jungle of high-rise buildings and an epic journey through a long tunnel under Hong Kong harbour.

Within minutes of leaving the tunnel, the limousine came to a sedate halt outside an impressive hotel.

Leaning forward in her seat to glance through the huge plate-glass doors, Maxine got a jumbled impression of gold carvings, bright chandeliers, expanses of black marble, tall ferns and even taller pillars. The hotel looked expensive, she decided, and way beyond her expectations.

A doorman, resplendent in red uniform edged with gold braid, momentarily blocked her view as he stepped forward to open the limousine door.

Waiting to greet Maxine was an immaculately groomed receptionist.

Maxine's palms moved down her wrinkled skirt in a self-conscious attempt to smooth away the ravages of travel.

The girl politely appeared not to notice her crumpled state. 'Good evening Miss Lowry,' she said in near perfect English. 'Welcome to the Mandarin Oriental Hotel.'

With a shock, Maxine came down to earth. There had been a mistake. The Mandarin Oriental was definitely not the name of the hotels she had committed to memory.

Her awed gaze assessed the wealthy, glossy guests who passed so confidently through the swinging glass doors and her thoughts turned towards the inadequate contents of her luggage. 'I don't think I have a reservation here . . . ' she said in a small, doubtful voice.

The receptionist smiled. 'I hope you don't mind, but there was a last minute change of plan. You're now booked in with us.' She paused, and then reassured, 'I'm sure you'll be very comfortable here.'

That must be the understatement of the year, thought Maxine, glancing at all the beckoning splendour. There were questions to be asked, she told herself as she watched her suitcase disappear with the porter, but now was not the time. She was too tired to think straight.

'If you'll follow me,' said the receptionist,

'I'll take you up to the Executive Lounge where you can register in comfort. Then I'll show you to your suite.'

The words *Executive* and *suite* were not lost on Maxine. This holiday was turning out to be full of surprises and each one better than the last.

As she crossed the marble foyer, into her mind's eye came the faces of Jonathan West and Adam Warwick, the two men who might have had a share in her good fortune. Eat your hearts out boys, she gloated silently.

*   *   *

Alone in the suite at last, Maxine kicked off her shoes, and enjoying the feel of thick pile beneath her feet, crossed the lounge to explore the perfectly designed kitchenette.

Locating the well-stocked bar, she helped herself to a Pepsi and ice and then padded back across the lounge to the large picture window that overlooked a vast harbour teeming with late afternoon maritime activity. The view was dizzying, ever-changing, and for a while, she watched a whole variety of craft, from small sampan to large double-decker passenger ferry, criss-cross the busy divide that stretched long and wide between island and mainland. A grey frigate passed, moving with slow caution towards the open sea. Beyond the harbour was Kowloon with its waterfront luxury hotels, modern Cultural Arts Centre — looking for all the world like an outsized ski slope — and a huge domed planetarium. Incongruously set against this modern backdrop, like a latter-day obelisk, was an old Victorian clock tower, a reminder of Hong Kong's recent colonial past.

Her interest shifted slightly to the left, to the sprawling, densely populated area that was a shopper's paradise. Reclining in the far distance, was the rugged mountain range of the Nine Dragons, and beyond, out of sight, stretching endlessly in all directions, was the rest of China.

Dragging herself away from the spectacular view, Maxine turned inward, towards the lounge with its exotic blend of colours and discreet combination of Western and Oriental designer elegance.

She set her glass down on a nearby table and sank into the pampering comfort of a plump, feather-cushioned armchair. Her long fingers lovingly stroked the rich brocade upholstery. Her eyes shone. Slowly, a complacent glow of pleasure spread across her face.

'I've arrived,' she was thinking.

For a moment she was content to luxuriate,

but curiosity soon got the upper hand and took her across the room to push open a heavy, panelled door. Beyond was a spacious and equally enchanting bedroom. Slowly, she advanced to its centre, and there, turning on the spot, she examined in detail every square inch of the interior: the solid, highly-polished furniture, the embossed carpet and colourful silks, the large hand-painted porcelains and the exotic watercolour paintings.

A huge smile spread contentedly across her face. 'And all this is to be mine for one whole glorious week!' she purred to herself. Crossing to the bedside table, she located and clicked on the radio. Pulsating music filled the air . . . and filled her with an overpowering urge to release the emotions that had for days been building up within. Catching at the rhythm, Maxine began an uninhibited dance of joy around the room, admiring and touching as she went.

'Simply the best . . . ' She sang joyously along with the voice of Tina Turner. Behaving like an over-grown child, aware of it and not caring, she jumped onto the king-sized bed and using it like a trampoline, bounced across the piped and quilted counterpane and off the other side. 'Better than all the rest . . . ' she continued, her singing growing louder and her dancing more abandoned by the second.

So absorbed was she in her emotional out-pouring, that she did not hear the en-suite bathroom door open, nor was she immediately aware of the man who had entered the room. Coming up against fine dark curls on a bare chest, her dance came to an abrupt and wobbly end.

Strong hands came up to steady her.

At this point it seemed as if her world decelerated into slow motion. She was aware of a towel around slim hips and the mingling sensual smell of soap and after-shave. Her gaze travelled up a lean, muscular torso and came to rest on a familiar face beneath wet tousled hair. With a shock, she recognised Adam Warwick.

'You!' she accused, jerking out of his grip.

Inwardly she groaned with embarrassment, for she was aware she had made a ridiculous spectacle of herself. From the amusement in his eyes, he obviously thought so too. Colour suffused her cheeks.

'Where did you come from?' she demanded, ungraciously.

'The bathroom,' he drawled, as if to say, silly question.

'I mean, what are you doing here?' she flustered, trying to make sense out of his sudden materialisation.

'I've been taking a shower . . . '

'I mean . . . ' she cut in.

' . . . and now I'm about to change.' With mock humour and a slight bow, he added, 'If that's alright with you?'

'B-but it's not alright with me,' she stammered. 'You can't do that.'

His eyebrows went up. He grinned. 'You mean you like me just as I am?'

'No. I mean . . . '

'In that case . . . ' he assumed an air of disappointment, ' . . . I'd better get dressed.' He moved with intent towards the wardrobe.

Maxine focussed on the neatly stowed clothes. Her eyes narrowed. 'What are your things doing in my wardrobe?' she asked.

'*My* wardrobe,' he corrected.

Maxine gasped at his audacity. 'That's *my* wardrobe and this is *my* room,' she said in a no-nonsense tone of voice, 'and I'm not sharing either with you.' Her gaze travelled to the large, inviting bed. To cover up the direction her thoughts had taken, she added, quickly 'And I'm not sharing that with you either.' She glared up at him, wondering why she had said anything quite so gauche, wishing she hadn't and now trying hard to keep her eyes from roaming over his thoroughly attractive chest.

'That's fine by me,' he shrugged. 'I'm quite

69

choosy about who I share my bed with.' With a sardonic grin, he added, 'Close the door on your way out.'

Maxine folded her arms and stood her ground. 'I'm not going anywhere,' she insisted now fully on her dignity.

'Make up your mind! A moment ago you didn't want to share a room with me,' he reminded her.

'And I still don't,' she stubbornly insisted. 'Reception gave this suite to me and I'm not budging.'

'And to me too, it would seem,' he replied. 'And since I got here first, I get first choice of bedroom, and I choose this one. You'll just have to be satisfied with the one opposite.' He indicated through the open door to another room on the other side of the lounge.

There was a stunned silence. 'You mean there's another bedroom?' Maxine asked, and then crossly added: 'Why didn't you say so?'

'You didn't ask,' he pointed out.

By now his shirt was on and fastened. Without hesitation, he reached into a drawer for a pair of boxer shorts. Maxine watched his large, supple hands move to the towel and suddenly realised he was not going to wait for her to leave. Turning her back on him, with more haste than grace, she slammed out of the room.

Maxine felt humbled and very foolish. There was no doubt that the better of the two bedrooms had been left to her. It was larger and more feminine, and it commanded a double-aspect view. From here, she could see not only the harbour and the mainland, but also a very large section of Hong Kong Island.

She had not expected to see so many skyscrapers, nor the acres of glass windows that glistened gold and pewter in the late afternoon sun. They mushroomed out of the older, smaller buildings like colossal mega-liths, tall and proud, each appearing to have been designed to outdo its neighbour in both height and architectural interest. Immediately below her window, many floors down, there was a park with palmed and shrub-lined walkways and on the other side of this park, the majestic buildings that were a reminder of Hong Kong's early colonial history.

She turned her back on the panoramic view and gazed thoughtfully at the connecting door to the lounge. If she had not been so angry with Adam Warwick for helping her to jump to the wrong conclusion, she might by now have shown some appreciation towards his generous gesture. Instead, the closed door and her hurt pride stood firmly between them.

She had long since unpacked her case and taken an invigorating shower. Pulling the hotel fleecy-white, towelling robe closer around her slender frame, she went to lie on top of the bed in the semi-darkness.

At dusk the city lit up like a Christmas tree: vibrant, colourful, inviting. From where she lay, Maxine could see a warm glow in the sky, and on her ceiling, the pastel reflections cast up from the city's bright lights.

Maxine had a lot on her mind, important questions she dearly wanted to put to Adam Warwick. Had he arranged her limousine transfer from the airport and been responsible for the change in hotel venue? Was he also responsible for the upgrade to this splendid suite of rooms? If so, by whose authority had he made these changes? More to the point, who was going to pick up all the extra charges that would undoubtedly appear on their bill? Why had he decided that he would, after all, fly half-way round the world to be with her when he had said quite clearly that a holiday in Hong Kong was not on his itinerary? Most importantly of all, who was this Adam Warwick and where did he fit into the equation?

Soft music carried through from the lounge

along with a variety of sounds that suggested Adam was working at the desk and at a computer.

Twice she heard the door of the mini bar open and close, followed by sounds of ice clinking against glass. She too would have liked a drink, but after making such an idiot of herself . . . albeit, with his help, she was still too embarrassed to face him.

The ringing of the telephone interrupted her thoughts. Already growing tired of her own company and pleased of a diversion, she rolled across the wide bed and reached for the handset.

'Hello,' she welcomed.

There was silence on the other end of the line.

An extension phone clicked. 'Hello. This is Adam Warwick. Can I help you?' intoned the deep, confident voice.

'Adam . . . I thought for a moment I had the wrong room,' answered the seductive, slightly accented voice of a woman Maxine took to be Chinese.

The call was obviously not for Maxine. But then, since she knew not a soul in this city, that was hardly surprising.

She was about to hang up when she heard her neighbour say, 'Must have been a crossed line, sweetheart.'

Maxine bristled at being so casually dismissed. Clearly, he did not want the girl he so blithely called by endearments to know he was sharing rooms with another woman. Adam Warwick, it would seem, was two-timing his girlfriend. He was no better than Jonathan West. Hoping to register her disapproval, she returned the phone none too gently to its cradle.

The telephone engaged light stayed on for ages. Sounds of laughter and muffled one-sided conversation floated through to Maxine's room. Curiosity almost took her to listen at the door, and at one stage she even put her head close to the telephone in the hope of being able to overhear what was being said. But, with the handset firmly in place, it was as dead as a dodo. Maxine was left to ponder over the identity of the girl and where she and Adam might have had time and opportunity to meet . . . *if* indeed this was Adam's first visit to Hong Kong.

Maxine glanced at the clock and noted the lateness of the hour. The excuses Adam had used at the ball for avoiding her company sprang to mind. He needed a *good night's sleep*, he had told her. Yet, despite the added disadvantage of jetlag, a *good night's sleep* was, it would seem, no longer top of his list of priorities. And what of those *other commitments* he'd referred to? Had he been eluding to a lover . . . a wife even? And did the woman at the other end of the phone know of these *other commitments*? Maybe she *was* the other commitment. But, if that was so, then what was her boyfriend doing in a hotel with another woman?

One thing Maxine knew for sure, Adam Warwick was not here, sharing this suite with her, because he was lusting after her body. He had already made it quite clear that she didn't interest him in that way. Whether she wanted to be or not, she was quite safe from the amorous advances of Adam Warwick.

So then, why was he here? She had no idea — the man remained a mystery.

Maxine yawned, crawled in between the crisp clean sheets and rolled onto her side. What did she care, anyway? She was no more interested in him than he was in her. Their feelings for each other were quite mutual and his love life was his own affair.

Succumbing to travel fatigue and time change, Maxine was asleep long before the light on her telephone extension went out.

★   ★   ★

Eleanor lay her book down on the bedside table. She had read the same paragraph over and over and still did not know what it said. Her mind was on Adam. Despite their telephone conversation, the riddle remained unsolved.

'Why are you staying in the Mandarin Hotel?' had been her first question on meeting him at the airport. 'Why are you not with me?'

'I *am* staying with you,' he said, evasively.

'Only for one night,' she reminded him.

'Convenience darling . . . there's so much happening right now . . . with the merger and everything. I need to be near the office,' he told her. But she did not believe this to be the reason.

'Ah Fong can get you to Central in half an hour, any time, night or day,' she reminded him. 'Why this sudden need to be closer?'

He had laughed at her possessiveness, but promised to be with her at every opportunity. After only one night at the house in Shek-O, Ah Fong had been ordered to take him to the Mandarin. Even the usually inscrutable Ah Fong had appeared to think it strange that Mr Warwick should want to stay in a hotel when he had a perfectly comfortable house to come to and a driver to negotiate the heavy rush-hour traffic.

Houses were a luxury in Hong Kong that few could afford. This one, with its white stuccoed walls and archways, had been in the same family a long time — by Hong Kong standards. It stood in secluded grounds well back off the road and was surrounded by a high wall. At one time it had been home to half a dozen servants. Now it housed only three. Ah Fong, his wife, Fong Quan, and a young Chinese gardener who went by the adopted Western name of Winston. All three were devoted to Eleanor's welfare, but none more devoted to their mistress than Adam.

★ ★ ★

Bright sunlight streamed in through the window.

Maxine stirred; her eyes flickered open. Vacantly, she gazed around the unfamiliar room. Memory filtered through. Feeling like the cat that had got at the cream, she smiled and stretched luxuriously. And then ... she remembered her neighbour and the questions flooded back into her mind. Why had Adam Warwick taken an earlier flight instead of travelling with her and when had he arrived? Had he worked into the night or gone out on the town with his late night caller?

She listened but no sounds of life came from the lounge. She glanced at the bedside clock. Seven-twenty it said. He was probably still asleep.

Quietly, Maxine entered the lounge and going to the fruit bowl, helped herself to its contents. She would have gone next to the kitchenette to make herself a strong black coffee had she not, just then, heard the sounds of movement coming from the other bedroom. Aware of her tousled appearance, not wanting to appear at a disadvantage, she beat a hasty retreat back the way she had come. Coffee, she decided, could give way to pride.

Behind her, a door opened.

'Good morning,' she heard Adam Warwick say. 'You're just the person I want to see.'

She muttered an oath under her breath and wished the feeling was mutual.

Maxine had no alternative but to turn. 'Good morning,' she managed to acknowledge despite the inconvenience of a mouth full of banana.

Pushing thick tangled hair back out of her eyes, she scrutinised him from top to toe. Showered and shaved, in a smart lightweight suit and carrying a briefcase, he looked the epitome of a successful businessman on his way to the office.

Her eyebrows rose. 'What ever happened to holiday casuals?' she asked.

Adam had no time to stop and talk. He was

due to chair a meeting in twenty minutes and he was never late for anything important. 'A couple of loose ends to tie up,' he said by way of explanation, then added, 'I'll be back in time for the outing. The car will be here at eleven. I'll see you in the lobby near the main entrance.'

Maxine frowned. 'What outing?' she asked. This was the first she had heard of an outing.

'Consult your itinerary,' he threw over his shoulder as he headed for the door.

'What itinerary?' she called after him, only too aware that she was beginning to sound like a parrot.

He stopped and with mock irritability retraced his steps. 'Here take mine . . . make a copy for yourself,' he said. From his briefcase, he took a sheet of typed paper and laid it on the desk near the copy machine. 'And while you're at it, take a look through those.' He indicated a pile of tourist literature on the coffee table. 'Street maps, entertainment guides . . . '

He was gone before she could ask any more questions.

Annoyed by his domineering, high-handed manner, Maxine glared at the closed door. 'Who said I was going anywhere with you?' she called out.

Damn the man. Why did she always sound

like a total imbecile when he was around?

Still scowling, Maxine went to sit on the sofa. Scanning the itinerary, she saw that a trip had been planned for each day of her stay in Hong Kong, beginning with a tour of Wong Tai Sin Temple where, if they wanted to, they could have their fortunes told.

5

The girl at his side had, so far, said very little on the journey. But then, Adam reminded himself, he'd hardly strung two words together himself. He had squeezed a whole morning's work into a couple of hours in order to be available to her on time, and unfinished business still dominated his thoughts.

Now, as Ah Fong expertly manoeuvred the car through the heavy traffic, Adam pushed those thoughts aside and cast his mind back to the evening of the ball, to the moment his eyes picked Maxine out of the crowd. He had thought her a frivolous, attention-seeking butterfly. Fascinating . . . but quite empty headed. Later, from her personnel file, he had learned that she was a graduate, had an unblemished employment record, was reputed to be good at her job and held in high esteem by her boss.

There was, he had discovered, far more to Maxine Lowry than he had originally supposed and for some reason this had pleased him . . . more than it ought to have done.

A couple of days later, however, quite by chance, he had tuned into a ludicrous tale of an ex-fiancé tricked into baring heart and soul to the entire Sales Department. According to the raconteur, the man had been caught with another woman, quite literally, with his pants down. Exactly when, where and with whom this had happened, the man had not said. Adam had been amused but not interested enough to ask questions . . . that was, until it suddenly became clear that the Maxine in the tale and the Maxine in the red dress were one and the same person. By then, it was too late to ask; the conversation had moved on to other things.

So, she'd had sense enough to end her engagement to this Jonathan West. Well, good for her. Only a fool would have turned a blind eye. But he found himself wondering about the circumstances that had compelled her to so publicly humiliate the man and in such an underhand way.

Covertly, he glanced at his fellow passenger, at the girl whose face was slightly averted, her attention absorbed in the hectic city life flashing past her window. Did she miss her errant lover, he wondered, did she have regrets? If so, then where were the signs of grief?

His thoughts moved on to question her

reasons for trusting to the luck of a draw when she could so easily have brought a friend on this holiday with her. Had she acted on impulse . . . an atmosphere and alcohol-induced impulse? Or, despite her denials to the contrary, had she been seeking the thrills of a blind date? Possibly, but more likely, this was all about revenge . . . an attempt to teach her ex a lesson. Again, he glanced at Maxine. Was the break-up final or would she return to Jonathan West after she had played him at his own game?

He'd find out soon enough, and in the meantime, he would escort her around the sights, even though he could think of a dozen more important things he should be doing with his time.

Working against the clock, he had accomplished all he could towards closing the deal with Comp-Dynamics so that, any day now, the legal papers would be signed and sealed. He had returned to Hong Kong to find the expected backlog of work awaiting his attention and had dealt immediately with those matters most urgent. Tonight and at every opportunity, he would whittle away at his overflowing in-tray until he was back in control of it. Between Maxine, Eleanor and his office, he was stretching himself very thin.

Adam exhaled a deep breath and felt some

of the tension melt away. Since he was already committed to a morning with Maxine, he might just as well relax and enjoy it. After all, it was not every day he took time out to see the sights with a beautiful woman.

The autumn months in Hong Kong were his favourites, when the skies were clear blue, the sun still hot, and there was none of that intolerable summer humidity that kept one confined to air-conditioning. He wondered if Wong Tai Sin Temple or any of the other attractions he had in store for her would be of interest. If his guess was right, her real interests inclined more towards clubbing. She'd be right at home in the nightclubs of Wanchai and Lan Kwai Fong, he thought. Beaches too, and shopping would have their appeal. Well, he was not averse to any of those things, and had added both to the itinerary, but there was a lot more to this, his Hong Kong, as Maxine was about to find out.

And since he had gone to a great deal of trouble to reorganise their travel, accommodation and itinerary, Maxine was going to oblige him by seeing Hong Kong the way it should be seen — the way he wanted her to see it.

Ah Fong brought the car to a halt as near to their destination as the narrow, congested roads would allow. With instructions from

Adam to return in two hours, the couple set off on foot to cover the remaining short distance. The pungent aroma of burning joss sticks filled the air heralding their close proximity to the temple. Within minutes, they turned a corner, and there stretching before them, were the many broad steps leading up to the pillared gateway of Wong Tai Sin. Beyond was the huge temple itself with its crowds of worshippers, vendors and sightseers.

Adam hung back a little in order to observe Maxine's reaction. He heard her intake of breath and saw her wondrous gaze move slowly along the sea of golden roofs with their upturned corners, over tall red pillars, turquoise friezes, ornate latticework and intricate carvings.

His gaze followed hers, and for a moment, it was as if he was seeing the temple anew, and he felt that same thrill he had felt as a small child long ago when seeing it for the first time.

'I've never seen a Chinese temple before,' she told him in an awed whisper, breaking the spell that hung over them. 'It's so big, so colourful, so . . . ' she searched for the right words, ' . . . so Chinese.' For a moment, lost in thought, her focus stayed fixed on the largest building. Then, she turned large, questioning eyes up to his, and asked, 'Will we offend anyone if we go inside . . . or is that only for Buddhists?'

Her attention was distracted by a busload of inquisitive Western tourists, who, following their Chinese guide, had ascended its steps and were now entering its colourful portals.

'Forget I asked that question,' she laughed. Then she added wistfully, 'We could do with a guide.'

'Will I do?' Adam offered with deceptive humility.

She cast him a sceptical look tinged with a hint of scorn. 'I meant a real guide. One who can give us accurate, detailed information.'

He raised a brow. There was amusement in his lively dark eyes. 'What would you like to know?' he asked.

She looked at him steadily, then at the huge complex and said with a hint of challenge, 'Everything!'

He regarded her thoughtfully. Lip service, he wondered, or is she really as interested as she makes out? His mind slipped back through the years to memories of the wise and gentle influence that had brought him many times to these sacred environs, to the teachings that had intrigued and enlightened his young mind. To Adam, the temple was sacred to the memory of a loved one and deserving of respect. Would this girl give it that respect? He wondered.

'Okay. If you insist,' he responded, suspecting she would be looking for other diversions long before he had done . . . but hoping she wouldn't. 'Tell me when you've had enough,' he added.

Eagerly, she followed him through the milling crowd, up a flight of broad stone steps leading into a new and mysterious world, a world filled with vibrant colours and sounds, philosophies, strange faiths, strange aromatic smells and even stranger tales.

'This is Wong Tai Sin . . . the temple's namesake,' he told her, drawing her attention to a painting of a shepherd boy. 'At fifteen, he was taught by an immortal the art of refining cinnabar into a medicine that was believed to be a cure for all illnesses.

'Cinnabar . . . ' she queried, 'what's that?'

He searched his memory, 'Mercuric Sulphide.'

Maxine was none the wiser. Sounds lethal to me, she thought, but let it pass.

'And there,' he said, drawing her attention on, 'is the mischievous Monkey God, expelled by the Taoists for creating havoc in heaven and hell.' She seemed genuinely interested. Encouraged, he continued, 'Later, he took his place among the divinities of the Buddhists.'

He took her to see the statues of Kwun Yam, the Goddess of Mercy and the martial arts god, Quan Ti, and took pleasure in filling her head, as Lai Ho Mai had filled his, with enchanting stories of their wondrous deeds.

He led her through the many halls resembling temples, each dedicated to some worthy use, each holding the carved statues of deities acclaimed by Buddhists, Confucians and Taoists. And over all hung the heavy pall of incense and the atmosphere of religious fervour and mystique.

Before the many altars, devotees, absorbed in prayer, bowed and shuffled on their knees towards their deities. Among them was a young woman, serene in silent prayer. Between her hands, she held a bamboo cylinder filled with dozens of bamboo slithers. The woman was shaking the cylinder in a jerky, rhythmic motion, causing the sticks to clatter noisily, like castanets.

Intrigued by the noise and strangeness of the ritual, Maxine hung back at a respectful distance to watch. Eventually, one of the sticks worked its way free from the others as it was meant to and fell out onto the floor.

A monk picked up the stick, and for a moment, studied it intently while the woman waited in silent anticipation.

Maxine turned to Adam for an explanation.

'Numbered fortune-telling sticks,' he said in a hushed voice. 'The monk will give an interpretation.'

By mutual unspoken agreement, allowing the worshipers their privacy, they moved out of the inner sanctum, back into bright sunlight, where, on the temple steps, they paused to watch more devotees waft the smoke from burning pieces of paper into the morning breeze.

'They're sending messages to their gods,' Adam explained.

Maxine watched in silence for a moment. 'Asking for cures . . . good exam results . . . promotion? That sort of thing?' she asked.

He laughed. 'More likely they're asking for this week's winning lottery ticket, or a windfall at the casino in Macao. The Chinese are inveterate gamblers,' he went on to explain. 'They'll bet on anything. I once watched two men on a train to Lo Wu betting on which raindrop running down the outside of the window would be first to reach the sill. Money changed hands a dozen times before they left the train. I swear it gave them as much pleasure as a day at the Happy Valley race course.'

With growing interest, Adam watched Maxine's fascination with the rituals of worship: with the bowing and chanting, and the placing of joss sticks in sand-filled cauldrons. He answered her questions about the food offerings to favourite deities placed on red paper mats on the temple steps. The intelligence behind her questions impressed him, as did her appetite for knowledge and the quiet respect she showed for the beliefs of others.

Once more he cast his mind back to their first meeting, to the lady in red who had been high on drink and atmosphere and whom he had judged an airhead. Overwork and jetlag must have marred his judgement, he now decided with wry humour.

And then, again, he remembered the punishment she had inflicted upon her fiancé, and his humour dissolved. Whether her actions had been justified or not, the very last thing he needed was involvement with a harridan capable of inflicting such public humiliation on another. And yet, here he was, on holiday and sharing a suite of rooms with the very woman herself. Was this not asking for trouble?

* * *

Maxine followed Adam along walkways lined with busy stalls selling all the things a worshipper could want from paper offerings

90

to souvenirs. This was where the cubicles of the fortune-tellers were to be found.

'The itinerary said we could have our fortunes told,' Maxine reminded him. Her sapphire eyes, bright with anticipation, searched for the stall of her choice.

'Yes, so it did,' he agreed, 'but be warned, there are a dozen different ways of having this done. Take a look at a few before you pick one,' he advised.

He was right. There were readers of palms, physiognomy, horoscopes and tarot cards, and there were interpreters of rune stones and dreams. Intrigued and discretely amused, Maxine paused to watch a reading taken from head and facial lumps and bumps.

'To the Chinese, every freckle, mole, wart and age-spot has a special significance,' Adam explained.

Next, she paused to watch a small bird, not unlike a sparrow, hop out of a bamboo cage and along a line of cards. Using its beak, it turned over one of the cards. Then, having received its edible reward, returned voluntarily to its cage. Two heads bent over the card: the teller and the listener. A serious discourse followed.

'Very sweet,' whispered Maxine, eyeing the bird. 'And, very clever, but I don't think I care to trust my future to the whims of that little fellow.'

'In that case,' Adam smiled, 'I recommend a visit to Fu Chu Ming. He's the best.' With a light touch on her arm, he steered her through the crowd until they came to a cubicle with the longest queue.

'Well,' she said, disheartened, 'It looks like you're not the only one who thinks he's the best.'

'Mmm . . . a half hour wait . . . at least,' Adam murmured, casting a sceptical eye along the line. 'Worth the wait?' he asked, leaving the decision up to her.

'If he really is the best . . . ' she said, turning hopeful eyes up to his.

With good-natured resignation, he joined her in the queue.

The wait gave Maxine time to take stock of the stall. With its detailed pictures of anatomy and physiognomy and its numerous painted signs, lines and symbols, it was not unlike so many of the others. There were horoscope charts and a pile of old tomes over which the soothsayer frequently bent his head of greying hair and long wispy beard. The flowing traditional Chinese robe added dignity and mystery to the wearer as, she supposed, it was meant to.

Since Maxine had no strong beliefs one

way or the other where fortune-telling was concerned, she would, she determined, keep an open mind on the subject. But, noting the shrewd, dark eyes that contrasted so oddly with the bland economy of facial expression, she decided to say nothing that would help to give insight into her past, present, or hopes for the future.

When, at last, it was their turn the couple took their places before Fu Chu Ming. In Cantonese, the man greeted Adam with unexpected warmth. Adam responded in kind.

Dumbfounded, Maxine looked from one to the other. So, not only did her self-appointed guide know his way around the temple, but also he was on friendly terms with its most popular soothsayer. Furthermore, Adam spoke this language with its strange up-and-down singsong tones like a native. This man never failed to surprise her.

'He would like to know how he can be of assistance,' Adam translated to Maxine. He indicated to the charts. 'Do you have a preference?' Seeing Maxine's indecision, he advised, 'Leave it to him? He'll probably tell your horoscope and throw in a little palmistry and physiognomy.'

She agreed and gave the time and date of her birth. While Adam translated, she watched entranced, as the soothsayer leafed through the pages of an old and much-used almanac. Although intriguing in itself, it was not so much the almanac that caught her attention, but his long fingers . . . or rather, the long nails that gave the illusion of long fingers. Any woman might be proud of such nails, she observed, but on a man, they looked strange. She had noticed other Chinese men with talons like these, mostly older men, and assumed that this was just one of the many cultural differences between East and West.

Finding what he sought, Fu Chu Ming read for a moment in silence while Maxine continued to watch the finger that traced the rows of calligraphy. Then, putting the book aside, he pulled a roll of rice paper towards him, and dipping a soft pointed brush into black ink, he began to paint with artistic sweeps, vertical rows of Chinese characters. He worked quickly for a minute or so, and then, laying his work aside, he took Maxine's hands in his own. He did not immediately look at her palms, but first, with narrowed eyes, he studied her face.

Slowly, phrase by phrase, Adam translated.

'He says . . . *You have been trusting to a fault*,' he began.

Spot on, agreed Maxine, remembering all

she had endured at the hands of Jonathan.

'*But have now dealt justly and firmly with your problem . . .*'

For Maxine there was the joy of remembering black bags in the gloom of a lonely stairwell and an indiscreet telephone call made public to an amused department.

The soothsayer dropped his penetrating gaze to her open palms.

'*But . . . your problem does not accept that it has been dealt with.*'

A wicked smile came to play on Maxine's face. 'Oh . . . I wouldn't say that,' she purred, satisfied that even Jonathan, with his colossal ego, could not fail to realise that he had been well and truly dumped.

At her words, Fu Chu Ming looked up, but did not ask for a translation. The intelligent gleam that appeared in his dark eyes suggested he already knew all her deepest secrets.

Unsettled, Maxine waited warily for the old man to continue.

'He warns,' said Adam, '*like the dying ember, it has the power to flare again . . . and devour all in its path*, and he advises you to *dowse the fire with cold water.*'

Maxine looked sceptical. If he really was referring to Jonathan, he'd got it wrong. She couldn't imagine him destroying all in his path. Banging on doors and making nuisance telephone calls was just about the extent of his rather limited activities . . . where she was concerned, anyway.

However, this time she did not air her opinion. Instead, she watched the old man trace a long nail across an astrological chart, and waited patiently for him to decipher its message.

'*You are entering a new phase in you life*,' Adam stated.

Such originality, thought Maxine. She glanced at the man at her side. Next he'll tell me I've come on a long journey to meet a tall, dark and handsome stranger.

'*You have come on a long journey to meet a tall, dark and handsome stranger with far reaching influence and power*,' said Adam.

Spot on! I'm in the wrong business, thought Maxine cynically, her eyes sparkling with good natured humour. And then she saw the mischievous smile that played across Adam's face and her eyes narrowed.

'Did he really say that,' she asked, suspiciously, 'or did you just make it up?

'Of course he said it,' he replied. 'He says it to all the girls.'

Maxine gave him a withering look and would have responded with a suitable quip, had not that hushed incantation with the strange tones begun again. Only this time, there was an almost sinister quality in the voice.

'*Solve the mystery of the dark couple shrouded in secrets . . . whose destinies are irrevocably entwined. Beware of deception . . . beware of an evil gift from a stranger . . . *'

A chill ran down the full length of Maxine's spine.

'God,' she murmured, glancing nervously up at Adam. 'Do I take this seriously?'

'Of course,' he replied.

She waited for the reassuring smile that would tell her this was just a bit of harmless fun, but Adam's face remained expressionless.

Fu Chu Ming took up the rice paper on which he had recorded her horoscope. He rolled it up, tied it with a narrow red ribbon, and with a polite incline of the head, he presented it to her. Then, with dancing eyes he turned to Adam and said a few words that made both men laugh.

'What did he say?' Maxine asked, suspiciously.

Adam translated, '*The tiger may banish the rabbit and teach the monkey good manners, but it is written he will lay down with the dragon.*'

Baffled, Maxine waited for an explanation. Adam did not explain. Instead, he rose from his seat and began the rituals of leave-taking.

Maxine hesitated to follow. 'Aren't you going to have your fortune told?' she asked him.

'I just did,' he smiled.

★   ★   ★

It was well past one by the time the car returned them to the Mandarin Hotel. Maxine fully expected Adam to suggest lunch, but as they passed through the busy lobby, he made no mention of it.

At the concierge's desk, she waited while Adam checked for messages and was surprised to see an envelope change hands.

Who could be leaving messages for him? she wondered.

While they waited for an elevator, he opened the envelope, and turning slightly away, he quickly read the enclosed note. A smile hovered on his lips.

An elevator was not long in coming. With the tinkling announcement of a bell, its doors slid back and Maxine stepped inside. Turning, she saw that Adam had not followed.

'Something's cropped up,' he said apologetically. 'I've a few things to do, but I'd like it if you would have dinner with me this evening.' The door was closing. 'Seven-thirty?' he suggested.

Although she was delighted to have been asked to dinner, Maxine was not at all pleased to have been abandoned so abruptly, nor was she overjoyed at the prospect of lunching alone. Not for the first time she regretted the impetuosity that had brought her on holiday with a total stranger. One tequila less and she might have had the good sense to accept the raffle prize in full, and then the fun-loving Carrie would be here with her now and lunch, swimming, shopping and clubbing would be very much on the agenda.

Irritably, Maxine tapped the Chinese scroll against the side of her leg. Its hollow sound brought her attention back into focus and reminded her of the wonderful enlightening few hours she had just spent at Wong Tai Sin. Such a visit would have been way down at the bottom of Carrie's list of sightseeing priorities.

Thanks to Adam, the temple had allowed her a glimpse of a strange new world. Adam, however, had been on familiar ground and comfortably at home in that world. How had he come by so much knowledge? Not from a guidebook, that was for sure. And the fluent Cantonese . . . where had that come from

. . . an English school? Unlikely, she thought, unless he had gone on to study Oriental languages at university.

Who *is* this man? she asked herself yet again, and what is his connection with Hong Kong? More importantly, what is his connection with Comp-Dynamics?

Tonight, she promised herself, over supper, I'll get the answers to those questions.

Maxine toyed with the idea of finding a restaurant, but resigned herself instead to ordering from room service. Severe jet-lag was beginning to set in, and if she wanted to stay awake long enough to enjoy a night out on the town, then she would be wise to put the shopping on hold in favour of a short siesta.

She thought of the clothes neatly stowed in the wardrobe and was aware that many were inappropriate for a holiday of this calibre. But then she had not known she would be staying at the Mandarin Oriental. Her bank balance was healthier than it had ever been, thanks to Jonathan and his constant reminders of a mortgage they would not now need. Her spirits lifted to an all time high. She was going on a monumental and long-overdue shopping spree.

The lift arrived at her floor. But just as the doors slid open, Maxine remembered having seen postcards on display in one of the lobby's smart kiosks. Hanging back, she pushed a button that returned her to the lobby.

In her mind, Maxine ran through the names of those she wanted to send cards to. Now let me see . . . there's Carrie, Janet and the folks, Nan and Granddad, and . . . yes, there's Auntie Grace . . . and Auntie Norah . . . and I ought to send one to the department. She began to search through the colourful assortment on the revolving rack. Having made her choice, she looked for someone to take her money. It was then that she saw the now familiar figure of Adam Warwick. He was in the flower shop opposite and had in his hands a generous bunch of assorted flowers, many of which were red roses. They were beautifully arranged in cellophane and tied around with a wide, shiny ribbon, the same vibrant colour as the roses.

Unashamedly curious, Maxine moved behind the card stand from where she could observe without being seen.

A thoughtful scowl creased her brow. Who on earth can he be buying those for? She wondered. For me? No, surely not. We hardly know each other. Nice thought though, she told herself, a little wistfully.

She remembered the telephone call of the

night before and wondered if the flowers were for the mystery caller. Had the message collected from the concierge also come from the caller? Was she his girlfriend and if so, then what was he doing asking her, Maxine, out to dinner tonight? Did he make a habit of two-timing his girlfriends and was this one aware she had competition?

Here, Maxine checked her thoughts. Competition? What on earth was she thinking of? She wasn't competition to anyone. After all the nonsense and aggravation Jonathan had put her through, she was not interested in another romantic entanglement, and was not likely to be for a very long time. And she certainly was not interested in an entanglement with a man as deep and devious as this one appeared to be.

She watched him pay for the flowers, move into the lobby and cross the wide marble expanse. From a distance, she followed. No harm in a little idle curiosity, she airily convinced herself.

Beyond him, through the tinted plate-glass doors, she saw a shiny red sports car glide smoothly to a halt. The hotel porter, splendid in braided uniform, stepped around the car to open the driver's door. Out stepped one of the most beautiful women Maxine had ever seen. She was fine-boned and as she moved, long sleek hair swung around her like a dark mantle. There was a hint of Chinese in the colour of her skin and in the almond shape of her lively dark eyes.

The main doors swung open for Adam. Catching sight of him, the girl smiled radiantly, ran up the steps and threw herself into his eager arms.

For a moment, his cheek rested against her hair. Then he drew back, and with a tender smile, placed the flowers in her hands. She bowed her head to their fragrance and was so obviously moved by his thoughtfulness. A few unheard words passed between them. The girl handed over a bunch of keys.

With Adam at the wheel, the car moved away taking them both into the dense, fast-moving traffic, and quickly out of sight.

Into Maxine's mind came the words of the soothsayer: 'A dark couple shrouded in secrets . . . whose destinies are irrevocably entwined.'

★　★　★

Maxine threw the scroll into the far corner of her room and cast herself down on the bed. Lunch, postcards, siesta . . . were all now quite forgotten — replaced by images of a loving couple and a jumble of mixed emotions.

Through curiosity, she now had the answers to some of her questions . . . only they weren't the answers she wanted. Adam did have a girlfriend . . . a beautiful girlfriend, and a girlfriend with whom, it was apparent, he was very much in love.

A knife twisted somewhere in the region of her heart. It was one thing to suspect he had a girlfriend; it was quiet another thing to know. The knowing hurt. Sheer physical attraction, she scoffed at herself. It's got to be. You can't possibly care about someone you know so little about.

This brought her round full circle to the questions she had already asked herself a hundred times. Who is he? Where does he fit into Comp-Dynamics? Maxine was sure she could identify all Comp-Dynamic's employees, including its overseas reps, and she was equally sure that, until the spotlight picked Adam out at the ball, she had not previously laid eyes on him.

For the first time it occurred to her that maybe he did not work for Comp-Dynamics after all. But if that was so, then what was he doing at a ball that was only for company employees and their partners? She wished she had paid more attention . . . seen the table he had come from and the partner to whom he had returned. The drink and party atmosphere had made her less observant than usual.

She sighed, rolled on to her side and tucked an arm under her head.

And what did she know of his moral character? What kind of man dates one girl for lunch and another for supper?

Her thoughts lingered on Adam's almond-eyed companion: exotically beautiful, demonstrative, young . . .

She brought a pillow over her head in an attempt to dispel the little green demons.

'I don't give a damn about you or your love life, Adam Warwick' she said aloud, as if words of denial would alter her feelings for him.

Maxine threw off the pillow and rolled on to her back. 'Liar,' she muttered at the ceiling. Okay. Okay. I admit it. He does mean something to me. He's very attractive. No . . . not attractive . . . he's positively bloody gorgeous. He has only to put in an appearance to set my pulse racing; he's constantly on my mind and to make matters worse, he occupies a room only two unlocked doors away.

She checked her wayward thoughts. None of that Maxine, she told herself sternly. You don't like two-timing men, remember?

Adam and his beautiful girlfriend were still

on her mind when she fell into a fitful, exhausted asleep.

★ ★ ★

Eleanor stooped to place the flowers on the mound before them. A tear trickled down her cheek. Adam took her hand in his.

'I miss her so much,' she murmured, turning dark, tragic eyes up to his.

'Me too,' he replied squeezing her hand gently. Adam glanced at the dates on the tall headstone and did a mental reckoning. Lai Ho Mai had been born in the sensitive, artistic year of the Goat and today was her birthday. 'She would have been forty-five,' he murmured. Still so young, he thought but did not say.

Eleanor sank to her knees.

For a while she would commune silently with her mother. Adam released her hand and stepped back. He watched her for a moment and then, turning away, strolled over to sit on a low crumbling wall to gaze across the vast cemetery to the ocean below and to the distant green hills of Lantau Island. The sea breeze ruffled his hair; the sun was warm on his tanned face.

He tried to picture Lai Ho Mai as she had been, before the cancer had taken hold and reduced her already slender form to skin and bone. He saw the perfect bone structure of a proud face, the long black hair swept back and tied at the nape of a graceful neck, the gentle eyes . . . and then he saw the pain that too often clouded those eyes . . . even before the onset of cancer. He had blamed his father . . . would always blame his father for her great loss of face, although he knew Lai Ho Mai had never blamed any one but herself.

Born a Taoist, it had been Lai Ho Mai who had introduced him to the wonders of Wong Tai Sin Temple and taught him Cantonese, and it had been her gentle homespun philosophies that had guided him through life, shaping the man he was today. But, when it came to instilling forgiveness, she had failed miserably. He never would forgive.

6

Maxine awoke slowly to the sounds of movement in the adjoining room, followed by muted male voices and the closing of a door.

She glanced at the bedside clock and was startled to see how long she had slept. She had worked out the time difference between England and Hong Kong and had meant to sleep for only a couple of hours, thus allowing Janet time to get to work. She had wanted to phone, to ask important questions about her secretive holiday companion, and Janet, being in Human Resources, was just the person to supply the answers. Then she had planned to explore the shopping malls and lanes only a few minutes walk away.

How had she managed to waste a whole precious afternoon on sleep? Jetlag had caught up with her, she supposed. She had lost a night's sleep on the flight over and the time change had not helped. Well, she was awake now, refreshed and ready for an evening out, but unfortunately, she had run out of time for a call to England. The long chat, the sharing of confidences, the questions and answers, they would all now have to wait until later.

How long had Adam been gone? She wondered. Had he spent the entire afternoon with his girlfriend, or had he returned soon after lunch?

Her train of thought progressed to whether or not she should accept Adam's invitation to dinner. Maxine mulled over the problem for only a moment and then made a decision. She had not come to the other side of the world to shut herself away in a hotel bedroom. She was going out on the town, and whether she went with him or alone, could be decided while she showered and changed.

Ready at last, leaving a pile of tried and discarded clothes on the bed, Maxine moved towards the door. Passing the mirror, she stole a last critical look at her reflection, and scowled. There was no time for another change, she reminded herself, and besides, until she hit the shopping malls, she had nothing more suitable for this unexpected classy life-style than the clothes she already had on. She was being paranoid about her appearance and knew it, but then, the man behind the door had that affect on her.

'You'll do,' she said in a no-nonsense voice to her mirrored image. She then pulled a comical face at herself and headed for the lounge.

Wearing a short, softly-draped skirt and a glitzy evening top, and with hair swinging freely and make-up immaculate, Maxine, exactly on time, made her entrance into the lounge. Her mind was made up — she was not going to supper with Adam no matter how much she wanted to. He had a girlfriend and too many other secrets besides. She would discover for herself the nightlife of Hong Kong. After all, she was a modern woman, free and independent, and quite capable of looking after herself.

An ice bucket had been brought into the lounge and Adam, devastatingly attractive in smart-casuals, was pouring champagne into crystal flutes.

He looked up at her approach, and she saw the appraising gaze that swept over her and the approval that came into his candid eyes. Her stomach did a funny little summersault of pleasure and a warm glow travelled up to her cheeks. Perhaps, if his smile had not been so warm, so appreciative, her resolve might not have weakened. Instead, she found herself returning the smile and meekly accepting the champagne, and all without the tiniest hint of resistance. The argumentative voice in the back of her mind gradually faded, and by eight o'clock, she was willing to follow him anywhere. The evening was cool. The restaurant, Adam had told her, was walking distance and several stages up a steep and very long canopied outdoor escalator. And so, they moved leisurely along busy streets ablaze with colourful neon signs.

Maxine had expected to see rickshaws, but not one crossed their path. Instead, she was surprised to see overloaded double-decker trams, running along fixed lines, their bells clanging noisily, and London buses painted blue and covered in advertisements. And it seemed to Maxine that every other car was a taxi, red, with horn blaring.

Shops, with lights and neon signs blazing, were showing no signs of closing for the night. They were doing a thriving trade and as the couple passed through a popular alley lined with lamp-lit stalls, vendors called to them in off-key singsong tones to stop and inspect their wares.

Maxine was easily tempted. But each time she hesitated, a light touch on her arm moved her on.

'Tomorrow . . . ' Adam said persuasively. 'There'll be plenty of time to shop tomorrow . . . here, if you like, before we go to Stanley, and again later at Stanley Market.'

Manoeuvring past a group of idling shoppers, they came to the end of the alley where they negotiated the tricky crossing of a busy road to join a stream of human traffic on the escalator moving from Central District towards the higher lights of residential Midlevels.

The escalator ran beside and sometimes high above, steep stone steps that were flanked by shops, office blocks and high-rise apartments. It crossed over congested illuminated streets and as it travelled up the hillside, the air cleared of traffic fumes and the pungent appetising aromas of commercial kitchens replaced the choking smells of the city.

Maxine had missed lunch. Thoughts of shopping dissolved as she focussed in turn on the variety of restaurants they passed. And then they came to a particularly attractive Bayou Restaurant.

'That one looks interesting,' she commented hopefully.

Adam smiled. 'I must be psychic,' he said.

They left the escalator at the next exit. But instead of turning towards the Bayou restaurant, he led her down a side street.

'First, we need to buy wine,' he explained.

Astonished, she asked, 'A restaurant that doesn't sell wine?'

With so many restaurants from which to choose, Maxine wondered what had possessed him to make a reservation at one that didn't sell alcohol. She would have put the question to him if he had not already entered a dingy hole-in-the-wall shop.

She followed him into the heady aroma of burning joss sticks, and when her eyes had adjusted to the smoky haze and the gloom of inadequate light, she saw that she was surrounded by floor to ceiling shelves closely packed with a very strange assortment of wares.

So this is what a Chinese medicine shop looks like, she told herself.

Her interested gaze came to rest on the nearest glass topped display counter, but most of its strange contents were, to her, unidentifiable. Curiosity and a couple of steps took her past a large open basket full of dried fungi to the next counter. There she eyed with growing interest and an equal measure of distaste, a row of animal horns, a variety of dead insects and frogs, and a number of gossamer thin parchments that were undoubtedly snake-skins shed by their former owners.

And are those what I think they are? she wondered, leaning closer to inspect a couple of large hairy balls that looked suspiciously like dead spiders. How can these have any medicinal value? Suddenly afraid they might still be very much alive, she took a wary step back, and another when it occurred to her that the spiders might have come to the cabinet of their own accord, and there, keeled over with old age. In which case, there could be a whole colony of their offspring lurking in dark corners. Maxine searched the walls, and afraid that one might have dropped from the ceiling and even now be making a home for itself amongst her curls, she swept a hand over her hair. Maxine loathed spiders. Just the thought of them made her skin crawl.

Why on earth had Adam brought her here?

'Not shopping for dinner, are we?' she asked him with a mix of suspicion and wry humour.

'Yes, as a matter of fact we are,' he replied.

Hastily, she moved further away from the gruesome displays and half afraid he might be serious, turned to catch his expression in the half-light.

He had moved towards and was studying the contents of a temperature-controlled glass-fronted cabinet. Stepping closer, she was relieved to see that it held rows and rows of bottles of wine.

'That will do . . . ' he said, reaching for a New Zealand, Cloudy Bay, Sauvignon Blanc.

'Wine in an Apothecary shop? Whatever next?' she murmured. 'And what has wine got to do with medicine?' she wanted to know.

'Ancient Chinese remedy,' he grinned. 'Sorts out the Ying from the Yang.'

'Befuddles the Ying and the Yang, more like!' she laughed.

Maxine followed him to the counter where her gaze came to rest on a large jar of preserved and very dead cockroaches.

'And they're pickled onions I suppose?' she said, moving in for a closer look at the round mottled brown bodies and the tangle of antennae and hairy legs.

'Much tastier. Want some?' he offered.

She shuddered and gave him a withering look. Maxine had seen and heard enough; it was time to go. 'I'll wait in the street,' she said, making a quick exit.

Determined to see nothing more that might further impair her appetite, Maxine deliberately stood with her back to the window display.

To one side, near her shoulder, something moved. She turned to focus on a large glass tank. Inside was a wreathing mass of silver grey snakes . . . all very much alive and waiting, she guessed, for the soup pot.

* * *

From the moment they entered the busy restaurant, it was obvious that Adam and the voluptuous Creole owner were on friendly terms. Leaving a table at which she had been engrossed in conversation, the sociable owner came over to greet him by first name and to lead them to a window table.

'Business looks good Naomi,' Adam commented, having observed that the tables were either occupied or reserved.

'Considering we've only been open three weeks . . . ' she replied in a rich Louisiana accent and with a satisfied smile.

'And the liquor license?' he asked.

'Not a sign of it . . . could be months,' she grimaced, then with a grin added, 'and in the meantime unofficial back-street off-licenses mushroom and flourish, and keep our customers happy for us.'

She relieved Adam of his purchase and handed it to a Chinese waiter.

Such a cocktail of nationalities thought Maxine, watching Naomi weave her way between the tables. She had heard Hong Kong referred to as the crossroads of Asia. Even so, she had not expected such a blend of East and West.

Her thoughts turned again to her mysterious partner. And where does he fit into the grand scheme of things? She wondered yet again.

Maxine curbed her curiosity until the wine

had been served, their orders taken and they were alone. 'You seem to know your way around Hong Kong pretty well,' she then remarked, fishing for information.

'Yes. I suppose I do,' he replied. 'But then, I've spent a lot of time in Asia.'

She waited for him to elaborate. When he did not, she asked, 'You're our rep in Hong Kong then?' She didn't wait for a reply; she was sure he was not. 'I thought I knew all our overseas reps . . . by name at least, but I don't think I've ever heard of you.'

'You haven't?' he said with mock surprise. 'And I thought my name was on everyone's lips. How disappointing.'

A smile played across his handsome features. Soon his name *would* be on everyone's lips at Comp-Dynamics. On his instructions, the official announcement was scheduled for next week.

She laughed and after a moment's pause, persisted, 'So . . . have you been with Comp-Dynamics long?'

He mulled the question over for a second. Loosely speaking, he was with Comp-Dynamics, although it would perhaps be more accurate to say that Comp-Dynamics was now with him. 'No, not long. Not long at all, actually,' he replied, thinking of the legal documents that had only recently been finalised. 'I'm the new boy on the block, you might say.'

That explains it, thought Maxine. He was not someone's guest . . . not some woman's partner. He's new to the company. Progress at last. Not much, but a little. 'And the Cantonese . . . Did you learn that here in Hong Kong?' she asked, thinking that anyone who could pick up such an impossible sounding language in anything short of a lifetime must have an abundance of natural linguistic talent.

'Yes,' he confirmed, 'and a little Mandarin and Japanese.' Seeing her look of astonishment, he added with modest nonchalance, 'Languages come easily to me.'

So it would seem, she thought, wishing she had just a fraction of such a wonderful gift. 'And will we be seeing very much of you at Head Office,' she asked, trying not to sound too eager. For some reason, the thought of seeing him regularly on a day-to-day basis sent her pulse into overdrive.

'Yes, quite a lot,' he confirmed, knowing that for the first few months of the merger, it would be necessary for him to share his time between Warwick International and Comp-Dynamics. Later, when he had filled a key position within the company and was sure of his staff, he would be able to limit his visits.

She hoped he would add to the scant information she had had to practically drag out of him, but instead he turned the conversation around to her and kept it there.

She told him about her parents and older brother, Tristan, and about life in Devon.

'Where it rains six days out of seven,' he quoted.

'Gross exaggeration,' she laughed. 'I've never noticed that it rains there any more than anywhere else . . . ' she saw his light scepticism and amended, ' . . . well not where I live, anyway. It usually bypasses the coast and empties it down on higher land.

'I love the moors . . . the gorse, the heather . . . the wild ponies . . . ' she rhapsodised dreamily.

She thought affectionately of her own pony, cared for in her parents' livery stables. Jonathan did not ride and had made no secret of the fact that he had no interest in country life. After a couple of disastrous visits, Maxine had preferred to go without him. She now wondered if those nights he had spent in her apartment had been spent alone.

These thoughts of Jonathan, Maxine kept to herself. But they prompted her to question several times throughout the evening her reasons for wining and dining with a man who appeared to be as devious as the man she had recently ousted from her life.

Again, she wished Adam would give some insight into his background and character, and most of all, she wished he would speak openly and honestly about his girlfriend. But, although the courses came and went and conversation flowed comfortably, he never once touched on anything remotely connected to his private life.

Finally, while they waited for the bill, unable to curb her curiosity any longer, Maxine asked as casually as such a question would allow, 'And have you got a girlfriend?'

At that moment the bill arrived to claim his attention, and he bent his head to sign it. 'No,' she heard him reply after a slight pause, 'I don't have a girlfriend.'

Maxine sat back in her chair. Caught you, she thought, remembering vividly the cosy scene on the steps of the Mandarin. Adam Warwick, you're telling lies.

★   ★   ★

Eleanor sat quite alone in the fine drawing room of her home. She had more than her fair share of friends to call on, but had no desire to be with any of them.

She knew that in her present mood she would be poor company and so she sat gazing at the television without seeing or hearing a thing. Her mind had moved to a different plane, and back in time.

There had been no secret about Eleanor's mixed blood, nor had she been spared the knowledge that it was regarded as tainted and brought shame on her Chinese connections. It was not in the blunt nature of the Cantonese to be tactful, and in any case, what was the point? She had only to look in the mirror to know the painful truth ... to see the startling differences between herself and her young Chinese friends. She was too tall, her eyes too round. Her skin tone was unusually warm and there was the tiniest hint of bronze in her almost black hair. That she was different was an unhappy and unavoidable fact of life and not one Eleanor had found easy to accept. In an attempt to distance herself from her foreign blood, in an attempt to identify with her friends, she had insisted on being called by her Chinese name, Lai Lan, and had stubbornly refused to answer to any other.

Then, at the time of her mother's death, Adam had come into her life and he had called her by her Western name.

'I am not Eleanor,' she had quickly corrected. Then, as if daring him to contradict, she had slowly and emphatically

121

added, 'I am Lai Lan.'

She remembered how he had cupped her chin in a gentle hand and forced her to look up into smiling, teasing eyes. 'To me sweetheart, you are Eleanor,' he had said softly in that deep velvet voice that had become so dear to her.

Her heart had melted and even now, her eyes misted with the joy of remembering. Fear of the *gwei'lo*, foreign devil, had evaporated along with her shame. From then on, she had become Eleanor and she wanted to be called by no other name.

Adam had become a regular and highly esteemed caller at the tiny low cost tenement apartment she shared with her grandmother. It was no secret that his interest lay with Eleanor, but he was kind to them both and always respectful towards her grandmother. He eased their lives with gifts, and their grief with laughter. And then, the unthinkable happened. Her grandmother, worn out before her time, had died in her sleep, 'Of old age,' the ambulance man told her with a careless shrug.

Eleanor reached for the glass of iced water on the table beside her. Her hands, she noticed, trembled slightly. Two deaths in as many years, even now, still had the power to move her to tears.'

Neighbours had come as she prayed they would, offered condolences, muttered over the many unfair hardships of life, but had soon gone away to worry about their own too numerous troubles. All through that first terrible night Eleanor had sat in the dark, tormented by the demons of grief and the fears of an uncertain future. The woman who had for a while become more mother to her than grandmother, had gone out of her life forever. Who now would love Eleanor, who would comfort her, who would be waiting each day for her safe return home?

After her mother's death, her grandmother had been the sole supplier of income for their meagre needs. Now her grandmother had gone, leaving her alone and still a minor. She feared she would have to quit her studies; that the authorities would take her away to live in an orphanage or foster her out to a family who would put her to work like a servant. Or worse, maybe she would be expected to take her grandmother's place in the fly-ridden meat market with its slippery floors and sickening smells of blood and death. And where was she to find the money for her grandmother's funeral?

The next day, Adam had come. He had opened his arms to her, held her close and stroked her hair. He would take care of her grandmother's funeral, and she would go with full honours to be with her ancestors, he had promised. Then, without hesitation, and despite fierce opposition, he had taken her from her humble beginnings to live like a princess in his palace.

Tonight, despite the ever-present servants, the palace seemed empty. Adam had not come home as she hoped he would. Where was he? Who was he with?

Eleanor's gaze circled the lonely room. Adam was her protector, her champion, the most important person in her life. She could live without the luxury he provided . . . if she had to, but she could not live without Adam.

★   ★   ★

At Maxine's request to see a little of Hong Kong's nightlife, Adam took her from the Bayou restaurant to the cobbled quadrant of Lan Kwai Fong. Again they travelled on foot. If her sense of direction was to be trusted, they had come two sides of a triangle and were not that far from the hotel.

Here, were dozens of bars and clubs packed into one small area of Central District. The air was thick with party atmosphere, the scene was multi-cultural and the language mainly English. Many chose to

124

drink and circulate in the narrow streets while others spilled out of doorways on to pavements, not by choice, but because the bars and clubs were filled to capacity. A cacophony of musical sounds pulsated jarringly, competing with each other for customer attention.

'I chose the restaurant,' Adam said to her, raising his voice in order to be heard, 'so you choose the bar. Which one will it be?'

'Which ever one we can get into, I guess,' she laughed, looking up and down the street. 'That one,' she said, indicating towards well-lit premises which seemed to beckon more encouragingly than the others.

'A good choice,' Adam approved, and Maxine was soon to discover why. Before they could push their way through to the bar, he had been heartily hailed several times in both English and Cantonese. Adam, it seemed, was on familiar territory and very much among friends.

7

'You did what?' spluttered Carrie into the phone.

At the other end of the line, Agnes cringed. 'I told him she'd gone to Hong Kong and where she's staying. What's wrong with that?' she whined defensively.

Before Carrie could tell her what was wrong with that, Agnes said hurriedly, 'Got to go. The switchboard's going mad.'

The line went dead.

'Silly bitch,' Carrie said angrily, banging the phone down.

Janet was waiting to go to lunch with Carrie. She paused in the process of applying a fresh coat of plum-coloured lipstick. 'What's she done?' she asked.

'She went out with Jonathan for a drink last night,' Carrie replied, staring at the black phone with the same expression of disgust one might accord a slug. 'Only ever seen him once but fancied the pants off of him ever since. Thought she had it made . . . anyone with half a brain would have known he only wanted to pump her for information.'

Janet giggled over the unintended double

entendre. A picture of Agnes, ten years older than Jonathan and all belly and bum came to mind. 'I don't expect he did much pumping. She's not in the least bit his type.'

Carrie was not laughing. Coming back on track, Janet asked, 'So . . . what's the problem?'

'She fell for the charm and told him all about Maxine's blind date . . . to the last detail,' Carrie explained.

'Good!' Janet grinned cheerfully. She put the cover back on the lipstick and dropped it into her over-sized bag. 'Won't hurt him to find out what his cheating cost him. Nor will it hurt him to find out he's been replaced.'

'True . . . but the silly tart told him the name of the hotel,' Carrie replied, her cockney accent becoming more pronounced as it always did when she was riled. 'He'll be making nuisance telephone calls again, and spoiling her holiday.'

'Not him,' said Janet. 'It would cost too much . . . he's far too mean to call Hong Kong.'

Janet returned her gaze to the small cheap mirror Carrie kept on the wall of her partitioned office, and ran her fingers through her dark unruly hair. It had a mind of its own and sprang straight back into its former tangle of curls. Exasperated, she sighed and turned away. 'He might use the office phone though,' she conceded. 'That's more his style.'

About to close down her computer, Carrie paused. 'I'd better warn her,' she said, and quickly rattled off an email to Maxine at the Excelsior Hotel.

★   ★   ★

All flights to Hong Kong were fully booked. Even as an employee of British Airways, there was nothing Jonathan could do to pull strings. Luck, however, was on his side. Because of a last minute cancellation he had been allocated a seat at the back of the aircraft, opposite the lavatories and near the clatter of the rear galley. An upgrade was out of the question, he had been told. Take it or leave it.

Of course he had taken it, but with bad grace made worse when he discovered that the bulkhead, being directly behind him, made it impossible for him to recline his seat.

To add insult to injury, the woman on his left declared she never slept on flights, and as if bent on proving her point, had prattled on non-stop through most of the night.

In a foul mood, he blamed Maxine for turning his world up side down. But, dear God, how he missed her. He'd only got himself to blame, he knew that, and in future he'd be more careful not to play around so close to home. In the meantime, he had less than a week to find her, talk her round, and be back in his office . . . and Maxine's flat.

A date in a local pub and a mountain of flattery had worked wonders on the switchboard operator. The Excelsior Hotel was where the woman had said Maxine was staying. He remembered the Excelsior from a company familiarisation trip he had made to Hong Kong the previous year. It was the hotel that so many of the airlines used for their crews — a good location for shopping and only a short walk from the bright lights of Wanchai with it's hundreds of nightclubs and raunchy bars. His spirits lifted. Yes, a few days in the Excelsior would suit him fine.

They had been making their descent into Hong Kong for some time. Soon he would be plying Maxine with apologies, soft words and promises. Soon he'd get her to cut the playacting and admit she was pleased to see him. Then with his ring back on her finger, all would be as it had been before.

★   ★   ★

Sorry to inform you that we have no guest by the name of Maxine Lowry registered at our hotel read the cryptic email on Carrie's monitor.

'That's nonsense,' muttered Carrie, and wondered briefly if she had made a mistake with the email address. She checked and found she hadn't. Taking a copy of the email with her, she went in search of Janet.

'Bloody hell!' said Janet who had just recognised a name in an important document that had not been meant for her eyes. She catapulted to her feet and was just swivelling her hips out from behind her desk when Carrie appeared in the doorway.

The reaction was quite out of character with the usually calm and placid nature. But then, Janet had just made an astounding discovery.

'I was on my way to see you,' she began, lowering her voice and casting cautious glances around her.

'Me first,' cut in Carrie, rustling the facsimile under her nose.

As Janet read, her excitement turned to agitation. 'But, she must be at the Excelsior Hotel,' she wailed. 'It was specified in the prize, she told us so.'

'Maybe the hotel's made a mistake,' suggested Carrie.

Janet frowned worriedly. 'This does present a bit of a problem,' she said, passing the email back to Carrie. 'I've just discovered something about Adam Warwick, something she really ought to know about. But how do I get the information to her if she's not at the Excelsior?'

8

Caught in a human tidal wave, Maxine moved as if without will of her own along the congested pavement. It was as well that she was targeting neither the department store nor the several designer shops she was forced to bypass, as it would have taken an enormous effort to extricate herself from this moving tangle of bodies and limbs. To step off the pavement was almost certain to prove fatal, for it seemed to her, that everyone and everything in Central District moved with the purpose of a life-saving mission. Clutching her bag to her, she gave up the struggle for independence and moved with the crowd until she was caught in a cross current that swept her into a lane that proved to be a shopper's paradise. Here, though equally as densely populated, the pace was quite leisurely.

More by chance than good management, Maxine had rediscovered those same bustling lanes she and Adam had passed through the night before. And here, displayed on carts, on tiered stalls and in hole-in-the-wall shops were a vast variety of retail goods to delight the soul of the most severely afflicted shopaholic.

Maxine did not have to look too hard to find the designer copies her travel-wise work colleagues had told her about. They were displayed quite shamelessly for the whole world to see. Within minutes, she recognised an authentic looking copy of a watch she had recently admired in a full-page advertisement of a glossy magazine. She picked it up and turned it between her fingers. This really did look like the real thing. There was even a serial number on the back to add to the appearance of authenticity. Maxine was more than a little tempted to buy it. Its interior would be vastly inferior to the real thing and would probably fall apart before the month was out, she warned herself, yet even so . . . it was handsome. She sighed, and began to return it to the stand.

The vendor panicked. Business this morning had been slower than usual and he'd no wish to lose a lucrative customer. Perhaps he had misjudged this *Gwai'por* — *foreign devil lady*. Maybe she was not one of the hundreds of naïve tourists that flocked everyday to his stand; maybe she was a Hong Kong resident who knew the score too well. Hastily, he took a chunk off the price.

Maxine had thought the price already more

than reasonable. The accent must have confused her; she had misunderstood. She put the watch down and began to turn away. In a clearer voice, the price came down again. It was now only half the original asking price. This time she knew, she had not been mistaken. How could she possibly resist?

Her next purchase was a bag. But at the ridiculously low price she paid for it, it was clearly not the designer product its label claimed it to be . . . neither were the two designer tee shirts, bought for her brother, any more the genuine articles.

After she had purchased a whole variety of casuals, she moved out of the lane to a row of small exclusive boutiques where she bought an expensive burgundy crepe dress, a cream silk evening suit, a pair of evening trousers and a couple of little mix-and-match tops. Now she had clothes suitable for all occasions and could hold her head up in any company.

Blissfully happy with her purchases and still with plenty of time left to inspect and admire the contents of her carrier bags, Maxine fought her way back to the hotel.

By the time Adam returned to the suite, she had freshened up, and from the newly-acquired additions to her wardrobe had selected to wear to Stanley Market a short cotton sundress with shoestring straps.

Again, there was that look of interest in his eyes, and yet, his manner remained as coolly aloof as on previous occasions.

'Give me a few minutes to change,' he said, and headed for his room.

While he was gone, Maxine helped herself to an iced drink from the fridge and went to sit in an armchair. Her eyes focussed on his closed door while her thoughts slipped back to the morning. By the time she had entered the lounge, although very early, Adam had been on his way out. From his smart appearance and from the briefcase he carried, she assumed that, just like the previous morning, he was on his way to work. Where his office was, she still had no idea. She had thought she knew all there was to know about her company's overseas dealings, but this was a mystery. She hadn't even known Comp-Dynamics had offices in Hong Kong. Clients yes . . . but not offices.

Her thoughts now turned, as they too often did, to Adam's beautiful girlfriend, and she found herself wondering how intimate was their relationship, and how serious were his feelings for her.

She wondered if, during those hours of absence, he made time to meet with her. Perhaps they breakfasted together. Yesterday, he had given her flowers, many of them red roses. Almost certainly they had lunched together, and probably they had spent the entire afternoon in each other's company. Why had he not mentioned it . . . why did he never mention her?

Although Maxine dearly wanted to ask a whole stream of questions, she knew pride would prevent her from doing so.

She shook her head over the strangeness of the situation. He has a girlfriend who he obviously adores, and yet, here he is sharing a hotel suite with someone who interests him hardly at all. Why is that? Maxine asked herself. It makes no sense.

Obviously the girl was the commitment he had referred to on the night of the ball . . . or was she? Maybe there was a girlfriend in England . . . a girl in every port. Well, why not? He was attractive enough, and if he could share himself between two, why not between three or four?

⋆ ⋆ ⋆

A red convertible, classy and new, was waiting for them at the main entrance of the hotel. Maxine immediately recognised it from the day before. So he *had* been with his girlfriend . . . had probably spent the morning with her. How else would he have acquired car and keys? And what excuse had he given for wanting them?

With much skill, Adam manoeuvred through the dense, fast-moving traffic. They spoke little until they were clear of the city, and then he described the geography of the island and the route that lay before them.

'Stanley's on the south side,' he told her. 'It's a quaint old fishing village . . . or was, before it grew. Nice place to live if you don't mind the commuting. Unspoiled hills and beaches.' He negotiated a sharp bend.

'It's got an interesting history,' he continued. 'It was once home to a famous pirate called Chang Po Chai. The bell that was used to warn of approaching danger is still there.'

She turned inquiring eyes up to his. The name Stanley Market was listed in the itinerary, but no information had been given.

'It sounds as if you're familiar with Stanley . . . like you've been there before?' Maxine said.

He had. In his teens he had shopped there many times with his friends for designer jeans and tee shirts.

However, 'It's all in the guide book,' was, however, all he offered.

Seeing a break in the traffic, he put his foot down hard on the accelerator and skilfully overtook an indolent driver. 'I thought we'd take the scenic route and make a couple of interesting stops on the way.' He glanced at the dashboard clock. 'We should make Stanley in time for lunch,' he said, 'and after, you can spend the afternoon in the market.'

Interesting, thought Maxine. He gets his information out of a guidebook and yet he can confidently find his way to the other side of the island without the aid of a map.

As they passed through the green hills of Pokfulam, they came across a large funeral cortege of decorated cars and lorries, and until it turned off the road, they followed in its wake behind a deafening cacophony of drums, gongs and any other instrument capable of making, what seemed to Maxine, an unholy racket. The coffin was so big it reminded her of an Egyptian sarcophagus. The mourners were not in black, she noticed, but wore rough cloth of stark white and the vehicles were extravagantly decorated with artificial flowers.

'The noise is to ward off evil spirits,' Adam shouted above the din. 'And, when they get to the graveside, a whole stack of artificial paper money will be burnt for the benefit of the departing spirit . . . for bribing obstructing ghosts and buying directions to the underworld.' Encouraged by her interest, he continued, 'The day

138

before a funeral, an assortment of large paper models are burnt: cars, boats, horses, blocks of apartments ... anything the deceased enjoyed in this life that will benefit him in the next and give him lots of face.' He glanced at her and grinned. 'Ghosts may or may not benefit from such a lavish send-off, but for sure the paper craftsmen do a thriving trade.'

She listened entranced, while he told her about the annual Ching Ming Festival, when the living honour the dead at the hillside burial grounds.

'They bring food offerings to the hungry ghosts and when they've washed their tombs and cleaned their bones, they sit down to a candle-lit feast with their ancestors.'

She shot a startled look at him. 'What do you mean *cleaned their bones?*'

'Just that,' he said. 'They remove and clean the bones of their ancestors.'

She shuddered. 'That sounds so macabre.'

'Not to them it's not,' he replied. 'To them it's a time for happy communion, a time for celebration.'

'And then they have a feast?' she asked incredulously. Her stomach was doing funny things.

'A pity to let all that good food go to waste,' he laughed.

They passed the sprawling hillside cemetery where headstones bore photographs of the deceased and were inscribed with red or gold calligraphy. Many were decorated with ribbons and rosettes and everywhere joss sticks were impaled in containers of sand.

'That's where they filmed Han Su Yen's *A Many Splendoured Thing*,' Adam said. 'And over there,' he drew her attention to the other side of the road where a part of a building was just visible between the trees, 'that's the hospital.'

'I read the book,' Maxine told him, remembering the bittersweet romance. 'It made me cry,' she admitted sheepishly.

They followed the coast road to the populated pleasure beaches of Deepwater Bay and on to Repulse Bay.

'Such English sounding names,' Maxine commented, knowing they were a legacy of British colonialism. She looked longingly at the sand, the sun worshippers and the glistening sea, and wished she had brought a bikini.

'There are less congested beaches . . . and more secluded,' he offered, reading her mind.

They passed a huge statue of an oriental goddess sitting cross-legged on a lotus flower and facing out towards the open sea.

'Tin Hau, the Queen of Heaven,' he told

her, 'and the protector of the fisher folk, and these days, of swimmers too.'

In Aberdeen, they turned off the main road, passed the open-air food markets teeming with life and continued on down to the busy waterfront. The humid air was heavy with the smell of salt water and fish and appetising aromas coming from the many popular cooked-food stalls.

Leaving the confines of the car, they crossed the pavement to stand at the water's edge and lean against the sun-warmed tubular metal rail. For a moment they stood in companionable silence absorbing sights and sounds of the hundreds of sampans and junks that made up the vast floating city. Among these vessels, and the centre of attraction, were two massive four-storey floating restaurants.

Maxine studied the golden lettering, the garish colours of the carved woodwork and the ersatz pagoda roofs. After a moment of silent wonder, she summed up these floating giants. 'Huge, gaudy and fascinating,' she murmured. 'It reminds me of the old Mississippi riverboat ... only decorated Oriental style.' A moment later, she asked, 'Which one featured in the James Bond movie?'

He satisfied her curiosity.

A fishing vessel slipped its mooring and headed along the watery highway towards the open sea. While his parents went about their business, a small child played contentedly on its grimy deck. A mongrel dog stood in its prow like a figurehead; its ears erect, its nose pointing into the breeze.

'Whole families and sometimes even live stock live out their lives on these little vessels,' Adam told her following the direction of her gaze.

'I'd be afraid to take my eyes off that child, even for a second, in case he fell overboard,' Maxine said, in a worried voice.

'There'll be a short securing line tied to one of his ankles,' Adam reassured, in a matter-of-fact voice.

Maxine looked shocked.

'A time proven method . . . essential in choppy weather,' he said, laughing at her disapproval. 'I don't see anyone complaining,' he added, 'least of all the child.'

He was right, of course. The child looked blissfully happy.

While they spoke, a sampan, propelled forward by a solitary oar, came along side.

An old lady in cotton tunic and trousers and the woven cane hat of the Tanka water-people, turned a smiling weather-beaten face up to them and called, 'Missy,

Master, you wan' sampan?' A gold tooth glistened in the sunlight. 'Not muchy money . . . I take you floatin' restaurant.'

Adam looked questioningly at Maxine, but she shook her head.

He declined in Cantonese.

The woman persisted, but eventually flashed her toothy smile and moved on.

Beyond the mouth of this sheltered haven, yachts in full sail with their brightly coloured spinnakers billowing, skimmed the glistening waters of the South China Sea.

Adam thought longingly of his own yacht, moored at the marina. He had taught Eleanor to sail and it was a passion they now shared, when time allowed. Seeing the eager interest on Maxine's face, he was about to ask her if she knew how to crew, but quickly changed his mind. He would have to take her to the marina . . . introduce her to his friends, and under the circumstances, he wasn't sure it was wise to let her into his private life. And so, he let the moment pass.

Returning to the car, they drove on to Stanley Village where trusting to the sea breeze to keep them cool, they chose an outdoor table at one of the little waterfront restaurants.

We could be in Europe; Maxine mused to herself, taking in the mix of English-styled

143

pubs and continental bistros, the wrought-iron tables and chairs and the predominantly Western clientele. On a board, under *Specialities of the Day* were the words — *fish and chips*. She pictured them wrapped in newspaper, laughed to herself, and returned her attention to the more sophisticated menu.

They took their time over a light lunch of chilli prawns and ice-cold Tsingtao beer, neither in a hurry to go anywhere.

'Such a contrast to Aberdeen,' Maxine commented, gazing out at the sleepy bay, empty of all but a few small yachts. She brushed an errant strand of hair back out of her eyes. After a moment's reflection, she added with nostalgia, 'I grew up near the sea. I miss it . . . the bays . . . the estuaries . . . the fishing villages . . . '

'The tourists . . . ' Adam finished for her.

Her face lit up with amusement. 'True,' she laughed, and in a broad West Country accent, replied, 'But mind . . . we d' call 'em *Grockles* down our way. And very welcome they be too, since trade do thrive on 'em.'

'Spoken like a native,' Adam grinned.

Maxine's thoughts turned to the lush fertile acres owned by her parents between the sea to the south and the moors to the north and she felt the familiar stirrings of conscience that had been bothering her of late. Her mood changed. She had not, in recent months, managed the journey as often as she would have liked.

After a moment's quiet reflection, Adam said, 'Berkshire to Devon . . . it's a long way?'

'I get home as often as I can,' she said a little on the defensive.

Although far too well-mannered to be anything other than hospitable, neither her parents, nor her easy-going brother had warmed to Jonathan. They had recognised his shortcomings and incompatibility with Maxine long before she had.

Jonathan had made no secret of the fact that he did not like the country, and that he went for her sake and under duress. Soon he was making excuses for staying home. His decision, and yet, her visits to Devon without him had resulted in feelings of guilt and unspoken recriminations. Gradually, putting Jonathan first, she had allowed her visits home to become fewer and had substituted missed ones with extra telephone calls. How could she have allowed herself to be pushed into making those kinds of choices? Later, she now promised herself, she would make it up to her family for those months of neglect.

Just before leaving England, she had called her parents. They had been almost as excited as she over the lucky prize draw and although they had said little concerning Jonathan, she could sense their relief over the break-up.

Silence infringed upon her consciousness making her aware that neither she nor Adam had spoken for a while. How long had he been watching her she wondered?

'Do I detect a touch of homesickness?' he gently teased.

She thought of the amazing good fortune that had come to her so unexpectedly through a tiny scrap of red paper. She thought of the flight that had brought her half way round the world, the luxury hotel, the temple tour and the reawakened joys of shopping without guilt. And then she thought of the heightened emotions this man aroused in her, and she smiled, a secretive little smile. Where else would she rather be than here with him?

'No, I'm not homesick . . . well, not at the moment,' she replied. She tore her focus from Adam and settled it again on the yachts manoeuvring in the bay. 'But I have to admit, I do miss the sailing,' she said, in an attempt to lighten the mood. 'I sail . . . ' she hesitated, then corrected herself, ' . . . I *used* to sail at every opportunity.' Her thoughts lingered for a moment on those happy, carefree weekends of racing in Torbay followed by clubhouse camaraderie. Yet another hobby neglected out of love and consideration for Jonathan's likes and dislikes.

The knowledge that Maxine sailed was of enormous interest to Adam. He had not missed the nostalgia in her voice and he wondered what had put a stop to a sport she had so obviously enjoyed. He wanted to ask a whole variety of questions and, for a moment, was again tempted to invite her to the marina and onto his boat where he could put her skills to the test. But again common sense prevailed and he pushed the thought away.

Don't start something you can't finish, he warned himself. Don't complicate your life . . . or hers.

⋆   ⋆   ⋆

So that Maxine would know her way to the factory-outlet shops and stalls, Adam had deliberately walked her through the market to the waterfront. It had not been his intention to accompany her on a shopping expedition. He had brought Eleanor to Stanley Market so many times that, for him, it was no longer a novelty.

He watched Maxine until she was out of sight and then, settling back with another beer, he returned his thoughts to Eleanor, his beautiful, wilful Eleanor in whose eyes he could do no wrong.

And what did she get up to when he was away, he wondered? She had become restless of late, showing signs of discontent.

Business often took him out of town, but his dealings with Comp-Dynamics had taken him away more often than usual, and for longer spells. She had begged to accompany him on his last trip, but negotiations for a successful merger required his full attention and a clear head, and so he had put her off.

'When I close the deal, I'll take you to London. We'll celebrate . . . do the restaurants, clubs, theatres . . . what ever you want,' he had promised her.

Only slightly mollified, she had accepted his ruling, as she always did.

Eleanor . . . dear, trusting Eleanor. Just as he had been her salvation in a crumbling world, so she had been his.

He remembered the pain that came with the realisation that his parents no longer lived together. Their marriage, he learned, had for years been no marriage at all but had been in the process of falling apart even before his mother had taken him, at the age of eight, to an expensive preparatory school in England. School holidays had found him either in Hong Kong with his workaholic father or in the family home in England with his mother.

His parents were seldom together and when they were, their attitude towards each other could best be described as 'politely tolerant'. He remembered their many plausible reasons for living apart, and had actually thought that he was one of those reasons: an opportunity for him to be with one of his parents during school exeats and half terms when time did not allow for the long journey to Hong Kong. He had felt both guilt and gratitude over the sacrifices he thought they were making for him.

The servants had known better, of course, as servants always do. They knew the cause of the marital rift, and they had also understood that they were not to gossip in Adam's hearing. Consequently, it was years before he became aware of the skeleton in the family closet.

9

'Check again,' Jonathan ordered, glaring at the hotel receptionist who was doing her best to hide her irritation. There were other guests waiting to be booked into rooms and this arrogant man who would not take no for an answer was keeping her from getting on with her job.

'I've checked thoroughly, sir. No one by that name has booked into this hotel.' Before he could ask again, she quickly added, 'Not at any time during the past week.'

Jonathan finally had to accept that Maxine had not booked into the Excelsior Hotel. That stupid woman Agnes had given him the wrong information. Someone at Comp-Dynamics was sure to know where she was. He could call in the morning but company policy would, he knew, prevent disclosure of Maxine's whereabouts. Instead, there would be the offer to pass on a message. He knew Maxine too well to forewarn her of his arrival. Feeling the way she did about him, she would not return his call. But somehow, he promised himself, he would find her, even if he had to phone every hotel in Hong Kong.

She had to be booked into one of them, but tomorrow would be soon enough to start. Right now, he was too exhausted; it had been a long and thoroughly uncomfortable flight and he had missed a whole night's sleep.

He smiled to himself. A few hours should just about set him up and then he would hit the high spots, or better still the low spots, and soak up some of that twenty-four hour entertainment he remembered so well. He wondered if Rosie Wai was still *Mama San* of the Full Lips Bar and whether, this time round, he would find her girls . . . and one in particular, quite so appealing. He doubted it. In their game, it didn't take long for the bloom to wilt.

Jonathan was aware that October was the height of the tourist season. Finding accommodation would not be easy. He had hoped to be able to talk his way back into Maxine's favour, and into sharing her room. He knew better than to expect her to share her bed — it was too soon for that, but surely, after all they had been to each other, she would not have denied him a blanket and some floor space. That she was not booked into the Excelsior presented a bit of a problem, but only a temporary one. When he caught up with her, one foot in the door was all he needed . . . the rest would soon follow.

The Excelsior receptionist met his request for a room with doubtful looks. Nevertheless, she returned her attention to the computer screen. There followed further rapid tapping of the keyboard and a brief over-the-shoulder consultation in Cantonese. A colleague joined her at the screen and more Cantonese followed.

'We've had a cancellation, Sir . . . one night only,' the receptionist finally informed him.

★   ★   ★

It was early evening and just growing dark when Ah Fong called to collect Eleanor from one of the antique shops on Hollywood Road owned by the prosperous Choi family. Patrick, the youngest of the three sons, was Eleanor's closest friend and had been with her through teens and University. He was taller than most of their Chinese friends and more broadly built, and behind the wire-rimmed spectacles, he was good-looking. He was a man quietly confident of his own worth.

Eleanor and Patrick often rendezvoused in one of the shops after work before going on to meet friends. This evening, however, Eleanor had not wanted to go out on the town. In the hope of finding Adam at home in

Shek-O, she had arranged with Ah Fong for an early collection.

Patrick kept his disappointment to himself. He was in love with Eleanor. He wanted to be with her every minute of every day. He wanted more than just friendship; he wanted her for life. His family would not object to him marrying a Eurasian girl: not this particular one anyway. She was beautiful, intelligent and more importantly, she was connected to a family as wealthy and as well established in Hong Kong society as his own. Eleanor, however, had no idea how deep his feelings were for her and had, so far, given no indication that she wanted anything from him beyond friendship.

Quelling the temptation to turn his lips to hers, he accepted the sisterly kiss she planted on his cheek, before she hurried out of the door.

When Eleanor arrived home, she was disappointed to find that Adam was not there. Instead, in the drawing room, dusting a precious and delicate collection of jade ornaments was the wife of Ah Fong.

'Master Adam borrowed your car this afternoon,' Fong Quan told her in Cantonese.

With loving care, the amah replaced a graceful figurine before glancing up at her young mistress. 'He said he would return it later, but couldn't say exactly what time. If you want to go out somewhere, Ah Fong will take you.'

Fong Quan returned her critical gaze to her housework. A picture, hanging too straight, caught her attention. Carefully, she dusted the unseen devils off the top of the frame, and then gave the picture a slight tilt so that new arrivals would slide off the end.

'Did he say where he was going?' Eleanor asked, making no effort to hide her disappointment. She was full of insecurities and begrudged every moment she and Adam spent apart.

'No. He didn't say,' the amah replied, her mind more on her housework than on her unhappy young mistress. Moving on to the next picture, she gave it the same treatment. Then, satisfied with a job well done, the amah stuffed the duster into a pocket and disappeared in the direction of the kitchen.

Eleanor scowled at the tilted pictures. 'Superstitious nonsense,' she muttered in English. She would have returned them to their former horizontal position, but the Chinese in her intervened.

It was all she could do to keep from stamping her foot: not over the pictures and their mischief making devils, but over her frustration with Adam and over the loss of an evening out with Patrick.

Where was Adam this time, why hadn't he phoned her to say he was taking her car and why hadn't he told her he would be out tonight?

She reminded herself that she had conducted a lot of business over her office telephone that day, including a couple of hour-long interviews for articles going into the next issue of Sing Tao Weekender, the magazine for which she was a reporter. Maybe he had tried to get through to her, and being unsuccessful, had finally given up. Yes, that was why he hadn't been in touch.

She reached for the phone and dialled his mobile number. When the recorded voice invited her to leave a message, she slammed the phone back on its cradle.

★　★　★

Adam returned Eleanor's car to Shek-O soon after midnight. The house was in darkness. He considered waking Ah Fong for a ride back to town, but decided instead to stay the night and go directly to the office the following morning. Ah Fong was not so young any more. He needed his sleep.

Adam smiled tiredly. He too could do with a good night's sleep. To create free time for

Maxine, he'd been keeping some very odd office hours. Soon his staff would be asking questions; by now they must be wondering.

Leaving the car in the garage, he walked slowly, thoughtfully up the drive. For once, he was oblivious to the shadows of the night, to the chorus of cicadas and the dark tropical foliage. He was thinking of the girl he had taken to Stanley Market, on to supper, and a short while ago, deposited at the marble entrance of the Mandarin Oriental Hotel.

Would Maxine be aware of his overnight absence? Would she be waiting up for his return? Probably not, he thought, and smiled at his wishful thinking. By now she would be asleep in her room, the door tightly shut against him and the world. She would awake late, and if she gave him a thought, would assume he had already left for the office.

The smile faded when he thought that soon, with or without his help, Maxine was going to find out about the merger and his lofty connection to her company. He wondered how she would react. He had not lied in answer to her few questions. No, she could not accuse him of that. But he was, he knew, guilty of being economical with the facts.

Some secrets, he could justify. But how could he justify his sharing a holiday . . . and a hotel suite, with an employee who hadn't the faintest idea that he was the new owner of the company she worked for?

Although not yet announced, the merger had become official at noon that day. He was free to tell her all and was aware that he should have done so over dinner. He had intended to, but somehow the moment had never seemed quite right because he knew that no matter what he said or how carefully he chose his words, she was going to be outraged that he hadn't told her sooner. She was going to be further outraged when she realised the awkward situation he had helped place her in.

Soon, everyone at Comp-Dynamics would be aware of the name Adam Warwick. It would only take one person to remember he had been the other lucky winner at the ball, and the grapevine would do the rest. Speculation would be rife and the gossips would have a field day.

He raked his fingers through his dark hair. A scowl creased his forehead. 'Hell,' he muttered irritably. 'Whatever possessed me to get involved with an employee? What a way to start a new business venture.'

And how would Maxine handle the inevitable questioning and ribbing? Would she laugh the whole thing off ... or would embarrassment compel her to resign? Would she want anything more to do with him, or would these few days be all he ever had to remember her by?

Adam stood still in the moonlight, surprised by the direction his thoughts had taken and the impact they were having upon his senses. Had she come to mean so much to him? Had he really become emotionally involved? He didn't know. It was too soon to tell.

He knew only, that from the beginning, Maxine had attracted him like no woman ever had. So strong was the attraction, he had gone against his better judgement and taken advantage of a heaven-sent opportunity to get to know her better. In doing so, he had acted way out of character and broken all his self-imposed rules. Worse, he had used his money, influence and position to manipulate the quality of her holiday, and all without a thought for her feelings or what she might want.

And what *did* Maxine want? He wondered, continuing his stroll towards the house. There was no understanding her. Her mood swings were mercurial: warm and spontaneous one minute, cool the next. No woman had ever baffled him quite like she did. Maybe that was half the attraction, never quite knowing where he stood with her. He wondered if she was aware that she was effortlessly turning his world upside down.

A smile came to play at the corners of his sensuous mouth. The attraction was mutual, he felt almost sure. There had been unguarded moments when her eyes had revealed her thoughts . . . and they weren't always pure. Those were the moments when he had almost reached out for what he wanted . . . almost, but not quite. Intimacy, he knew, would only add to their problems.

His thoughts moved on to the relationship Maxine had recently terminated. Was it permanently over, or would she return to her ex-fiancé? So far, she had said not one word, good or bad, about him, nor had she shown any obvious signs of unhappiness over her loss. Did she prefer to do her crying in secret?

Adam remembered again, the sparkle in her clear blue eyes and the invitation they sometimes put out to him before the veil dropped. He smiled. She did not look like a girl who cried herself to sleep at night.

Still smiling, he quietly let himself in through the front door.

*   *   *

Next morning at the breakfast table, Eleanor hardly said a word to Adam. Correctly assuming Ah Fong would be driving them both into town; she saved her questions for the journey.

'Who is she, Adam?' she asked the moment they gained the main road.

Adam did not reply immediately. He had his briefcase open on his lap and was scanning a list of reminders and appointments. Eventually, closing the lid, he turned his attention to Eleanor.

'*She?*' he teased. 'Why *she?*' When Eleanor refused to reply, he said, 'A work colleague, sweetheart, and I'm looking after her while she's in Hong Kong.' After a moment he added, 'All part of a day's work . . . '

'Is she young and beautiful?' Eleanor asked, her eyes searching his for information.

'An old crow,' he laughed, and after a short pause, asked lightly, 'Happy now?'

Eleanor was slightly mollified. 'Will I see you tonight?' she wanted to know.

Adam thought about that. He had already committed himself to an evening with Maxine. 'No. Sorry. Duty calls. Will tomorrow do?' he asked.

Her face dropped. 'Friday night . . . Oh Adam, I've made arrangements to go clubbing with friends.' Eagerly, she added, 'I can cancel.'

'Which clubs and which friends?' he asked, keeping his voice light.

'Nowhere and with no one you wouldn't approve of,' she replied quickly.

He regarded her in silence for a moment, and then said, 'Have fun.'

* * *

Soon after breakfast, Maxine crossed the walkover leading from the hotel into Princes Building and there, in the arcade, spent a leisurely couple of hours wandering around the shops. Aware that they would pack flat against the bottom of her case, she bought for friends and family, several exquisite Chinese watercolour paintings on silk. After she had deposited these treasures in her room, Maxine left the hotel and found her way to the harbour waterfront promenade. With the sea breeze gently tangling her hair and the sun on her face, she strolled for a while and then, she stopped to lean against the rail and watch the passenger ferries criss-cross the watery divide.

A smile played across her lips. She felt as if she had recovered from a long, debilitating illness. Shedding Jonathan was rather like shedding an irritating rash — his departure from her life was a blessed relief.

Her thoughts turned next to Adam . . . it seemed they were never far from this handsome enigmatic man. She relived the previous evening when they had dined in a revolving restaurant and looked down on a spectacular carpet of nightlights. If her guess was right, this glistening, sophisticated world was home to him and had been for a long time. He was comfortable with all the things that were to her so unfamiliar — the mixed society, strange customs, languages and dialects.

This was his world and she was to be a part of it for only a very short time. Gazing at him in the half-light, she had found herself wondering how it would be if she were to become a permanent part of his life. But what exactly was his life? What was she wishing herself into? Maxine didn't know. She still only knew about him what he wanted her to know, and that was next to nothing. Why was he so secretive? Was his life so dull that he could find nothing of interest to relate? Somehow, she doubted that. The man with whom she was sharing her holiday was far from dull.

Maxine remembered how, on the journey back to the hotel, she had fantasised over nightcaps in the intimate setting of their suite. She had imagined their natural progression to his bedroom and, with a clarity that had set her nerve-ends tingling with anticipation, had gone on to imagine a night of uninhibited passion.

Disillusionment had followed when, with some mention of returning the car to its owner, Adam had dropped her off at the Mandarin. He had not asked her to wait up for him and neither had he elaborated on where he was going.

Maxine had again lain awake listening for the sounds that would herald his return. Only this time, he had not returned. In the morning, the door to his room was ajar, as he had left it, his room empty, the bed untouched. He had stayed out all night.

Through those long dark hours of waiting, her imagination had run riot, conjuring up intimate scenes of him in the arms of his girlfriend. Maxine had tossed and turned and then, at dawn, she had fallen into an exhausted fitful doze and dreamed of Adam and the beautiful exotic girl . . . a disturbing dream that was reminiscent of their meeting on the hotel steps. The phantoms had gone eagerly into each other's arms. Jealously, Maxine had watched as they exchanged whispered secrets that she was not supposed to hear. Over and over, she had called Adam's name, but he had been oblivious to all but the girl in his arms.

It was only a dream, Maxine consoled herself, but even so, the pain she had brought into wakefulness had stayed with her through most of the morning.

Now, recalling the dream, she sighed and found herself wishing he would take her, Maxine, into his arms and look at her that same way. But of course, he was unlikely to do so. He was not interested in her and had more or less told her so. And had not she also, from the beginning made it abundantly clear that she was not looking for romance? And so she hadn't been, on the night of the ball. But, how was she to know her feelings would change so dramatically and in so short a time?

Maxine turned from the rail and began to retrace her steps.

No good torturing yourself over things beyond your control, she counselled herself firmly. Regrets and wishful thinking won't change a thing. He already has a girlfriend, and one that looks as if she had just stepped off the front cover of a fashion magazine.

They look perfect together, made for each other . . . as if they are soul mates. Her footsteps faltered. '*A dark enigmatic couple . . .* ' she murmured under her breath, ' *. . . whose destinies are irrevocably entwined.*'

Maxine skipped lightly up the hotel steps and into the lobby. Nothing and no one was going to spoil this holiday for her, not unpleasant memories of Jonathan West, nor troubled nights listening for the return of Adam Warwick.

If she was very quick, she could pay a visit to the Roman pool and still be ready in time for her noon date with Adam. He had suggested a ride to the top of the Peak in the funicular tram, and had promised her lunch among the gods and another spectacular panoramic view — this time in the sunlight and under a clear blue sky. And why not keep the date? After all, they weren't doing anything his girlfriend could object to, nothing she couldn't write about on an open postcard.

So focussed was she on her thoughts, that Maxine was unaware of the tawny haired man who followed her from the lobby to the lift, and who, obscured by other guests, sidled into a corner.

When Maxine exited, he followed, keeping a little distance between them, and did not come forward until she had slotted her security card in the door of her suite.

'Maxine,' he said, running his hands

familiarly over her shoulders and assuming the voice and air of long-lost lover.

Maxine jumped as if severely stung, and swinging around, raised startled blue eyes to Jonathan's unwelcome face.

'You!' she gasped, stepping backwards and almost falling into the room. 'What are you doing here?'

He smiled affectionately and ran approving eyes over her sun-kissed face and limbs. 'I can tell you're delighted to see me.'

'Think again,' she snapped. She moved further into the room with the intention of closing the door in his face.

The smile slipped. 'I only want to talk to you Maxine,' Jonathan said, jamming the door with his foot. 'I've come half way round the world to see you ... surely you could spare me a few minutes of your time?'

'No, not even one minute of my time. I didn't ask you to come half way round the world,' she reminded him.

'Please Maxine,' he pleaded.

It was not like Jonathan to plead. She weakened, and loathed herself for doing so.

Her hesitation, though slight, gave him confidence.

'That's not too much to ask, is it?' He paused to look vulnerable and then asked, quietly, 'Can I come in?'

She was warning herself not to fall for it, but still, again, she hesitated. Then, with a shrug and a toss of her long hair, she turned her back on him and walked through the hall and into the lounge. 'Don't think you're staying,' she threw over her shoulder. 'A few minutes are all that you asked for, and a few minutes are all you're getting.'

A smug little smile passed fleetingly across Jonathan's face. Round one to him, he was thinking as he flipped the door closed and followed.

In the middle of the lounge, chin up, expression distinctly hostile, Maxine turned to face him. She saw his interest in the room, saw the admiration and envy. Triumphantly, she watched and heard him murmur, 'Not bad. Not bad at all.'

She crossed her arms and waited for him to speak, aware that he was searching his mind for plausible explanations and apologies. He could have his say, but she was not going to make it easy for him.

His first sentence was a big mistake.

'It wasn't the way it looked, Maxine,' he said.

Maxine's brows shot up. 'Oh, I see. You and Annie were merely discussing the weather. How silly of me not to have realised,' she said with biting sarcasm. 'Of course, I only imagined the grunting, the heavy breathing, the bare flesh and the creaking springs. Well, silly me.'

'No. I didn't mean . . . ' He stopped, and then tried again. 'I mean, I don't . . . I never cared about Annie . . . not the way I care about you.' His tone and the irritable scowl implied that she was making a mountain out of a molehill.

There was a flash of anger in Maxine's over-bright eyes. She was not going to allow him to sweet-talk her round with his special brand of nonsense, not this time.

'Great,' she snapped. 'Now let me be sure I understand this. 'You took my best friend to bed, but that's all right because you didn't like her as much as you like me? Is that supposed to make me feel better . . . make everything all right between us?' Her voice now shook with suppressed rage.

'No, of course not,' he hastily responded, taken aback by the strength of her emotions. He preferred the malleable, all-accepting Maxine he was used to. The good-natured flatmate he had for months been allowed to take for granted. But then, she had never before caught him out big time. He tried again. 'I mean, it wasn't meant to happen . . . it was a mistake. She came to the apartment . . . uninvited, and I . . . ' He searched desperately for the right words, and failing to find them, said unhappily, ' . . . I don't know how it happened.'

'Somehow you managed to get Annie from the front door to the bedroom, and you don't know how it happened?' Maxine asked, now in a deceptively quiet voice.

'I'd had a few too many,' he explained, lamely, ' . . . well you know how these things happen?'

His eyes, she noticed, no longer met hers, and she wondered how often, exactly, did *these things happen?*

'A few too many . . . that's the story of your life,' she accused, wondering how she could have been a slave to Jonathan and his warped way of thinking for so long. 'And no, I don't know how these things happen . . . and I don't want to know.' Jonathan opened his mouth but before he could speak, Maxine interrupted. 'I've heard enough. Your few minutes are up. I think you'd better go.'

With nowhere to go, Jonathan hadn't any choice but to stand his ground and try again. 'God, Maxine, I'm sorry. I wish I hadn't done it . . . what else can I say.'

'Good-bye?' she suggested.

He looked hurt. 'Can't we at least be friends?' he asked, reproachfully.

'Sure, we can be friends,' Maxine said in a

voice that lacked enthusiasm. 'Where are you staying?' she asked, with absolutely no intention of looking him up.

He looked sheepish. 'Well actually, I'm not staying anywhere,' he replied. 'The Excelsior could only give me a room for one night, so I brought my bags over here. They're with the concierge.'

She stared at him through narrowed, disbelieving eyes. 'What are you saying, Jonathan?'

'It's the height of the season . . . it's not easy to find accommodation,' he said defensively.

He avoided looking at the sofa. If he made that suggestion, she'd have him out the door before he could finish the sentence. The suggestion had to come from her.

Slowly . . . feel your way, one step at a time, he cautioned himself.

Maxine felt the onset of nerves begin to gnaw at her stomach. By fair means or foul, he meant to worm his way back into her life. He would not accept that it was over between them, that he was no longer wanted. Well, she wasn't going to be manipulated by him, not ever again. He was not coming back into her life. If he had nowhere to go he could just get on the next plane back to London.

As if reading her thoughts, Jonathan sighed

and asked, 'Can I use your phone to call around the hotels?' He was playing for time and did not mean to try too hard to find a room, not when Maxine and her perfectly luxurious accommodation were right here.

At the mention of calling around the hotels, Maxine brightened. Here was a little ray of hope. It was no hardship for her to allow him the use of a telephone, and if he succeeded in his quest, she would be rid of him. She pushed the telephone directory towards him.

Maxine, suddenly aware of the passing of time, looked at her watch. Soon, she would be meeting Adam in the lobby and she wanted to look her best for him. The sea breeze had blown her hair into a tangle and heightened her colour. It was time to freshen up and time to bring this conversation to a close. Turning her back on Jonathan, she went off to her room. With a bit of luck he'd have the solution to his problem by the time she returned to the lounge.

Half an hour later, Jonathan was still working his way through the list of hotels.

At her approach, he glanced up; his eyes mirrored his appreciation. 'Wow. You look great,' he said with enthusiasm.

There was a time when Maxine would have thrilled to such a compliment, but not any more. Now she knew that Jonathan wanted nothing so much as those things he could not have. He enjoyed the chase. Breaking off their engagement had made her more interesting, more desirable, and the longer she held out the more irresistible he would find her.

Maxine did not acknowledge the compliment. Instead, she asked coolly, 'Found anywhere yet?'

Nettled by her lack of response, he frowned, and replied belligerently, 'No I haven't. And if you hadn't gone off with the first guy to cross your path, it wouldn't be necessary for me to be looking.'

Maxine was stunned by the injustice of his words. He was making it sound as if she was the guilty party. She was about to retaliate, but before she could find her voice, he muttered, 'If you'd given me a chance to explain . . . to put things right between us, it would be you and I sharing all this.' His envious gaze swept the room.

She remained silent. He had understood nothing.

Jonathan mistook that silence as an invitation to continue. 'Bloody hell, Maxine! You here with another man . . . how do you think that makes me feel?' he demanded. 'You're my fiancé.'

'Ex-fiancé,' she corrected sharply. 'And did

you give my feelings a moment's thought when you decided to take my best friend to bed?' she asked, again growing angry.

'So that's what this is all about. Revenge,' he accused. 'Well, you've had your revenge. Now throw him out . . . whoever he is.'

By now, Maxine was almost certain that, somehow, Adam was responsible for getting them moved from the Excelsior Hotel to a suite in the Mandarin. It was not for her to throw him out, even if she wanted to. But she was not going to tell Jonathan that, nor anything else that no longer concerned him.

Just then, Jonathan noticed something he had not noticed earlier. The suite comprised of two adjoining bedrooms. He felt a surge of relief that Maxine was not, after all, playing him at his own game. A complacent smile spread slowly across his face. 'I knew I could trust you darling,' he purred.

Maxine had followed his gaze and knew to what he referred. It took a great deal of self-control to ignore the comment.

'Let's call it quits,' he suggested. He dug his hand deep into his trouser pocket and pulled out the engagement ring. 'Be sensible and put this back on your finger where it belongs.'

Maxine was speechless. He was behaving as if nothing had changed between them

... making light of his betrayal and her reaction. Showing none of the guilt, shame or remorse one might expect from one caught in the act. In his own eyes Jonathan had done no irreparable damage to their relationship. He simply could not accept that he deserved to be dumped.

Maxine gazed scornfully at the offering he held out to her. Slowly, she turned her back on it and began to walk towards the door. 'Help yourself to the telephone,' she said as she left the room, ' . . . and let yourself out when you've finished.'

★　★　★

Jonathan helped himself liberally to the beers in the fridge while he worked his way through a long list of hotels. So far, only a small hotel in the heart of Kowloon could accommodate him; a place referred to by a back-packer he had chatted up in a bar the previous evening, as a 'fleapit from hell — definitely to be avoided'. Unless his luck changed, it looked like this fleapit was to be his lot . . . at least until he could turn Maxine around.

Thoroughly discontented, he sighed at life's unpredictability, and he wondered how she, the woman he had lived with for the past six months and promised to spend the rest of his life with, could be so unforgiving. How could Maxine be sharing this holiday, this suite, with another man, and all because of one little slip-up? Having separate rooms didn't mean she and this Adam Warwick hadn't been in and out of each other's beds. Quite likely the little hypocrite was doing to him precisely what she was blaming him for doing to her.

No woman had ever finished with Jonathan nor fooled around behind his back. Well, not that he knew of. He hadn't taken his eviction from her flat too seriously . . . not at the time, anyway. But her involvement with another man had come as a nasty shock and a bitter blow to his pride. He had panicked, and that panic had now brought him hard on her heels, all the way to Hong Kong.

He had hoped to find Maxine lonely and grieving for him . . . a lost soul in an alien city. He had hoped to be forgiven and welcomed back into open arms. Instead, he had found a woman thriving on independence and positively radiating health and vitality. Apparently, she had regained her zest for life. His eyes narrowed with suspicion as a new possibility came to mind. Could it be that Maxine actually fancied herself in love with this fellow?

Viciously, Jonathan hurled an empty beer

can at a nearby bin. She was his, and he was not returning to England without her.

Another question arose in his mind, demanding an answer. How would he feel if he knew for certain that Maxine was sleeping with this man? Would he still want her back? For a minute, he tossed the question around in his head. The thought of Maxine having sex with another man made his stomach churn. He would ask that question again, at a later date, when his ring was back on her finger. If she had cheated on him, and if he could not live with the knowledge, then this time, he would be the one to do the dumping.

Jonathan was still smouldering with resentment when there was a knock at the door. Fed-up with his own company and the seemingly endless task of phoning hotels, he welcomed the interruption.

Expecting nothing more exciting than Housekeeping, he pulled back the latch and threw the door open wide. The Oriental vision framed in the doorway took his breath away. Her tantalising apparel was a far cry from the sombre uniform he had expected to see.

In an instant, boredom evaporated. Slowly, deliberately, his gaze moved down her fine-boned frame and then back up again. The surly expression was replaced by a smile

. . . boyish and appealing.

He saw the surprise in dark almond eyes and the movement of sleek black hair as she turned for a quick glance at the door number.

'Adam Warwick . . . is this his room?' she asked, in an almost flawless English accent and not in the least put out by the frank, admiring stare.

'I believe so, but I'm afraid he's out,' Jonathan replied.

Eleanor was disappointed. Nightlife in Hong Kong did not really get started until very late. She had made her plans so that there would be time for a drink with Adam before meeting up with Patrick and friends from their university days, Mai and Andy.

'I'm Jonathan West. Will I do?' Jonathan asked, treating her to a hopeful grin.

Eleanor had been instantly drawn to this man with the candid grey eyes and honey tongue. Typical of so many *gwai'los*, his nose was too big, the Chinese in her observed. But in this case the defect was only slight and did no more that add strength and character to features already pleasing.

She returned the smile but ignored the question. 'Do you know when he'll be back?' she asked.

He had no idea when Adam Warwick would be returning, but he was not going to admit it. He wanted this beautiful distraction to stay.

'Soon,' Jonathan replied without hesitation. 'Why don't you come in and wait,' he stood aside to let her pass.

The girl hesitated, but only for a moment. Adam was a good judge of character. If he had allowed this man the use of his suite, then obviously, he could be trusted, she decided.

Jonathan followed her into the middle of the lounge.

'I'm Eleanor,' she introduced herself, turning to face him.

'Well then Eleanor,' he acknowledged, 'why don't you make yourself at home while I get you a drink.'

Jonathan was beginning to enjoy himself. If Adam Warwick could entertain his woman, then he could entertain Adam Warwick's. Fair exchange, he told himself, pleased to have found a way to strike back at the man who had come between him and Maxine. Seeing Maxine go off so willingly, eagerly even, to meet another man, had added insult to injury. Her behaviour had been out of character and there hadn't been a thing he could do about it.

'Do you know where Adam went?' Eleanor asked, breaking into his thoughts.

Jonathan took a beer out of the mini-bar and held it up for her approval. She shook her head and asked for an orange juice.

'He's lunching with Maxine and then I assume they're going sightseeing . . . didn't say where exactly,' he replied.

'*Maxine?*' she asked, latching on to the name and wondering if this Maxine and Adam's *old crow* was one and the same person.

Out of the corner of an eye, Jonathan saw the puzzled scowl that suggested this girl knew little, if anything, about Maxine.

He brought the drinks across the room and set them down on a table beside several already empty cans. Dropping into a chair opposite Eleanor so that he could see her reaction, Jonathan asked, 'You don't know do you?'

'Know what?' she countered, the scowl back again.

He paused for effect, and then slowly, resentfully told her, 'Your Adam Warwick is here with my fiancée.'

She stared at him. 'With your fiancée?' she repeated, understanding the implication and not liking it. 'But she's a business colleague, isn't she? Adam told me about her.'

'Do colleagues share suites?' he asked, bitterness creeping into his voice.

He saw her gaze move fleetingly around the room and settle for a moment on the open door to an adjoining bedroom.

'Maxine and I were supposed to be coming to Hong Kong together,' he continued, 'but at the last minute, we had a little misunderstanding and she broke off our engagement.'

'I'm sorry,' Eleanor said, simply.'

'She accused me of being unfaithful . . . didn't give me a chance to defend myself. The moods and tantrums I can forgive, but her bringing another man to Hong Kong in my place . . . a complete stranger . . . ' he let his words trail off.

'This Maxine . . . she's here with Adam?' Eleanor asked. Then, as if a mystery had just been explained away, she said, 'so that's it . . . that's why . . . ' Suddenly, the reasons for Adam's absences from home had become crystal clear. So, he had booked into this hotel with a woman. He was having an affair with this man's fiancée. No wonder she had seen so little of him. Eleanor was angry. She had been misled.

'She'll come back to me, of course, when she's had her revenge and made me suffer.'

'You mean, this is all about revenge,' Eleanor asked.

'Of course,' he replied. 'Well, it can't be about anything else, can it? She doesn't care

180

about this fellow. How can she? She hardly knows him. She's just leading him on so that she can get at me . . . make me jealous.' The wronged lover fell silent waiting for a show of sympathy.

Eleanor, however, was not feeling in the least bit sympathetic. Silently, she was congratulating him on his lucky escape from the claws of such a scheming, vindictive woman and wondering how a man as worldly-wise as Adam could have allowed himself to be taken in.

'Your Maxine is not a very nice person,' she commented, dryly. After a moment's pause, she asked quite logically, 'If she's sharing this suite with another man, what are you doing here?' Her eyes were bright with curiosity and challenge. 'It doesn't sound as if you've been invited . . . not by Adam anyway.'

'You neither,' he said, quite sure her visit had not been expected.

She did not reply. Instead she persisted, 'Does Adam know about you?'

He doubted it. If he were in Maxine's shoes, he would not own up to a romantic attachment, not if he fancied his chances elsewhere. 'Probably not,' he told her. He drained the beer from the bottom of the can, and after a pause, went on, 'I came over to try to make it up with Maxine . . . before I knew she was here with someone else,' he lied. 'I've been phoning around trying to get into one of the hotels.' He pushed the open telephone directory towards her. 'So far this is the only place that can give me a room.' He ran his finger along the page.

Eleanor leaned forward to look. Horror spread across her delicate features. 'You'd have to be desperate to stay there,' she gasped.

'I am desperate,' he replied.

'Maybe I can help . . . not me personally,' she quickly amended. Beneath the hard exterior Eleanor was soft-hearted, but not so soft-hearted that she would take in a stranger, and particularly not this stranger. Patrick would help out. He'd do anything for her.

'I mean one of my friends might be able to put you up . . . until you get your fiancée back.' She was prepared to do anything to get Adam out of the clutches of this man's fiancée.

★　★　★

By the time Maxine and Adam returned from the Peak, the suite was empty. As a parting gift, Jonathan had left behind half a dozen empty beer cans, an ashtray full of cigarette butts and a couple of crumpled cushions. There was no note to say where he had gone, and for this Maxine breathed a sigh of relief. She did not want to know. Neither did she want to have to explain to Adam Jonathan's visit to their suite, nor for that matter, his presence in Hong Kong.

Dirty ashtrays and empty beer cans were a part of everyday life with Jonathan. An inconvenience she had learned to put up with. Now she turned up her nose in disgust. It did not occur to Maxine to wonder about the glass that held the remains of orange juice, nor did it occur to her to wonder about the second crumpled cushion. But Adam looked thoughtfully at the telltale signs of a cosy tête-à-tête and did not much like the picture they presented. At sometime during the morning, while he was at the office, Maxine had been entertaining a visitor . . . and there was not much doubt in his mind that the visitor had been male.

He made no comment to Maxine who volunteered no explanation.

Housekeeping was sent for, and while all traces of Jonathan's visit were cleared away, Maxine went off to prepare for an evening in one of Adam's favourite nightclubs.

Through the crack in the connecting door, she could see his handsome profile at the workstation. This holiday was so obviously not all fun for Adam. He was juggling work with pleasure and snatching sleep in his girlfriend's bed when he could. Again, she wondered what his position was within the company. Smart and intelligent, and at a guess, very ambitious, he was no ordinary link in the chain, of that, she was now quite sure.

By the time Maxine had showered and returned to the bedroom, all noise coming from the lounge had ceased. He had made his phone calls and sent his e-mails, she assumed, and gone off to his own room.

Maxine turned her attention to her newly-extended wardrobe. When the time came, how was she going to cram all these extras into her case? She would have to add a handgrip to her purchases, she supposed, or somehow accomplish the impossible.

After pulling out several dresses for inspection, all figure-hugging and suitable for the most sophisticated of nightclubs, she settled on a shiny silver grey treasure with shoestring straps. Not a lot of it, she mused happily, admiring the flimsy fabric, but worth every dollar that passed across the counter. She added pearl-drop earrings and pendant and put on a pair of very high heels. Perfume, a touch of lipstick, the finishing touches to her hair, and she was ready to take on the world.

She heard the opening and closing of the fridge door. That was quick. Was he ready so soon or had she been an age? A last look in the mirror and she headed for the lounge.

Adam had been preparing tequilas. Hearing her approach, he turned, and like a lover's caress, she felt his gaze cover her from head to toe. 'God . . . you look gorgeous!' he exclaimed softly.

Maxine flushed with pleasure.

Holding her gaze with his own, he offered her one of the glasses. His eyes did not leave hers as she walked towards him. With not a thought for the other woman in his life, she would have walked straight into his arms . . . if only they, instead of the tequila, had been on offer.

★　★　★

It was a room designed to heighten the senses: dimly lit, smoky and crowded. Live music, sensual and atmospheric, gently pulsated from beyond the dance floor. Adam and Maxine moved between tightly-placed tables to one of the last few still available. A couple of times, Adam paused to introduce her to acquaintances, but he did not accept their invitations to draw up chairs nor did he linger to talk. His attention was all for

Maxine and tonight he meant to keep her to himself.

They had not long been seated in their secluded corner when Maxine's gaze was drawn to a small group of five who were showing signs of vacating the nightclub. Her gaze might have moved on had she not recognised one in the group. That Jonathon should cross her path again so soon, exasperated Maxine beyond endurance. There he was, apparently, life-and-soul of the party, with an arm casually draped around a young girl.

Only this afternoon he had proclaimed his undying love for her, Maxine, and now here he was with someone else. There had been other women, of course. She knew that now . . . probably a long line of others. How could she not have suspected? She marvelled at her naivety.

Maxine made an effort to shrug off the bad feeling invoked by the sight of him. She didn't want to bear grudges. Life was too short. Besides, Jonathan was history. What did she care what he got up too? The girl could have him, and with her blessing.

These thoughts were followed by feelings of foreboding. If he saw her, might he get it into his head to come over and cause trouble?

She shrank back into her seat and behind

the latticed fronds of an exotic pot plant. Only then did she become aware that Adam's attention was fixed on that same table. His focus, however, was not on Jonathan but on the girl at his side. For one of Jonathan's companions, Maxine suddenly realised, was Adam's girlfriend.

With a heavy heart, Maxine watched Adam come slowly to his feet.

'Excuse me,' he said, not taking his eyes off the girl, 'I see someone I want a word with.' Moving with purpose between the tables, he caught up with her before she could follow her friends through the door.

Maxine saw the surprise and pleasure that brightened the lovely features, and when the girl uninhibitedly threw her arms around his neck, Maxine's stomach did a sickening lurch.

After what appeared to be the exchange of a few fond words, the girl's almond eyes came to rest on Maxine. Apparently, she did not like what she saw, for the smile faded and was replaced by a disapproving scowl. The conversation continued, but it seemed to Maxine the tone had changed. A couple of times Adam shook his head in what seemed to be patient denial. It appeared to Maxine that he was explaining her, his date, away to an irate lover.

'He's been caught out,' Maxine told herself, and wondered what excuses he was giving for his two-timing activities.

Waiting just beyond the doorway, Jonathan lingered silently watching and listening, an unpleasant smirk on his face. Suspiciously Maxine wondered what part Jonathan was playing in all this and how he had come to meet this of all girls after only one night in Hong Kong.

From across the room, Jonathan's gaze met hers. He grinned complacently as if to say, 'You see . . . you've been wasting your time. He's already got a girlfriend.' He raised his brow and tilted his head, inviting her to come with him and his new friends.

She remembered the words of the soothsayer: *Dying embers can still start a fire* and wondered if Jonathan, out to cause as much trouble as possible, had somehow managed to engineer this disastrous meeting.

Pointedly, she averted her face and when she looked again, the girl and Jonathan were nowhere to be seen, and neither was Adam. Anxiously, she searched the crowd for his familiar face, but she searched in vain.

That Jonathan had gone with the girl worried her not one jot, but that Adam might also have followed, hurt more than she cared to admit. The evening that had started with so much promise now suddenly lay in ruins.

From the beginning she had known that Adam had other commitments. In a moment of honesty he had told her so, just that one time, and never mentioned it again. Well, it was time to stop being piggy-in-the-middle. Tonight, on her return to the hotel, she would lock the connecting door between her room and the lounge and in future use the corridor entrance to come and go. The raffle prize had entitled her to a room, and a room was what she would have. Her welfare and entertainment would, from now on, be no one's responsibility but her own.

Her thoughts returned to the present. She was in the humiliating position of having been deserted for another woman, left alone in a nightclub where she didn't know a soul, in a city that was not her own. Should she meekly accept defeat and slink off back to the Mandarin, or should she stay on in the club where there were other singletons, and try to make the best of a sorry situation?

A light touch on her arm broke into her thoughts. She looked up.

'Dance?' asked a swarthy stranger.

Maxine made a snap decision, took a deep breath and replied, 'Yes, why not.'

Why shouldn't she stay and why shouldn't she dance? Unlike Adam, she was free and independent. She was on holiday and entitled to have a good time . . . with anyone she liked, if that was what she wanted.

Head high, she followed the man onto the dance floor. Aroused by a multitude of conflicting emotions, the foremost of which was anger; emboldened once more by Tequila, which she knew she should never touch, Maxine began to dance a little more provocatively than she might have done under normal circumstances.

Encouraged, her Latin looking partner responded. The music slowed, he pulled her into his arms, and swaying to the rhythm, began to kiss her neck. Maxine didn't stop him. Who was there to care if she got steamy on the dance floor? Nice to know she still had what it took to put somebody's blood pressure up.

When he tried to kiss her lips, however, she pulled away, laughing and teasing a little to ease the rejection. Persistently, he tried to hold on to her, but her mood had changed. She was no longer interested in him, in dancing, in clubbing; in anything except a quick exit into the night. She wanted to be alone.

From the moment Adam left her side, the evening had been irretrievably spoilt, she realised, and no amount of play-acting could put that early magic back into it.

Murmuring her thanks, Maxine began to move away. She would return to the hotel and to hell with everyone and everything.

Just then, the band struck up a lambada. Her hand was suddenly reclaimed and she was swung back into the overeager arms of her persistent dance partner. As he manoeuvred her back into the circle of strobe lighting, suddenly she saw Adam. Her heart skipped a beat and then began to race too fast. Had she misjudged him? Perhaps he had not left the club after all, or if he had, he had come back for her. The two newly ordered drinks on their table suggested he had been doing battle at the crowded bar.

How long had he been sitting there, she wondered, and had he seen the intimate way she had danced with this stranger? Had he seen the passionate kisses trailed along her neck? What thoughts went on behind those penetrating eyes that missed so little? Jealous ones, she hoped, for she would like to be capable of making Adam Warwick jealous . . . very jealous.

The tempo quickened. Her partner was again holding her close . . . so close their bodies seemed fused into one. She had danced the lambada many times before, but never been subjected to quite so much

191

sensual gyration and so little expertise. She was embarrassed to be under Adam's watchful eye, but short of making a scene there was no way to loosen so firm a grip.

Out of the corner of her eye, she saw Adam come to his feet, and it appeared to her that he moved like a predator, slowly in her direction. At first, she could not make out the expression on his shadowed features but as he came closer, she saw by the flickering lights of the dance floor the purposeful gleam in his dark eyes. She hoped his encounter with his girlfriend had not put him in an ugly mood and that he was not looking for a quarrel. Wondering what he was going to do, knowing that he was going to do something, she held her breath.

'Ah, there you are darling,' he drawled. 'I was wondering where you'd got too.' His long fingers circled her wrist. 'Mind if I have my wife back?' he asked her dancing partner, taking Maxine firmly from his arms.

'Wife?' the man questioned, clearly startled by the unwelcome intrusion. His eyes went quickly to Maxine's left hand. 'She's not wearing a wedding ring,' he challenged, malice seeping into his voice.

'Really?' said Adam, quizzically. He held the hand up for inspection. The mark left by Jonathan's ring was still slightly visible.

'Taken it off again, I see,' he chided the astonished Maxine. 'Can't take my eyes off her for a second,' he confided to the man.

'She didn't say she was married,' the man grumbled.

Adam grimaced sympathetically. 'Never does,' he replied. Turning amused eyes back to Maxine, he continued to admonish, 'And I suppose, sweetheart, you've left all our little darlings at home again, with the *amah*?' He tut-tutted her and gave a long-suffering shake of the head.

The man was now looking at Maxine as if she was a leper. 'You want to keep your wife under better control, he muttered,' and without a backward glance, moved off in search of more acceptable company.

A threatening fit of the giggles rendered Maxine temporarily speechless. Before she could find her voice and ask for an exact headcount of their *little darlings*, Adam had swept her into his arms, and holding her very close, proceeded to lead her into an extremely sensual and expert lambada.

★   ★   ★

Eleanor's friends had gone ahead and were waiting for her and Jonathan on the other side of a busy road.

'He said she was an *old crow*,' Jonathan heard Eleanor mutter crossly to the pavement as they covered the short distance to the controlled crossing.

Jonathan sidestepped to avoid being elbowed by passing pedestrians. It seemed to him that the streets of Hong Kong were as densely populated by night as they were by day. Did no one ever sleep in this city?

'Is that what he called Maxine . . . an old crow?' he asked, grinning broadly. 'A crafty bugger, your Adam Warwick, and under different circumstances he'd be a man after my own heart.' He turned the verbal knife. 'Bet he only called her that to throw you off the scent.'

Eleanor transferred her glare from the pavement to Jonathan. 'You didn't tell me this Maxine of yours was beautiful,' she accused.

'You didn't ask,' he reminded her, still grinning. 'And in any case, it wasn't me who misled you. It was that two-timing boyfriend of yours.'

Eleanor stopped and turned to stare at him. At first, she wore a puzzled frown, and then understanding dawned. Very slowly, as if talking to a half-wit, she said, 'He is not my boyfriend . . . he's my brother.' She saw his disbelief. 'Half brother actually,' Eleanor clarified. Her chin went up proudly. 'We have the same father.'

It was Jonathan's turn to stare. 'But, I thought . . . ' he began.

'You thought wrongly,' she corrected, then warned challengingly, 'And be very careful what you say about my brother.'

The lights turned green. With a toss of her long, sleek hair, she preceded him across the road.

'I don't like the sound of your fiancée,' she said belligerently, 'and the sooner you take her back to England the better.'

Jonathan was in full agreement. 'That's fine by me,' he responded. Catching up, he fell into step with her. 'If you want to get shot of Maxine, I'm just the person to help you do it.'

Eleanor brooded in silence. She was remembering her first impressions of the girl with the vivid blue eyes and mane of tumbling golden curls, and her brother's invitation to meet her. This girl was neither old nor ugly; in fact, she was quite the opposite. She had scolded her brother over his misleading description of his colleague — if indeed she truly was a colleague. Adam had laughed at her rebuke and added nothing new to her knowledge of the situation so that Eleanor was now convinced that her brother was indeed having an affair with another man's fiancée.

Was Adam aware that the woman was merely using him as a pawn in a petty game of revenge? She was sure her brother didn't know and, by not introducing Jonathan West, she had missed an opportunity to tell him. But soon, Eleanor promised herself, she would make sure that he knew as much about his new lover as she did.

It was not in Eleanor's nature to be downcast for long and by the time she joined Patrick, Mai and Andy and with them negotiated a path through the night-time revellers to one of the many side-street lantern-lit *dai pai dong* food stalls, she had almost returned to her ebullient self.

There were three stalls in a row on the pavement, all with fresh produce on display that was meant to entice clientele to the make-shift tables and stools. On the counters were dried fungi, sea food and a variety of colourful vegetables. From overhead beams hung strings of fatty sausages, dried ducks, squids with their tentacles hanging down like ribbons, and all manner of unidentifiable foods, the sight of which stripped Jonathan of his appetite. With all the flair of the Master Chef, cooks were at work over their chopping boards and their woks, from which delicious aromas filled the night air.

From the beginning of the evening, out of

courtesy to Jonathan, all four of his new acquaintances had conversed in English punctuated only occasionally with the odd Cantonese word.

'What will you have?' Patrick asked, regarding Jonathan over the top of his glasses.

Jonathan scanned the stall for something familiar, but the food was as foreign to him as the smells and sounds of Hong Kong. Eyeing the wok with suspicion, he hesitated. Nothing appealed to his fastidious tastes. If the cooked-food stall had not been Patrick's idea, he would have vetoed it in favour of a conventional, sit-down air-conditioned restaurant. But Jonathan would not risk upsetting the man who had earlier offered the hospitality of his apartment . . . and a very spacious and luxurious apartment it was too. He continued to examine the unpalatable display.

'I'll choose for you,' Eleanor offered. Like Patrick, she had seen the look of revulsion that had passed fleetingly across Jonathan's handsome features.

Patrick wondered if he should intervene. Friends since early teens, born in the same year as Eleanor: the year of the Monkey, he knew how her mind worked, and there was definitely mischief in the making. Thoughtfully, he pushed his glasses back up the bridge of his nose and smiled. He was not comfortable with this *gwai'lo*, and it had something to do with the amount of interest and familiarity he was heaping on Eleanor. He decided to let Eleanor have her way.

Leaning forward, Eleanor gave her order and Jonathan's in Cantonese.

'Not too much,' Jonathan said warily. 'I'm not hungry . . . I've already eaten.'

'That must have been hours ago,' she chided gently. 'You must be starving by now.'

While they waited, they discussed which club to go on to next. Mai favoured taking a taxi to Lan Kwai Fong. Because the quadrant covered a much smaller area than Wan Chai, they were more likely to run into friends. Her less sociable boyfriend, Andy, was against the idea. Patrick was happy to go along with whatever would make Eleanor happy. Eleanor was undecided.

Food was eventually passed to them, money changed hands and Jonathan received his portion along with a pair of wooden chopsticks. On a bed of grease proof lined paper lay what appeared to be a couple of gnarled witch's hands. The long, yellow fingers were complete with talons.

Jonathan regarded the grisly offering with distaste.

Four pairs of eyes watched him take a claw

between finger and thumb and raise it for closer inspection.

'Eh . . . what's this?' he inquired of no one in particular.

'What does it look like?' Eleanor asked, sweetly, while the others looked on, amused.

'A chicken foot?' suggested Jonathan.

'That's right,' Eleanor confirmed. 'Delicious. Try it,' she said, nibbling at her own tasty snack.

She and her friends were well aware that *gwai'los* do not eat chicken feet; they dispose of them along with other unwanted parts. The Chinese, on the other hand, waste nothing that is edible.

Jonathan watched for just a moment. 'You can have mine if you like,' he offered to anyone who would take it from him.

Grinning broadly, Andy obliged.

'I'll get you something else,' Patrick offered.

'I'll do it,' Eleanor stepped in again. 'What will it be? You'll like those,' she said, pointing to something unidentifiable that looked as equally unpalatable as her first choice.

Jonathan was not going to be taken in a second time. 'A couple of those,' he replied, pointing to a row of sizzling innocuous chicken breast kebabs.

More Cantonese, money and food were exchanged.

'Much better,' Jonathan said, pulling the succulent pieces of meat off a stick with his teeth. After a moment, he took from his mouth a couple of very small bones that did not in the least resemble any part of a chicken's anatomy. He inspected the tiny perfect miniatures, then, turning suspicious eyes on Patrick, he asked, 'What am I eating?'

'Barbecued frog,' Eleanor chipped in knowledgeably.

Jonathan headed for the nearest bin.

'Don't you like that either?' she giggled. 'Perhaps I could order some sea-slug congee for you,' she offered.

'Sea-slug congee?' queried Patrick in Cantonese, looking with renewed interest at the food-stall. 'Is there such a thing?' he grinned.

A few minutes later, Jonathan returned, minus food but with a can of coke bought at one of the many late night shops. The next port of call was again under discussion. Since Jonathan knew only a few bars and clubs, all unsuitable for these two particular women, he had nothing to contribute. He was willing to go where led.

Leaning against a wall, he waited — and while he waited, he brooded on Maxine. He wished he could believe she was just playing hard to get, but he was no longer so sure. It was beginning to look as if she really did want him out of her life. Worse still, she appeared to have rebounded into the arms of the first good-looking man to cross her path. He had seen the way she looked at Adam Warwick . . . in that special way once reserved for him, Jonathan, in those early days. Her eyes had betrayed her in the nightclub when their gaze had followed the man across the room. And again, they had betrayed her feelings when Eleanor had greeted her brother with such open and tactile affection.

Only now did it occur to Jonathan that Maxine must be unaware of the couple's true relationship to each other. She thought they were lovers. He smiled at the revelation. Good, let her continue to think so and with the collusion of Eleanor, he'd turn her ignorance to his advantage. Maxine might not yet be lost to him.

Rejection and damaged pride worked together to convince Jonathan that, more than ever, he wanted Maxine back. She had loved him once; she would love him again, surely. But, if not . . . if he couldn't have her, then he'd make damned sure Adam Warwick didn't have her either.

In the meantime, he'd bide his time with this Eleanor. She excited him and he enjoyed a challenge. Added to that was the attraction of knowing that messing around with the sister was bound to cause aggravation to the brother.

★ ★ ★

At first, Eleanor had been flattered by Jonathan's interest. That was until she noticed his interests were not confined to her alone but extended to any reasonably good-looking woman that happened to catch his eye. It was as if he had an insatiable need to be noticed, to be found attractive. His attention was not now quite so flattering after all.

Added to this shortcoming was Jonathan's lack of humour . . . or rather his inability to laugh at himself. And then again, there was something not quite right about a man who helped himself so generously to his rival's room, fridge and telephone, or about a man who was fussy to the point of rudeness over what went into his mouth, but not so circumspect over what came out of it.

There was no denying that he was physically very attractive, but there was something not altogether likeable about Jonathan West. But then Eleanor would have found fault with any man who criticised her brother.

Despite Jonathan's fall from grace, she knew she would help him to get his fiancée back. Not for his sake, but for Adam's. The girl did not deserve her brother ... she was nowhere near good enough for him.

The slight movement of a pair of long, hair-fine antennae caught Eleanor's attention. A large mottled-brown cockroach with thick hairy legs had found its way onto Jonathan's shoe. Her eyes sparkled with mischief. Nature, she told herself, could not be offering a more irresistible joke.

Eleanor put her foot in front of Jonathan's and sharply tapped the pavement. In sudden panic, the cockroach scuttled for darkness, as she knew it would, and shot up Jonathan's trouser leg.

'Oh ... I missed,' squealed Eleanor, arranging her beautiful features into a mix of horror and concern. 'There was a big cockroach on your shoe ... I meant to step on it,' she fibbed.

There was mild censure in the tilt of Patrick's head and in the look he cast over his glasses at Eleanor. Now, that's enough, he seemed to be saying.

But Eleanor was set on having fun. A giggle escaped her lips and carried contagiously to Mai.

Jonathan did not need to be told a large

insect had run up his leg. Although he had not known what it was, he could feel it and was clutching at the folds of his trousers trying to halt its upward progress. Frenzied stamping, shaking and jumping on the spot failed to dislodge the intrepid intruder. Against all the odds, the insect found its way, unharmed, down the other trouser leg where it fell out onto the pavement.

For a moment it lay on its back, its legs frantically clawing the night air. Then, righting itself, it made a frenzied zigzag dash for the darkness of a nearby alley. With murder in mind, Jonathan stamped after it.

Having lost both battle and dignity, Jonathan became aware that, attracted by the commotion quite a crowd had gathered to watch and were finding his extraordinary antics highly entertaining.

'Oh my God . . . the look on your face,' gurgled Eleanor, wiping tears from her eyes.

There was nothing Jonathan could do but laugh sheepishly along with his audience, but he felt foolish and inwardly, he seethed.

Eleanor had played one trick too many. Before too much longer he'd find a way to pay her back in full — along with that brother of hers.

★ ★ ★

By the time Maxine and Adam left the dance floor, the passionate intimacy of the lambada had successfully blasted away all their carefully cultivated reserve. The couple had not needed to speak of attraction and desire, their bodies had, in that short space of time, communicated to each other far more than words ever could.

Over their reclusive little table there followed the meeting of minds and fingertips, and the evening passed in a romantic haze of softly spoken words and laughter.

Although Maxine willed him to do so, Adam did not mention his earlier unexpected meeting with the dark-haired beauty. And so, as the candle burned lower, the incident blurred and eventually receded into the background of Maxine's consciousness.

By the time they left the magic of the nightclub, dawn was a promising glow on the horizon and Maxine was convinced that at the end of their taxi ride, in the privacy of their hotel suite, their blossoming relationship would break new ground. But, somewhere between Wanchai and the Mandarin, Adam's mood sobered, and although he held doors open for her to pass through, he no longer reached out for physical contact.

Confused and disappointed, Maxine had to accept that for some reason, maybe because he was still in a relationship, Adam had decided not to take romance into the bedroom.

* * *

In Kowloon, on Signal Hill Meteorological Station, the black warning symbol 'T' had been hoisted.

10

Maxine picked out a string of pearls from among the many ropes. They were of a good size, evenly matched and whiter than the others. She ran their cool smoothness through her fingers, looking and feeling for flaws, knowing there were bound to be some irregularities, but hoping they would be slight. She loved the soft satin glow of pearls and their ability to enhance the tone and texture even of sallow skin, and she loved the versatility that made them wearable with almost anything.

'This one,' she said to Adam, hoping they would not cost the earth. 'I'd like this one.' Then she asked in a whisper, 'But, how do we know they're real?'

When buying pearls from Patrick's shop for Eleanor's eighteenth birthday, Patrick had demonstrated a simple test.

Adam raised the pearls to rub gently against his teeth. 'If they feel slightly gritty, they're genuine,' he said.

'And?' she asked.

'These feel like the real thing,' he replied.

Is there anything this man doesn't know?

Maxine wondered in awe. Without understanding a word, she listened in quiet fascination while Adam haggled with the shrewd-eyed vendor over the price until he was quite sure it was as low as it was likely to go. Even so, Maxine caught her breath when she heard the value put upon the pearls.

'No,' I don't think so, she said regretfully. 'I've already spent enough on myself.'

Adam ran a discerning eye over the other strings and came back to the favoured one in his hand. 'You've got good taste . . . you've picked out the best,' he complimented.

Maxine glanced again at the less expensive ropes, but none could compare. The one she had chosen stood out beyond the rest and she knew she would not now be satisfied with anything less.

'Oh well, I can't have everything, I suppose,' she said, with a whimsical smile. 'Thanks anyway,' she added, and with an apologetic shrug aimed at the vendor to ease his disappointment, began to turn away.

'Let me buy them for you . . . a gift,' Adam offered. The price of a rope of pearls meant nothing to him. And besides, he had a sudden desire to make this girl happy.

Out of the blue, the words of the soothsayer returned to haunt Maxine: *Beware of a gift from a stranger.* Did Adam still qualify as a stranger? Yes, she supposed he did. There was still so very much to know about him.

'Oh no, don't do that,' she replied a little too quickly. 'I mean . . . thanks for the offer, but no thanks. I couldn't possibly . . . '

Adam was about to insist on her acceptance; was even tempted to pun 'no strings attached', but then he saw the worried frown and thought better of it. Secretly, he was pleased with her refusal. He admired her independent spirit and lack of avarice.

Together, they moved on and went deeper into the Jade Market. At every turn there were stalls stocked with beautiful, breath-taking ornaments. There were vases and bowls in colourful cloisonné, aged bronze and fine porcelain. There were fragile figurines intricately carved in coral, amethyst, tur-quoise and blue lapis lazuli streaked with gold. And everywhere there were artefacts in translucent jades, varying in sizes, qualities and colours. This was the precious and versatile stone revered by the Chinese and from which the market took its name.

Maxine's attention was arrested by a set of ornaments: twelve animals intricately carved out of ivory . . . or were they carved out of bone? Maxine didn't know, she couldn't tell the difference. But it was here she stopped to look and for a moment, she was still. A puzzled frown creased her brow. These animals belonged together rather like the pieces of a chess set, but these had nothing to do with chess. She reached for the only mythological animal in the set, the dragon, and turned it slowly, carefully between her fingers and then she reached for the tiger. Her eyes looked for and found a monkey and a rabbit.

'What are these?' she asked Adam, who, also recalling the parting words of the temple soothsayer, had been watching her with interest.

He moved forward to stand at her side. 'They're the animals of the Chinese zodiac,' he explained. 'The years run in cycles of twelve and each year is represented by an animal.'

After a thoughtful moment, she asked, 'And what year were you born in?'

'The year of the tiger,' he replied. And then, remembering the date of birth she had given for her horoscope reading, anticipating her next question, he added, softly, 'And you were born in the year of the dragon.'

Her eyes met with his and for a moment held. And he knew without a doubt that the words of Fu Chu Ming were chasing through her mind, as they were through his own: *The tiger may banish the rabbit and teach the monkey good manners, but it is written he will lay down with the dragon.*

★   ★   ★

Eleanor's gaze passed over the brooch several times before it claimed her full attention. It was not beautiful. It was not even particularly interesting . . . until she took the trouble to read the enamelled calligraphy.

It was nearly ten-thirty. Shops closed late in Hong Kong, especially at the height of the tourist season. She waited impatiently for the last of Patrick's customers to leave the shop, and when the doors had been bolted for the night, she asked if she could handle the object of her interest.

Her request took Patrick by surprise. But after a moment's hesitation, he removed the brooch from the display cabinet and laid it in front of her on the glass-topped counter.

Eleanor picked it up and held it to the light for closer scrutiny. Slowly, a sphinx-like smile spread enigmatically across her face. 'Does it say what I think it says?' she asked, raising inquisitive eyes to Patrick.

'You know it does,' he replied, then added, 'It's genuine you know . . . over a hundred years old . . . from Shanghai. It came in with

211

the last shipment.'

'I must have it,' said Eleanor. 'You've got to sell it to me.'

He regarded the abomination with disapproval. 'Now what would you want with a thing like this?' he asked, reaching out a hand to take it from her.

Possessively, she withheld the brooch from him. 'Its not for me silly,' she laughed, 'It's for someone . . . ' she hesitated, searching for the right words, ' . . . for someone who deserves it.'

His eyebrows arched, 'Then I pity her,' he said.

'Oh please Patrick,' she wheedled, turning dark imploring eyes on him that now positively danced with mischief. 'You have absolutely got to sell it to me.'

★　★　★

The next morning, soon after daybreak, on Signal Hill, the black warning symbol **T** was inverted.

11

With the setting of a blood-red sun, Maxine and Adam had found their way to a row of traditional seafood restaurants perched on bamboo stilts over the water's edge. Lanterns cast a thousand colourful, dancing lights over them and over the few remaining customers who had not caught the earlier ferry back to Hong Kong Island. From all around came the sounds of water lapping against wood and the whisperings of a fresh sea breeze that blew in from the South China Sea.

They had spent the morning walking in the lush, green hills of Lantau Island. Lunchtime had seen them in the austere dining-hall of a monastery, spooning bland vegetarian soup prepared for visitors by resident monks. After lunch, they had followed an endless stream of devotees and chattering tourists up innumerable steps to a plateau high on a hill top on which sat a giant, awe-inspiring bronze Buddha. Later, in the afternoon, when the sun had lost its power to burn, they had dived through breakers and after, thrown themselves down on the warm sand to sunbathe on a beach almost deserted because it was only accessible on foot or from the sea.

Each passing hour and each new adventure had helped to relax the barrier that stood between them. And then had come the moment when, climbing up jagged lava rocks, Adam had reached down for her. She had not needed his help, not really, but had taken it and enjoyed the sensations aroused by the strong masculine hand . . . his hand. When those rocks lay far behind, her hand was still in his, their fingers entwined like casual, familiar lovers.

There had followed a lull in their conversation when she felt sure that a problem was weighing heavily on Adam's mind. As if coming to a decision, he had eventually turned to face her, and then he had hesitated. It seemed to her that he was searching for the right words. But evidently the right words had not come, for after a moment, he had tenderly pushed a wayward lock of her hair back off her face, and looking away, had moved their attention on to other things. The moment of revelation had been lost leaving Maxine strangely disconcerted and with a burning curiosity to know what it was he had wanted to say.

Now, in the restaurant, looking over the top of her glass, it struck Maxine anew how quickly she had fallen under the spell of this secretive man, and how much pleasure it gave her just to be in his company. She remembered vividly the lambada of the night before, the feel of his strong arm around her waist and those long sculptured fingers in the curve of her back, holding her tightly moulded against the taught muscles of his body.

Maxine came slowly out of her reverie to the realisation that Adam's attention was as much fixed on her as hers was on him and that there was a hint of a gentle, knowing smile in the curve of his lips. Had he been reading her thoughts?

★ ★ ★

On Signal Hill, the inverted **T** symbol was replaced by an ominous black triangle.

★ ★ ★

The waiter returned to replace an empty centre dish with a steaming bowl of mussels. His easy-going smile had been replaced by a fretful scowl and he did not hover to chat good-naturedly with Adam as he had before. Thoughtfully, Maxine watched him hurry off towards the kitchen, his rubber flip-flops slapping the soles of his feet as he crossed the rough bare floorboards.

Probably had a disagreement with the cook, she thought, and transferring her attention to a passenger ferry that was entering the bay, she promptly forgot about the waiter and his problems.

There was restless movement among the diners and some were already making their way off the veranda and along the nearby pier. She and Adam would also soon be leaving, she supposed sadly . . . but not yet, she hoped. She wanted to linger a while longer over the variety of excellent seafood dishes Adam had ordered. Then they would catch the last ferry back to Hong Kong Island, and it would be the end of their perfect day.

★ ★ ★

'No Eleanor, he didn't come in today,' said Adam's secretary, into the office phone. 'You could try his mobile.' She had been working late and the night-watchman had come, especially to tell her the latest bulletin. Now, understandably, she was in a hurry to be gone and Eleanor could detect the hint of anxiety in her voice.

Eleanor hung up the phone. A little worry line formed between her eyebrows. She had already tried her brother's mobile but had failed to raise even his answering service. Over-use of the network; too many panic calls, she supposed. She would try again later.

Somewhere in the background, she could hear the sounds of wood banging against wood and was reassured that Ah Fong was securing heavy shutters into window frames. She moved away from the television and went to the window for a last look out at the world before Ah Fong got around to her side of the house. Winston, with hair blowing in the wind, hurried past on his way to stow garden furniture in the garage. Removable pots and other storable items had already been taken to safety.

Probably all quite unnecessary, Eleanor brooded fretfully. After all, it was October . . . a bit late in the season for anything to get really worried about, surely? Experience warned her, however, that it was better to be safe than sorry. And even as she peered out into the darkening night a few heavy drops of rain began to mark the flagstones.

On the other side of the house, the old *amah* was bringing in the wind chime that had, despite its many hours of melodic fuss, failed to repel the dragon that was circling in the South China Sea. With another swish of its vicious, far-reaching tail, the angry dragon had twisted its gigantic body around so that its fire-breathing head was now facing Hong Kong.

★ ★ ★

A thoughtful frown creased Adam's brow as he watched the last few passengers cross the gangplank and the ferry crew's practised maritime activities. A prolonged blast heralded the vessel's departure. It pulled slowly away from the pier, picked up speed, and was soon beyond the bay, diminishing rapidly in size. It had robbed the restaurant's communal veranda of all but Adam and Maxine, and one other couple, who were now also preparing to leave.

Adam's gaze shifted to the last few hurricane-lamp-lit vessels moving with urgency towards an already crowded enclosure at the farthest point of the bay.

While Adam began to suspect the reason for the sudden mass exodus and the rush of the *Tanka* sea folk to safety, Maxine continued to puzzle over the vacated tables. It seemed odd to her that so many customers should end their evening at this early hour when there was an alternative ferry a little later.

Already, and with efficient haste, staff were

stacking and securing tables and chairs on their sections of the veranda. Others were placing protective shutters over kitchen windows.

For a moment, Adam watched the lively activity, and then, laying down his chopsticks, he summonsed a passing waiter.

A few rapid words of Cantonese passed between them and she heard the words *dai foo* mentioned several times. The waiter then hurried off to get their bill, leaving Adam to frown thoughtfully at the sky, and seaward towards the departing ferry which, having picked up speed had become no more than a distant bright light.

Somewhere near, a car engine started up. The veranda was now empty of all customers except for themselves . . . and yet, the evening was still young.

Only now did Maxine notice the approaching canopy of unfriendly clouds. The sea had grown a little rougher and the breeze was no longer playful but had become ominously aggressive.

'What's wrong,' she asked Adam, aware of growing tension, but not sure she fully understood its cause.

'There's a storm on its way,' he replied, careful to avoid the word *typhoon*. 'It's been brewing off the coast of Hainan for days.'

Maxine was used to coastal storms — even storms that materialised as unexpectedly as this one. She was not overly concerned, as long as it didn't stay long enough to spoil their holiday.

'Tropical Storm warning number one was hoisted a couple of days ago,' Adam told her. 'Nothing unusual in that . . . happens all the time . . . when there's a storm within a certain radius. This one looked as if it was going to blow itself out before it could do any damage. But, according to the waiter, it intensified unexpectedly this morning and has turned its sights on Hong Kong.'

The storm had, in fact, whipped itself up into a frenzy so that now it was a fully-fledged typhoon and one that was hungry to devour all in its twisting, capricious path. But Adam was not going to frighten Maxine with the details. If the typhoon passed directly over Hong Kong, she would know soon enough, the devastation it could cause.

'Apparently, warning signal number three was raised this morning . . . while we were in the hills. It's been gathering momentum all day and the radio's just announced the hoisting of signal number eight.'

Even to Maxine, who knew little about typhoons, this information sounded ominous. From the row of little kitchens came the low monotonous hum of radios, all presumably tuned in to the weather forecast. Only now did they infringe upon her consciousness.

'So?' Maxine asked after a moment's silence.

He looked her directly in the eyes. 'So, all transportation has just been suspended until further notice.'

He saw her glance go quickly to the receding light that was now a tiny speck far out to sea, and knew that she understood there would be no late night ferry back for them tonight.

Maxine remembered the long bridge that linked Lantau with Kowloon. 'Can we phone for a taxi?' she asked.

'*All* transport has been suspended . . . ' he repeated.

'That bad?' she asked, still not overly concerned, but surprised that bad weather could be the cause of so much disruption.

'Could be,' he replied, knowing that, by now, everyone was running for cover and battening down the hatches. Life all around would come to a complete standstill while the populace, through television and radio, tracked with fascination the menacing approach of the *dai foo*. There was, however, still a chance that the eye of the typhoon would bypass Hong Kong, but if it came in for a direct hit, on Signal Hill, the threatening black cross, the number ten sign, would be hoisted.

His thoughts turned to those whose welfare he cared about deeply. The damage caused by a typhoon of this vicious intensity could be catastrophic. They had been known to cause floods and mudslides, level dwellings, leave the harbour in a shambles and kill and maim hundreds of people. When a bad one struck, especially out of season, hardly anyone escaped unscathed.

Adam reached into his shirt pocket and pulled out a small mobile-telephone. 'Damn!' he muttered when twice he failed to get a signal.

Intrigued, Maxine watched him stow the phone deep within the dry and secure interior of the canvas pack that held all his and her requirements for the day. She wondered to whom he had made the call, but suspecting she already knew the answer, refrained from asking.

Instead, blissfully unaware of the dangers they could be facing, she inquired lightly, 'What do we do now? Are we going to be stuck here for the night like castaways on a desert island? Shall we gather foliage and make a shelter on the beach? Shall we light a beacon and write a giant SOS out of seashells?' She glanced over the rail to the wide strip of sand below that stretched away to her right and saw the ominous, scuttling shadows of a family of rather large crabs. She focussed on a pair of beady eyes and vicious looking pincers and shuddered. 'Perhaps not . . . ' she grinned, 'the beach is out. They're cute little fellows, but not my idea of cuddly slumber toys.'

Adam forced himself to smile. 'We'll have to do a lot better than that,' he said. 'We need to get a roof over our heads. We need a hotel.'

He turned to search the hills for life, but no lights of hospitality beckoned from their dark shadows. With equal interest and as much success, he searched the bleak curving headlands.

Maxine savoured the word *hotel*. It had been a long, tiring day and it conjured up visions of a hot bath and a comfortable bed. A *double bed*, perhaps . . . Her pulse quickened . . . but then it calmed. Wishful thinking, she told herself. She had shared a hotel suite with this man for nearly a week. He'd had plenty of time and opportunity to take advantage of the situation, if he had wanted to.

Let's face it Maxine, she told herself, he's not interested in you and his feelings are not likely to alter just because of a change of venue.

The bill arrived, and while Adam settled it, he exchanged rapid Cantonese with the waiter. The distinctive words *tai tai* were uttered by the waiter, accompanied by a glance in her direction. She wondered what *tai tai* meant.

'There's a guesthouse within walking distance,' Adam told her. 'It's just over the headland and owned by a Mrs Woo. A bit of a trek, and accommodation may not be up to much . . . ' he glanced up at the rows of hanging lanterns, now dancing a crazy jig in the gusting wind, 'but the weather's closing in fast and I don't see that we have much choice.'

Adam reached for the canvas pack, and coming to his feet, slung it over a broad shoulder.

Maxine hesitated only long enough to assess her weariness against the distance and the height he meant them to travel. The sea was growing angry causing the stilts and boards beneath their feet to groan in protest. Adam was right. It was time to move out.

★　★　★

The walk along the beach was the easy bit. The climb up narrow, overgrown trails that wound around boulders and through dense undergrowth, thick with tall thrashing bamboo was much more of a challenge. In the dark, with neither stars nor moon to guide them, they groped blindly upwards, in danger of being lashed by thrashing shrubs and in constant fear of losing the way. Then, nearing the top of the ridge, lightening split the sky apart, illuminating the landscape in a series of sizzling flashes as far as the eye could see. A volley of thunder rolled overhead and the heavens opened. Within seconds Maxine and Adam were soaked to the skin and the dry rough trail was transformed into a treacherous slope of slippery mud. By the time they reached the crest of the headland, the weather had deteriorated to such a degree that howling gusts were threatening to take them off their feet.

Adam had called this a tropical storm, but this was not like any storm that Maxine had ever experienced before.

'Are you sure this isn't a hurricane?' she shouted above the shrieking wind and the roar of breakers that far below crashed mercilessly against treacherous, jagged rocks.

'It's a *typhoon* . . . in this part of the world, that's what it's called — a *typhoon*,' he shouted back.

She stopped to stare at him, and was momentarily caught off guard by a powerful gust that took her perilously near a steep incline. Adam grabbed her by the wrist and kept hold of her until they were over the exposed ridge and on the slightly more sheltered downward track. For the remainder of their slippery nightmare journey, he kept a very protective eye on her.

The battle for balance and forward momentum sapped Maxine's strength and worked her muscles until they screamed for rest. To anyone else, she might have shown exhaustion and a healthy degree of fear, but not to Adam. She was with the man she most wanted to be with . . . most wanted to impress. She would have followed him, uncomplaining through any amount of danger and enjoyed the challenge, just to be in his company. She was, however, tremendously relieved when, through the torrential rain, the blurred outline of bricks and mortar came into view. And there, in the middle of some weekend bungalows was the welcome sight of the guesthouse, a building larger and a more reassuringly solid-looking than all the rest.

This outcrop of dwellings stood back out of reach of tides and waves on higher safer ground, but even so, it was clear they were taking a severe battering. Climbing plants, once firmly attached to sturdy trellises had been wrenched loose. Trees were bowing dangerously low, their branches thrashing noisily in the howling wind. Green foliage, once handsome and lush, was being brought down in a broken tangle of leaf and limb to be swept along this way and that until banked up against immovable obstacles. Plant pots had toppled off walls and verandas and lay smashed, spewing their contents onto the ground to be washed away by floodwater. From nearby there came the clatter of a sliding roof tile, followed by a crash as it shattered on the path below. Other tiles would soon follow.

Battling their way closer, they saw that the guesthouse was square, flat topped, with balconies and shutters that were tightly fastened. It was grander than it's modest, moremodern neighbours, and even in these treacherous circumstances, Maxine could tell that it was a house with a great deal of romantic charm.

Its proximity to the ferry point, restaurants and beach would, under favourable conditions, make it an ideal retreat for lovers. For the first time, Maxine questioned whether Adam had previously known of its existence. But for the lack of light, he might have led the way with easy familiarity and not once faltered where paths divided.

Had he brought a girlfriend here: the beautiful Eurasian, perhaps?

Maxine reminded herself that Adam had asked the waiter for directions. But then, she also reminded herself that, for all she had understood of the conversation, the men might have been discussing tomorrow's menu.

With an effort, she called her thoughts to order. Why should I care what Adam gets up to? she asked herself moodily. After this holiday, I'll be lucky if I ever see him again.

* * *

The house, when they came to it, was in darkness, or so they thought. And then they noticed the tiny glimmers of light showing between the cracks of the closed shutters. Maxine sent up a silent prayer of thanks . . . and another more fervent prayer that Mrs Woo would be able to take them in.

At Adam's side, she huddled into a corner of the porch for protection. Their hair was plastered flat to their heads and their clothes clung, wet and cold, to their bodies. During their fight for survival, she had not noticed the awful discomfort. But now, she found she was shivering violently, her teeth chattering like the fortune-telling sticks in the temple.

When had the temperature dropped so low? she wondered. Hugging herself for comfort, she huddled even closer into her sheltered corner.

'Mrs Woo's not going to like being disturbed in the middle of the night by a couple of half-drowned strangers,' she managed to say.

Adam laughed at her concern. 'Strangers? By a couple of paying customers you mean.' He banged determinedly on the door. 'She'll be thrilled to see us. Bet she does a roaring trade out of desperate fugitives.'

*　*　*

Despite the pools of water the unexpected arrivals were dripping on her polished parquet floor, Mrs Woo was, as predicted, all concern and eager hospitality. Her first task, however, was to secure the door before half the garden could follow her guests across its threshold, and this she managed, with Adam's superior weight and strength.

Muddy footwear was then removed, towels gratefully accepted and put to use, and negotiations in Cantonese were conducted. While Maxine waited impatiently, she heard again those strange recognisable words, *tai tai*, this time said by Adam, and her thoughts shifted from hot bath and dry fleecy towel to ponder once more over their meaning.

'There's only one room available,' Adam eventually paused to inform her. There was, he knew, no question of turning down this safe, dry haven. Nothing was going to oust either of them back out into such an evil night. Even so, he raised his eyebrows in question. The suggestion that they share the room must come from her.

At Adam's words, the prediction of Fu Chu Ming leapt instantly back into Maxine's mind: *the tiger will lay down with the dragon.* Her pulse quickened to a delicious thrill of anticipation and her throat went suddenly dry.

Striving for just the right amount of nonchalance, she gave a careless shrug and said, 'Only one room? Then, we had better share it.'

★   ★   ★

Maxine cast an inquisitive eye over cane furniture and pale Chinese watercolours and then her focus came to rest on mosquito netting that cascaded down over the solitary bed. She was quick to notice that there was nothing else remotely suitable to sleep on, unless one could count the cane armchair.

Adam followed the direction of her gaze and read her mind. Neither of them would be sleeping in an armchair tonight. They were going to share the warmth and comfort of that rather small bed that had been passed off as a double.

Teasingly, however, he said, for her ears only, 'I'll toss you for the chair in a minute.'

Laundry arrangements were discussed before Mrs Woo hurried away to investigate a worrying crash that rang out from a distant part of the property.

Maxine watched Adam close and lock the door. He slipped the backpack off his shoulder, propped it against the wall and then turned critical eyes on their surroundings.

'Not quite the Mandarin,' he commented wryly, breaking the highly-charged silence that hung between them. 'But tonight,' he gave a quirky grin, 'anything's better than sleeping *al fresco*.'

As if on cue, another roll of thunder crashed across the sky, and in its wake came sizzling streaks of lightening that flashed brilliant shards of light through the narrow cracks in the shutters. The overhead bulb blinked ominously several times, but stubbornly refused to go out.

'No, not quite the Mandarin,' she agreed, referring more to the shortage of beds and the diminutive size of this one. As if directed by a will of its own, her focus shifted from bed to armchair.

Keeping a straight face, Adam took a coin from his pocket. 'Toss or share?' he challenged.

Maxine hesitated. Neither one of them would find comfort in that chair. And as for the wood-block floor, even cushioned with some of the bedding, it would be unbearably hard. Worse still was the suspicion that an army of cockroaches lurked in dark corners just waiting for the lights to go out. A mosquito, driven in by the storm, buzzed near her ear recalling her attention to the protective netting. Without it, they'd be eaten alive. Was there still malaria in this part of the world? she wondered.

She searched his face and saw the challenge in his eyes. Her chin went up. 'I remember you telling me you were fussy about who you were willing to share your bed with,' she reminded him.

'I still am . . . when circumstances allow,' he teased.

She frowned, hesitated, not sure how to take such a response.

'Well?' he asked, after a short pause. 'What's it to be?'

Where there had been only one mosquito,

there was now a whole squadron of them and it seemed to Maxine that they were all on the same flight path and heading for her. She slapped at her arm. Too late, she already had the itchy swelling of a direct hit.

Maxine was shivering again. She was wet and cold and the bed looked so warm and inviting. What if she lost the toss? Making a snap decision, she answered, 'Share . . . ' and then, so as not to seem too obvious, quickly added, ' . . . just for sleeping.'

He smiled, and with an infuriating raise of the eyebrows, murmured, 'Of course. What else did you have in mind?'

Maxine had lots in mind that would raise both their temperatures faster than a sauna bath, but she was not going to say so. Since their first meeting, she had waited for this moment, and now that it had come, she felt as tongue-tied as a teenager on a first date.

Her eyes met with his; a peculiar kind of tension beamed between them. For a moment they were silent; neither moved. Slowly, his focus travelled down to the firm, pointed breasts, their nipples clearly outlined through the wet clinging fabric of the thin shirt. He saw Maxine shiver and knew that this time the shiver was more a reaction from desire than from the cold. He was tempted to reach out for her . . . but remembered in time that she must be the one to make the first move. He was already guilty of too much.

Dispelling the sexual magic, he tore his gaze from her, and taking control of the situation, went to the bathroom and turned the taps on for her.

★   ★   ★

Maxine helped herself to a sachet of hotel shampoo, and dropping her wet clothes onto the tiled floor, lowered herself into the hot, therapeutic water. She laid her head back against the rim of the bath, closed her eyes, and gave herself up to thought.

Had she imagined it, or had Adam been on the verge of reaching out for her? If so, what had stopped him? He wanted her, she was sure of that . . . or was she simply letting her imagination run away with her?

All day, Maxine had been happy to forget the existence of Adam's mystery woman. Now she found herself wondering if Adam had held back because of her. Was she still a part of his life and waiting for his call, somewhere on Hong Kong Island. Was she, at this moment, wondering where he was and worrying over his safety?

Despite the dangers, Maxine had welcomed a typhoon that had conveniently materialised at just the right moment to cut her and Adam off from the world. And now, here she was, sharing a room . . . a bed even, with a man who had for days played tantalising havoc with her emotions.

Where now was that commonsense that had warned her to keep him at arm's length? Maxine smiled to herself. Somewhere out there on the headland, it had been blown away by a gale force wind.

The warnings of Fu Chu Ming checked the flow of her thoughts. What a fool she was to even think of intimate involvement with a man like Adam. For, if the soothsayer's warnings were to be believed, if the couple *shrouded in secrets* were indeed *irrevocably entwined*, then she could have no hope for a future with him.

Last night, in the nightclub, Maxine had got the impression, or rather, had wanted to believe that he and his girlfriend had argued and agreed to part company. He hadn't told her so. Well, not in so many words. But if that was not the case, why else would he have returned to her, Maxine, and like a possessive lover, removed her from the arms of another? If Adam had still been romantically attached elsewhere, would he have held her so close . . . so intimately? And today, would he have kept her hand in his, or quite so tenderly pushed back a flyaway lock of her hair? Would his voice and look have held so much warmth? And out on the headland, would he have shown so much concern for her welfare?

Had she misinterpreted the body language and read too much into acts of friendship and man's natural instinct to protect?

There were far too many questions still to be answered, and until she had those answers, how could she be sure that she meant more to him than a passing fancy . . . more than just a one-night-stand? How could she be sure, that at the end of this holiday, Adam would not walk out of her life forever?

★   ★   ★

Outside, the rain drummed on remorselessly and the wind howled inland, whipping the sea into giant crashing breakers. Adam listened to the raging gale. Instinct and experience warned him that the worst was yet to come. There had not yet been that unnatural stillness, that dull and eerie silence that declared they were in the eye of the storm. It would come soon now, and then would follow the ferocious backlash of the swishing giant tail of the *dai foo* as it moved off in search of new prey. This typhoon was a bad one and he wondered just how much havoc it would leave in its treacherous wake before it finally blew itself out.

He inspected the catches on the shutters. They appeared secure enough. The house was old and of solid stone; it had endured the test of time. He and Maxine were safe, no need for concern — and Eleanor too, he hoped, but had no way of knowing.

Again, he had tried unsuccessfully to get a signal on his mobile telephone, and when he eventually ran Mrs Woo to ground, she had informed him that the guesthouse had only one phone and that the typhoon had long since rendered it useless. Must have brought a line down somewhere, she suggested.

For as long as he was stranded on Lantau, there was nothing more he could do. Eleanor would be all right. She was a survivor. And besides, provided she was at home, she was in the capable hands of Ah Fong and Fong Quan, the two people he most trusted with her welfare.

A shiver brought his thoughts to his own needs. He removed his rain drenched clothes and crammed them into the laundry bag provided. Shaking the folds out of a towel, he rubbed himself down vigorously and then reached for the long, black Chinese happy-coat provided for visitors by the guesthouse. He put it on, wrapped it tightly around his hips and secured the belt low on his waist. Then he reached for the bottle of brandy he had managed to commandeer from Mrs Woo, and poured generous helpings into two very ordinary glasses. Adam sighed at the incongruous tumblers, but both brandy and glasses were the best that Mrs Woo could provide. Under the circumstances, he was not complaining.

He settled into the armchair to wait, and as he waited, he sipped the golden liquid. While its medicinal powers went to work on him, he conjured up an image of Maxine, lying naked in the bath, not four paces away from him.

Until today, he had been convinced that physical attraction alone summed up his feelings for her. He had felt the strength of that attraction from the moment he picked her out of the crowd at the Comp-Dynamics ball. He had wanted to take her to bed and still did. But physical attraction alone was not enough to justify involvement with an employee, and if all he wanted was uncomplicated sex, he would do better to look elsewhere.

Along the way, however, his feelings for Maxine had grown, so that now, he knew sex was not his only interest in her. He wanted far, far more.

Today, he had been allowed to see the real

Maxine, in all her many moods, uncomplicated and stripped of inhibitions. He had
watched her long hair tangle carelessly in the
wind, and taken pleasure in her childish
delight over the fantasy-castles they built in
the sand. He had felt her alarm when a large
wave reached beyond the others to cancel out
their magnificent works of art. And tonight,
he had witnessed her determination to gain
the summit of a treacherous climb; her
courage in the teeth of a vicious typhoon; her
satisfaction in achievement, and then had
come the realisation that he had, quite
simply, fallen in love with her.

Adam thought of the Mandarin suite they
had shared for nearly a week; of the divide
between their rooms; that no-man's-land
through which they came and went but never
crossed into each other's territory. And he
could not help but be pleased by the typhoon
that would quite likely keep them on Lantau
for at least another day.

From behind the closed door came the
sounds that told him Maxine would soon
appear, and his pulse quickened. With a hand
that trembled very slightly, he raised the
brandy to his lips and felt the liquid spread its
warmth through his veins.

They would make love, he promised
himself, but their peculiar circumstances

demanded that the initiative must come from her.

★ ★ ★

After such an exhausting day, the last thing Maxine expected was to have trouble sleeping. It was not the narrowness of the bed or the hard mattress, nor was it the angry noises of a stormy night that were keeping her awake. It was Adam Warwick. To be more precise, it was his broad back and the soft rhythmic breathing that proclaimed he was asleep. How could he possibly have fallen asleep under such intimate circumstances? Why had he not reached out for her when she could think of nothing she wanted more than to be pulled into his strong arms? She sighed with exasperation. Was there something wrong with the man? Had he taken vows of celibacy?

Surely the very short happy-coat should have had the power to turn on even the most ascetic of men. Perhaps she had put out the wrong message. After all, she had not exactly flaunted herself at him. She had been too self-conscious for that. In fact, she had accepted the brandy on offer and gone as discreetly as possible to sit in his vacated chair. And then, she had watched him disappear into the bathroom without a backward glance.

Still optimistic, she had downed the brandy in one, in much the same way a child might swallow an unpleasant medicine — brandy was not her drink — and then she had given thought as to whether or not she should keep the dressing gown on in bed or take it off. She would keep it on, she decided, so as not to appear too willing. Besides, one little shrug would easily remove it. And then, since the fine fabric of the gown was no protection against the chilling drafts that found their ways through shutters and ill-fitting frames, she had thought it a prudent time to slip modestly between the sheets.

Impatiently, she had waited, and nervously too . . . although why the nerves, she could not imagine. After all, she was not by nature a shrinking violet.

She did not have to wait long. Pretending sleep, she followed the sounds of his movements as he circled the bed. But pretence, she soon discovered, was a big mistake, for although she willed him to reach out for her, he switched off the lamp the moment he was between the sheets, and turning his back on her, went straight off to sleep. For all the attention he had given her, she might just as well have been an unwelcome bedbug.

How can anyone fall asleep that quickly and particularly under such intimate circumstances? Was she that unappealing? Had he really thought her asleep or had he taken the closed eyes to mean *don't touch*? Then, another thought chased through her mind. Could he have been waiting for her to make the first move? Well, if that was so, he would have to wait a very long time.

Huffily, she turned her back on him and put as much distance between them as she could, which, considering the width of the bed, was hardly any distance at all.

She remembered that first day in the Mandarin: the moment when she had blundered into his arms. And she remembered the hard expanse of bare chest, the amusement that sparkled in his dark eyes, the smell of soap and expensive after-shave — and inwardly she groaned. No wonder she was suffering from insomnia. With such memories for company and the man himself only a breath away . . . well, how was she, a *normal* red-blooded female, expected to sleep?

But sleep she did, eventually, if one could call such a fitful doze sleep.

★　★　★

At some time in the night, Maxine became aware that she was snuggled up to a warm masculine back. At first she thought she was dreaming. She liked the dream, smiled contentedly and snuggled up closer.

Then, slowly, she became aware that the dream was too lucid, the feel of flesh too real. This was not a dream. Was it Jonathan? Her fingers moved inquiringly over the bare muscular flesh. Thank God, this was not Jonathan. She had not been that stupid. No, this was a larger, more powerfully built man, whose sleep-tousled hair was thick and dark and whose skin was tanned nut-brown. This was . . . Adam. Her arm was draped over him and his strong fingers, halting the progress of her hand, had moved to curl possessively around her wrist. Shock and embarrassment snapped her to full wakefulness.

Gentle rhythmic breathing suggested he might still be asleep. Maxine lay very still, hardly daring to breathe. If she could move away without disturbing him, he need never know she'd been practically groping him.

Slowly and very carefully, she began to withdraw her arm.

He stirred. His hand tightened on her wrist and then, gently, his thumb began to stroke the back of her hand. Adam, it would seem, was not such a deep sleeper after all.

He rolled onto his back, his eyes seeking hers in the grey dawn light. 'Good morning' he said softly in a quiet, sleepy voice, 'Awake so early?'

'I'm sorry,' she mumbled, edging backwards, trying to put space between her and the body she now knew to be completely naked, 'I was asleep . . . '

'I'm not complaining,' he responded softly, almost tenderly.

His fingers, still curled around her wrist, held her hand to his chest.

Her blood stirred. She wanted to move her palm over the muscles, to run her fingertips lightly along the angular line of his jaw and trace a path across the sensuous curve of his mouth. But instead, she lay still and watchful in the halflight, afraid to reach out, unsure of the man who shared her bed.

For a moment, she was silent. And then, again, she tried to withdraw her arm. 'I didn't mean to . . . ' she began.

'A pity,' he murmured, 'I hoped you did.' Still he did not release her hand.

She stared questioningly into the dark eyes, and there saw mirrored that same hungry desire that had for days been her constant companion.

And yet, still Maxine hesitated. She wanted far more from Adam than just one night of passion. She was offering love . . . now and forever. How could she possibly be content with less in return?

The eye of the typhoon had passed over them while they slept and was now moving away with a backlash of renewed violence. Lightning flashed its warning, and the thunder grumbling crossly, seemed to be saying, 'Don't be a fool. Here and now . . . that's all he'll give you, and like the *dai foo*, will be gone tomorrow.'

Memory winged Maxine back to Wong Tai Sin. 'Then I will have to settle for the *here and now*,' her thoughts replied, as she moved into his arms, 'for the fates have already decided that *the tiger will lay down with the dragon*.'

★   ★   ★

At dawn, the eye of the typhoon was directly over Hong Kong and its outlying islands. For a short while a surreal hush settled over everything. The wind ceased its howling, the rain turned into a drizzle and the sea grew calm. And then as it passed, the peace was once more shattered, this time by the vicious backlash of the *dai foo* as it turned its back and began to move slowly away leaving further destruction in its wake.

Now, several hours later, Adam awoke to a storm that had lost a little of its fury. He suspected that the signal on Telegraph Hill would soon be devalued to a Tropical Storm warning. Hong Kong would assess the damage, lick its wounds and return life gradually back to normal. By evening, transport would be up and running again.

Adam glanced at his watch on the bedside table and was surprised to see the lateness of the hour. Deceived by the shuttered darkness of the room, he and Maxine had slept the morning away.

His gaze travelled to the girl lying close beside him. Her hair had dried in the night and now sprayed out across the pillow in a heavy tangled web of spun gold. Her eyelashes were so much darker than her hair, he noticed. Her generous lips were slightly parted. He touched a shiny tendril, allowed it to curl around his fingers, and smiled. She made a pretty picture. Then, remembering their night of love, the smile slowly faded to be replaced by a thoughtful frown. It was not that he regretted making love to her. No, he had fully intended to do that, although he was not sure at what stage precisely in the past few days he had reached that decision. It was the knowing that first he really ought to have told her exactly who he was.

'Damn,' he muttered under his breath. He had some explaining to do and had no idea how she was going to react. The storm without might be abating, but within, he suspected, another storm was gathering momentum.

At his side, Maxine stirred and opened her eyes. As memory flooded back, she smiled a sleepy, confident smile, and moved closer to him.

Adam could not resist. Inwardly, he groaned at his own recklessness, but still he pulled her into his arms and once more made love to her.

⋆ ⋆ ⋆

Eleanor gazed out of the drawing room window at the devastation the typhoon had made of the garden that was Winston's pride and joy. Branches were down, shrubs flattened, a heavy bench over-turned, and at the furthest end of the property, an old well-established tree had been uprooted. While Ah Fong disappeared into the garage to check on the safety of the cars, Winston rolled up his sleeves and went to work on the felled tree with a hefty saw.

Eleanor watched progress for only a moment and then she turned her attention to a curio that was of far more interest to her than mere storm damage. From her jacket pocket, she took out the innocuous looking brooch acquired from Patrick's shop, and holding it to the late afternoon light, she re-read the calligraphy enamelled on its surface. Once again she smiled with secret delight.

There was a sound behind her. Swinging round, Eleanor came face-to-face with Fong Quan. The unexpected presence of the old *amah* took her so much by surprise that she nearly dropped the brooch. She looked guilty, like a child caught in the act of doing wrong.

'What's that you've got there, Missy?' asked Fong Quan. The scowl of disapproval on her lined face told Eleanor only too clearly that the old *amah* had not only seen the brooch, but had been quick enough to read the calligraphy, and understand its meaning. 'I hope that obscenity does not belong to you.'

'Of course not,' said Eleanor, all innocence. To herself, she said, well not for long anyway. 'It's very old Fong Quan. I'm just admiring its antiquity.'

Fong Quan peered at Eleanor through narrowed eyes. She was not fooled by the honeyed tone. 'And I hope its antiquity is your only interest in it,' she said, and there was a warning in the stern voice.

Fong Quan was aware that the Master's half sister had been born in the year of the monkey. Monkeys were tricky creatures, especially this one. She should know; she'd had a hand in raising the child and it hadn't been easy.

'Don't let me see it in this house again or I'll tell your brother,' Fong Quan threatened. Inwardly, she sighed, as she so often did, over the passing of Lai Ho Mai. The girl needed her mother, especially now. She was a handful and in her opinion the master allowed his sister far too much freedom.

Still grumbling, the *amah* left the room. She had work to do. They had been far luckier than most, but still the typhoon had not left them totally untouched and first on her list of priorities was a call to the glazier. A broken shutter and a shattered windowpane needed immediate repair.

Alone again and unperturbed by the threats of Fong Quan, Eleanor returned to the rosewood coffee table where, with great care and artistry, she gift-wrapped the brooch. And then, for a moment, her pen hovered over the tiny card.

'Now what shall I write?' she murmured to herself.

Several unsatisfactory sentences chased through her mind, and then, in a neat hand,

249

she wrote, '*The measure of my esteem.*'

She put no signature, thus leaving the recipient to guess the identity of the sender. Feeling pleased with her handywork, Eleanor smiled. Then, remembering that time was in short supply, she glanced at the cloisonné clock on the bureau.

Half an hour had passed since Adam's telephone call. She had not seen him for two whole days, and although his first words had been those of inquiry and concern, he had said not one word about where he had been. With whom he had spent the night, she could easily guess, of course. Eleanor had suggested they meet for dinner.

'I've already got an evening appointment,' he had replied apologetically.

'Who with . . . *the old crow?*' she asked, annoyed but trying hard not to sound so.

He knew her too well. His laughter had come down the line. 'Yes, as a mater of fact. Why don't you join us? Apéritifs in the Captain's Bar at seven-thirty followed by supper at Jimmy's Kitchen.'

Eleanor wasn't keen on *gwai'lo* food. It was heavy and indigestible. She would have preferred a Chinese restaurant, but she didn't complain. 'Sounds good,' she agreed.

This time, she was eager to meet her brother's beautiful employee who, if Jonathan was to be believed, had no one's welfare at heart but her own. With revenge in mind and a malicious desire to make her fiancé jealous, *the old crow* had deliberately lured Adam into a holiday romance. But, she would not have it all her own way, Eleanor would see to that.

In a flash of inspiration, she phoned Patrick's apartment and got his houseguest, as she knew she would.

'You're invited out tonight,' she told Jonathan. 'My brother wants to introduce me to your fiancée. Thought you might like to come and make your presence felt.'

'Er . . . did your brother say you could invite me?' Jonathan asked.

'No, not exactly,' she replied, then quickly assured, 'but he won't mind if I bring a friend.'

'He would if he knew who the friend was,' Jonathan replied.

'True . . . ' Eleanor happily conceded.

'And you want him to know?'

'That's the idea,' she agreed.

There was a short silence at the other end while Jonathan turned the matter over in his mind. 'Okay,' he agreed. 'What time and where?'

'Be at the Captain's Bar in the Mandarin at seven-fifteen.' Quickly she outlined what she wanted from him. Simple but effective, she thought as she returned the handset to its cradle, if he plays his part right and on cue.

She glanced again at the clock. Time was passing and there was still this little trinket to be delivered. Scooping up the present, she headed for the door.

★   ★   ★

Within the lofty portals of the Mandarin Oriental Hotel, the sleek uniformed receptionist accepted the gift from Eleanor along with her explicit instructions.

Satisfied, Eleanor crossed the marble lobby to the grand staircase leading up to the Clipper Lounge. There, on the wide sweeping balcony, among the elite of Hong Kong, Eleanor ordered Chinese tea.

It was the bewitching cocktail hour when the hotel guests came and went in an interesting flurry of well-dressed activity. From her well-chosen position over-looking the foyer, Eleanor watched and waited for her little drama to unfold.

★   ★   ★

Maxine was awakened by a knock at the door. Tousled and sleepy, she threw on a robe and still wrapped in that same cloud of romantic euphoria that had kept her company since Lantau, she padded through the lounge. Perhaps it was Adam, she told herself hopefully. Maybe he's mislaid his security card and needs me to let him in.

It was not Adam, however, but a young bellhop who handed her a small package, beautifully gift-wrapped, together with a message, for which she signed.

Who could be sending me presents? she wondered. Not Jonathan, surely? She turned the package over in her hand while she analysed the unlikely possibility. Noting the care that had gone into selecting the paper and ribbon, she knew that this was definitely not his style. Jonathan had neither the artistic talent nor the patience for such detail.

She crossed to the sofa, and tucking one leg under her, settled into the plump feather cushion. First, she read the message. It asked her to be downstairs in the Captain's Bar twenty minutes earlier than previously arranged. She did not recognise the writing and there was no name on the note, but she guessed that, although it was not his writing, it could only have come from Adam. He must have phoned the message through to reception. Fleetingly, she wondered why he had not had the call put through to her room.

After all, he knew where to find her, she had told him during lunch that she was going to spend some time in the hotel pool and gym, and then catch up on lost sleep. Probably didn't want to wake her, she concluded and smiled at his thoughtfulness.

So, he wants to bring our meeting forward. Glancing at her watch, Maxine saw she had enough time to shower and change. She turned her attention to the little package on which was printed: 'The measure of my esteem'. From Adam too, no doubt. A thrill of pleasure ran through her. With fingers made nimble by excitement, she undid the bow and then the wrapping, exposing a jewellery box. Raising the lid revealed an enamel brooch. It was not quite what she would have expected from Adam. She had discovered enough about him to know he had exquisite taste. She leaned closer towards the lamp to examine it in brighter light. It was not unattractive, just not . . . beautiful.

It occurred to her that there might be something significant about the calligraphy — a message especially for her. She would ask him. And then she remembered that, although Adam spoke Cantonese and Mandarin he had admitted to little, if any, understanding of calligraphy. Still, he must know what it says, she told herself. He would

254

hardly send such a gift without knowing its meaning.

Beware of a gift from a stranger, the soothsayer had warned. A smile touched her lips. The warning could not possibly apply to Adam . . . not any more. He no longer qualified as a stranger.

★   ★   ★

Ah Fong returned the car to the garage and let himself in through the kitchen door. Before he had even removed his jacket and hung up the car keys, he knew something was troubling his wife.

She was muttering and moving things around the worktops with more forceful clatter than the job required. He watched her fill his bowl from the steaming wok and place it, with a pair of chopsticks, on the table. The pungent aroma filled the kitchen. He felt his stomach rumble with anticipation. She was a good cook; a good wife, he was a contented man. He reached for the bowl and began to eat hungrily, forgetting for the moment to respond to her many cues.

It was not until she began to refill his empty bowl that he asked: 'What's she been up to this time?' They both knew to whom he referred.

'I don't know, and that's the problem,' she grumbled. 'But she's up to something, I know she is. I can always tell.'

Fong Quan reached for a porcelain teapot and placed it on the worktop. For a moment she stared at the hand-painted chrysanthemums on its shiny surface. But what she was seeing in her mind's eye was the brooch. 'Must be the foreign devil in her . . . ' she said, then added irritably. 'He should be firmer with his sister. He should be here, keeping an eye on her. She doesn't listen to me.' She poured boiling water into the pot, but this time the fragrance of the tea failed to please. 'And so many airs and graces . . . ' she muttered belligerently, ' . . . she forgets her mother was an *amah*.'

Ah Fong was silent. He had heard it all before. He didn't want to be drawn into a discussion about his employer, nor did he want to discuss his employer's spirited half-sister . . . no matter what she'd done. He had a soft spot for the child. Yes, she was mischievous, but she was loyal to those she cared about, and she had a warm heart. And behind the lack of humility were insecurities nurtured by rejection. They understood each other; he and the girl he thought of by the Chinese name her mother had given to her. Lai Lan called him Uncle

Fong and it pleased him.

Fong Quan sensed his unreceptive mood and decided to say nothing to her husband about the brooch . . . for now. Instead, she grumbled, 'And where is he when he should be home?'

'That's his business, not ours,' Ah Fong grunted, tucking once more into his supper. 'He's a good man to work for and that's all that should matter to us.' He paused, chopsticks waving in the air. 'If he chooses to stay in a hotel, you can be sure it's for a good reason.'

Fong Quan wasn't listening to him. 'There's sure to be a woman involved,' she grumbled. Her thoughts turned back in time to the naïve and vulnerable young *amah* the older Mr Warwick had brought to work in the house while his wife and son were visiting family in England. On her return, Mrs Warwick had accepted the beautiful Lai Ho Mai without question, but then Mrs Warwick had been too trusting for her own good. She hadn't known the darker side of her husband's nature — not then, anyway.

'Do you think Adam is like his father?' she asked Ah Fong. 'Do you think he's a womaniser?'

Ah Fong doubted that Adam was anything like his father, but he did know for a fact that there was a woman involved. Had he not driven Adam and his lady friend to Wong Tai Sin temple and to several other destinations besides? Had he not been delivering and collecting Eleanor's car when instructed to do so?

'And what if he is womanising?' Ah Fong replied, with a careless shrug. 'He's young, he's single, he's normal.'

Fong Quan scowled. 'Next we'll hear he's got some girl pregnant and doesn't want to know.'

'Not all sons are like their father,' Ah Fong countered.

Her scowl faded. Her husband was right, of course. Not all men would take advantage of an employee's infatuation, and few would take advantage of one as young and innocent as Lai Ho Mai had been. But then Adam's father had been a selfish man, taking what he wanted without scruple or thought for the consequences. Maybe Lai Ho Mai had been a willing partner; maybe she had been forced; maybe she had feared for her job. Since Lai Ho Mai had never confided in her, Fong Quan didn't know. Five months into Lai Ho Mai's pregnancy, her secret could no longer be kept.

By this time, Adam was already safely away from it all, boarding in an English school.

There had been a blazing row, one far worse than all the other rows, after which, Mrs Warwick had packed-up and gone to live in England to be with her son during holidays and exeats, or so she said. But, she never returned to Hong Kong, not when her son came to spend the summer holidays with his father, and not even later when Adam eventually came to work in his father's company.

Lai Ho Mai went to live in her mother's little flat in Mongkok on the pretext that her mother was ill and needed her. By the time she returned to work, several months later, the master had lost interest in her. Probably, by then, there was someone else in his life, thought Fong Quan. Lai Ho Mai was noticeably happier. She never mentioned the baby or what had become of it, but Ah Fong learned, though he couldn't remember from where, that she had given birth to a girl.

In Fong Quan's opinion, giving Lai Ho Mai her job back had been one of the few decent things the older Mr Warwick had ever done. Maybe it was his way of supporting his unacknowledged daughter, or just maybe his conscience had troubled him . . . if he had had a conscience. She doubted it.

Ah Fong was right, of course. The young master was not like his father. He had proved himself honourable. She felt a surge of pride when she remembered the day he had stood up to his powerful father and benefactor. With so much to lose, a lesser man would not have had the courage.

★ ★ ★

Eleanor was on her first cup of tea when she saw Jonathan, right on cue, enter the lobby and head for the steps leading down into the dimly-lit interior of the Captain's Bar. She had just poured her second cup from the dainty Chinese pot when Maxine, coming from the opposite direction, did likewise. At a glance, Eleanor saw with satisfaction the colourful enamel brooch pinned to the lapel of Maxine's cream silk jacket. Her eyes danced and the corners of her lips turned up.

After a quick glance at her watch, Eleanor paid the bill and descended once more into the lobby to await the arrival of Adam.

At seven-thirty, almost to the minute, the tall plate-glass doors swung open and her handsome brother, immaculate in dark tailored business suit, entered the hotel. He picked her out of the crowd and hugged her affectionately. 'Been waiting long?' he inquired.

'Just arrived,' she replied, stretching the truth a little.

She viewed him critically and thought he looked tired. 'Too much work and too little sleep,' she criticised. 'You should be with those who know how to look after you.'

'Those who know how to over-indulge me, you mean,' he countered with a grin. With a light touch, he steered her towards the Captain's Bar. 'And what have you been doing with your day?'

'Nothing of real interest,' she shrugged. 'I interviewed a bird-brained starlet this morning then spent the rest of the day trying to make her sound intelligent. My article's a masterpiece of subtle invention,' she gaily boasted, 'and the girl's too dumb to realise she never said the half of it.' Eleanor saw the quizzical rise of her brother's brow and the smile of sympathy that was all for the starlet. On paper, his sister's humour could be wicked.

'I wrote only good things,' she quickly assured, then pouted, 'No choice, I'm under orders . . . friends in high places, and she's probably sleeping with my editor.'

Listening fondly to Eleanor's amusing chatter, Adam slipped a guiding arm around her slender waist. Together, making a handsome couple, they descended the steps leading into the Captain's Bar where they were greeted by soft music and the steady hum of conversation. It took a moment for Eleanor's eyes to adjust to the dim lighting, and then, over the top of a carpet of heads, in a not too distant corner, she spotted Jonathan and recognised the golden haired beauty that was his fiancée.

The couple sat at a small table at right angles to each other. The cocktail glasses in front of them were almost empty, testifying to the fact that they had been together for a while.

As instructed, Jonathan had been watching for the appearance of Eleanor and her brother. With perfect timing, he placed a hand over Maxine's and leaning intimately close whispered something humorous into her hair. His few words were neither tender nor romantic, but, even so, they drew the desired response. Maxine tossed her head and laughed.

Adam, following the direction of Eleanor's gaze, took in the cosy scene and frowned.

'I know him,' said Eleanor brightly, her eyes on Jonathan. 'He's a tourist I met a few days ago.'

Adam recognised the man from the nightclub. At that time, there had been no particular reason to notice him, but now, his eyes raked over him with real interest. He remembered empty beer cans and dirty ashtrays, and asked himself if this was the man Maxine had entertained in their suite.

'His name's Jonathan West,' volunteered Eleanor, 'and the woman must be his fiancée.'

It took only a moment for Adam to recall the name and all he had heard about the man. His eyes narrowed. So this was Jonathan West, the ex who unwittingly went live on the office intercom, the man who bared his soul to Maxine and in so doing, made a monumental ass of himself. Adam watched him raise his glass to Maxine, and over the rim, look deep into her eyes. The comfortable familiarity suggested that Jonathan West was not going to be quite so easy to get rid of as Maxine might have supposed . . . if indeed she really did want to be rid of him, and of that, he was now beginning to have his doubts.

Eleanor broke into his reflections, saying knowingly, 'Jonathan told me she got the wrong end of the stick over some triviality and broke off their engagement, so he followed her to Hong Kong, to put things right. Looks like they're back together again,' she added cheerfully.

Strange, Maxine had said not one word to him about Jonathan West being in Hong Kong, neither had she mentioned his visit to their suite. And although she could not have failed to notice this man's presence in the nightclub, she had given no indication of having seen him. Surely, if she had nothing to hide, some sort of acknowledgement would have been in order. But there had been none.

Adam searched for signs of a replaced engagement ring. Maxine's hand, however, was still hidden under Jonathan's and she was making no attempt to remove it.

'I suppose we should say hello to him ... and be introduced, but they look so happy it would be a shame to disturb them,' Eleanor said, hanging back.

Just then, Maxine glanced in their direction. For a moment her eyes met and held with Adam's, and then they went to Eleanor. He saw the radiance die out of Maxine's smile. The message was clear, Eleanor was right. Their company would be an unwelcome intrusion.

Showing none of the pain that comes with betrayal, Adam turned away. 'You're right. It looks as if they'd rather be alone,' he said in a controlled voice. If that was the way Maxine wanted it, then he would not get in her way. His eyes searched for another vacant table as far from Maxine and her companion as possible.

'Now then, where's *the old crow* you wanted me to meet?' Eleanor asked.

'She has a prior engagement,' he murmured distractedly. 'She won't be dining with us after all.'

'Pity . . . I was looking forward to meeting her.' Eleanor responded with an air of innocence. Then, glancing up, she smiled, and with a change of tune, added, 'Actually, I'm pleased she can't make it. I'd much rather have you to myself. I've hardly seen you since your return from England.'

'In that case,' he said, giving up the fruitless search for a table, 'why don't we skip the aperitifs and go on to the restaurant?'

'Suits me,' approved Eleanor, happy to beat a hasty retreat while still ahead of the game. She did not want to be introduced to Maxine as Adam's sister. It was not part of the strategy. Being thought of as his girlfriend served a far more useful purpose.

Jonathan's own needs, however, were characteristically uppermost in his mind. He had seen the cool look that passed between Maxine and his rival and was aware that they had jumped to the wrong conclusions. Or rather, they had jumped to the right conclusions . . . depending on which side of the fence you were sitting. Where there had been trust, there was now suspicion, and that suited his cause very well.

'Look cosy . . . ' Eleanor had told him.

'Hold her hand, have your arm around her, kiss her . . . anything that suggests you're back together again.' He'd known better than to get *too* cosy. Maxine, he knew, was not ready for that. But she'd responded to his prepared short, sharp joke and did not appear to notice that his hand was covering hers. Now, a few well-chosen references to their intimate yearlong attachment would do no harm to the furtherance of his cause.

Jonathan came quickly to his feet. 'Eleanor,' he called, cheerfully, 'come and join us.' This was a greeting not easily ignored. Eleanor, however, would have turned down the invitation, had not Adam, for reasons of his own, decided to accept it.

★ ★ ★

Maxine could not have felt worse if Adam had thrown a glass of iced water in her face. He had known she would be here waiting for him. The meeting time and place had been his idea, and there had been no mention of bringing a third person.

If he wanted to be with his girlfriend, why invite me out for supper? Maxine asked herself. Then it occurred to her that perhaps he had not invited his girlfriend — that she had invited herself. But, if that was so, why

266

hadn't Adam done the three of them a favour and simply cancelled his date with her, Maxine?

She remembered the note. Maybe he'd tried to do just that. Maybe that was what the note was all about . . . his reason for wanting to meet her earlier than arranged. Perhaps he had wanted to explain and cancel.

No, that was not likely, she told herself. If he'd wanted to do that, he would simply have said so in the note . . . or better still, made a phone call to their suite. There was no need for them to meet like this.

Maxine puzzled over the various possibilities and then pondered the likelihood of his girlfriend turning up unannounced, catching him completely by surprise and giving him no time to act. It seemed the most likely explanation, but it didn't make her feel any better. The facts remained unchanged — Adam still had a girlfriend and she was here, hanging devotedly on his arm.

In silent misery Maxine had watched him bow his dark head to catch the words of his companion. She had seen the frosty look aimed her way, the search for another table and his initial reluctance to accept Jonathan's eager invitation. Then, on the verge of panic, she watched the couple's approach, and while she waited, her thoughts momentarily slipped back to Lantau, to those early hours when she and Adam had made beautiful, tender, romantic love.

In her happiness, she had assumed that, by some miracle, he was free and available to begin a new romance. The arrival of the brooch had seemed to confirm that hope. Now she knew that the gift was a bad conscience gift, just like all of Jonathan's. She had taken too much for granted. Obviously, Adam was still very much attached, for here he was, flaunting his girlfriend as if to say: I just want you to know Maxine that despite Lantau, nothing has changed.

Well, maybe for him it had been just sex and nothing more than a casual fling, but Maxine had hoped she was at the beginning of a new and lasting relationship.

Inwardly she groaned at her own stupidity. Why hadn't she had the sense to ask all those questions that had for days been rattling around in her head? The truth was, she supposed, she had been afraid to take a chance on the answers. She had not wanted to hear about the other woman in his life, a woman with prior claim whom he adored and who clearly adored him.

Now, watching them together, threading their way between the tables, Maxine not only felt sick with apprehension and jealousy, but with guilt and self-loathing too.

Jonathan had called the girl Eleanor. Knowing her name made Maxine feel terrible. Introductions, she knew, would make her feel worse. Somehow, it personalised the betrayal she knew herself to be part of.

And how would Adam introduce them? This is my long-standing girlfriend . . . meet my one-night-stand, might be appropriate. She flinched at the thought.

'Jonathan,' purred the beautiful Eurasian, taking his outstretched hands and kissing him affectionately on the cheek. 'You're beginning to find your way around Hong Kong, I see.'

Glancing beyond Jonathan and the girl, Maxine's eyes again met with Adam's. But his gaze remained cool and indifferent, and his interest soon returned to his girlfriend and her acquaintance with Jonathan. Where this girl was concerned, he was, Maxine decided with a sinking heart, a possessive lover.

'Jonathan . . . this is Adam Warwick,' Eleanor quickly said, before Adam could introduce himself as her brother. Then, looking at Maxine, she purred, 'And this must be your fiancée, Jonathan?' Without allowing Maxine time for a negative response, Eleanor hastened to add, 'I'm so pleased to meet you.'

Eleanor's smile was warm and not what

one would expect from a jealous girlfriend harbouring resentments. Clearly, Adam had told her nothing about his overnight stay on Lantau Island. Suddenly, Maxine felt angry and very sorry for the girl.

'Jonathan has told me so much about you,' Eleanor said to Maxine.

This comment and the innuendo she thought she detected in Eleanor's voice startled Maxine. When and where had this girl and Jonathan met, how well did they know each other and more to the point, what untruths had Jonathan been telling her concerning their romantic involvement? Remembering the warnings of the soothsayer, Maxine looked suspiciously from one to the other and wondered what plot might be hatching.

Again, leaving no time for questions or contradiction, Eleanor said to Maxine, 'Jonathan's arrival in Hong Kong must have been a wonderful surprise.'

Anything but wonderful, thought Maxine, bitterly. A disaster, more like.

From across the table, Adam watched and waited for her answer. Under different circumstances Maxine would have immediately put matters straight. But why bother? Why give Adam the satisfaction of knowing her true feelings towards Jonathan?

Last night had meant everything to her, but to Adam, apparently nothing more than a temporary diversion. Well, they could both play at that game. Wanting to hit back, Maxine smiled carelessly and let the moment pass in silence.

She thought she saw puzzlement in Adam's dark penetrating eyes, and resentment too. But when she looked again, his attention had turned to Jonathan.

A waiter came to take their orders, and while he waited for Maxine to decide, he looked with curiosity at the brooch pinned to the lapel of her jacket. A hint of amusement passed across his erstwhile expressionless features. A few minutes later, he returned with their orders. This time, his interested gaze travelled from the brooch up to her face.

Maxine was used to attention, she was a good-looking woman, but there was something strangely disturbing about that look . . . that slightly quirky smile. Covertly, she watched the waiter return to the bar and say something to the bartender who then glanced with interest in her direction. He looked highly amused, as if he had just understood a very good joke.

For a moment, Maxine puzzled over such odd behaviour, but Jonathan's hand possessively on her arm, and his disconcerting words, soon returned her attention to her companions.

'We got engaged a year ago . . . almost to the day,' Jonathan was saying. 'We should be celebrating our anniversary, shouldn't we darling,' he laughed and raised his glass in salutation.

Maxine noticed that Adam left his glass where it was, as did she. After a slight pause, Jonathan contented himself with touching his glass against Eleanor's.

Unabashed, Jonathan continued, 'We always said we'd honeymoon in Hong Kong. Our visit's a bit premature . . . but who's complaining?' He turned to smile at Maxine, the kind of adoring smile she had not received from him for a very long time. She returned his smile with a suspicious frown. Instinct, she suspected, had warned Jonathan that he had a rival, although she couldn't for the life of her think what had given her and Adam away, for so far, they had exchanged only a handful of disinterested words and not one friendly look.

The prediction of the soothsayer came back to haunt her. *Dying embers can still start a fire. An uncontrolled fire destroys all in its path.* At the time, Maxine had not taken the warning seriously. The only fire Jonathan was likely to start was at the other end of a cigarette . . . or so she had thought. The suggestion that he would stir himself on her behalf had seemed ludicrous. Now, she realised, that was precisely what he was doing. His words had been especially chosen to mislead and destroy any relationship that came between him and what he wanted.

Dowse the fire with cold water, had been the soothsayer's advice. But what was the point? If she were to tell Jonathan to go to hell, would it make everything right between her and Adam? He was Eleanor's and had been Eleanor's from the start, and between them was the kind of comfortable rapport that comes with time and the meeting of souls. Maxine was deeply envious of Eleanor and knew she could not hope to compete.

Conversation continued around her but Maxine was not a part of it. Her wits seemed to have slipped out of gear so that she could think of nothing intelligent to contribute.

Adam's attention was focussed mainly on Jonathan, who seemed to be doing most of the talking. He always did like the sound of his own voice, Maxine observed, moodily.

Feeling like an outcast, paying only partial attention, she lapsed into thought, recalling the moment when the evening had first begun to go so terribly wrong. Finding Jonathan in the bar had been an unwelcome surprise . . . and a baffling coincidence. He had insisted she join him, just for a moment. She had not wanted to, but neither did she want a fuss, and Jonathan, as she well knew, could be unpredictable in his behaviour. Besides, to refuse his company would have seemed churlish. It was over between them, but that didn't mean they could not be friends. An introduction to Adam would be unavoidable, but then she would have the pleasure of explaining Jonathan away to everybody's satisfaction . . . well, to everybody's satisfaction except Jonathan's. Only, it had not worked out like that . . . it had not occurred to her then that Adam would arrive with company of his own.

'Unless you have other plans, perhaps you'd like to join us for supper,' Adam was saying. 'I've booked a table at Jimmy's Kitchen.'

These words snapped Maxine back to the present. Again all attention, she frowned and kicked Jonathan under the table. She wanted him to finish his drink and go away. Furthermore, she had no masochistic wish to play gooseberry to Adam and Eleanor. Her evening was in ruins and she wanted it to come to a speedy end so that she could escape to her room.

Contrary as ever, Jonathan failed to take the hint.

'Yes, thank you. We'd like that very much,' he replied, accepting for them both and oozing charm in a way that only Jonathan could.

Maxine shot him a poisonous glance. Her fighting spirit leapt to the fore. 'Jonathan has other plans, haven't you Jonathan,' she said rather pointedly. 'He's leaving.'

Slightly taken aback, Jonathan hesitated, but only for a moment. 'I cancelled them,' he replied, a triumphant gleam in his eyes. 'I'm free to accompany you to dinner, darling.'

★ ★ ★

The basement restaurant on Theatre Lane was almost full. Overhead, fans oscillated, gently moving the air-conditioned atmosphere and adding to the charm of the old-world decor. Its clientele was multicultural and everything about it from its leather bound menus to its dark wood panelling suggested it was expensive.

The party of four were shown to a corner table, the reserved card was removed and they were seated. The special deference accorded to Adam, and because of him, also to his guests, did not at all surprise Maxine. A week in his company had taught her to expect only the best.

She still did not know who he was, nor did she know where he fitted into Comp-Dynamics. They had covered extensively many subjects, but Adam had not talked a great deal about himself, and on the rare occasions Maxine had tried to draw him out, he had adroitly steered the conversation in another direction. But she had eyes and ears, and it didn't take a great deal of intelligence to deduce that, in Hong Kong, he was someone with a certain amount of status. Jimmy's Kitchen was filled with the kind of people who made a difference to the world, and he was comfortably one of them.

It was a simple matter for the waiters to pull up an extra chair for Jonathan and to arrange another place setting. While this was being done, a number of puzzling questions ran through Maxine's mind. It was clear that the table had been booked for three. Adam, therefore, had known in advance that he would be bringing a third person. Why, Maxine asked herself again, would he deliberately bring the woman he loved to meet a woman with whom he had just spent an illicit night on Lantau? This was weird behaviour; something about it was very wrong.

And something else that was not quite right, Maxine noticed, was the inordinate amount of attention her brooch was receiving from the Chinese waiters. It seemed to attract their covert glances like a magnet.

The atmosphere in the restaurant was uplifting and under a different set of circumstances, Maxine might have enjoyed the evening immensely. But Adam's devotion to Eleanor, demonstrated with not a thought for Maxine's feelings, was painful to observe. Maxine's reaction was to retaliate in kind by treating Jonathan to a superficial show of affection, the like of which she had not lavished on him since catching him out with Annie. And even when Jonathan, rising to the occasion, placed a proprietorial hand on hers, she made a supreme effort not to recoil from his touch.

Adam, she was sure, missed nothing that was going on around him. From time to time his thoughtful gaze came to rest on her, but although she searched his face for some measure of understanding, Maxine could find no loving message there for her — just the polite interest of a good host.

Resentment grew, tying her tongue in a knot and prohibiting her from the natural flow of conversation . . . with all but Jonathan, the one person she had hoped never to have to talk to again. Her ease with him came from months of habit, she supposed, but mostly because Jonathan no longer figured in the emotional equation.

Keeping pace with the shifting tides of conversation, Maxine smiled, ate, sipped her wine, and then, smiled some more. But, all she really wanted to do was cry. Adam had been her lover, yet he belonged to someone else. He was an opportunist who had cheated on both her and Eleanor.

Maxine wondered if, behind the cool composure, he felt any guilt, at least, where Eleanor was concerned. She thought not. To feel guilt, you had to have a conscience, and if Jonathan was anything to go by, men did not have a lot of that commodity. She, on the other hand, felt enough guilt for the both of them.

Well, it was over between her and Adam. The whole experience was best forgotten. Eleanor, she vowed, would never learn about Lantau from her. A lump came to her throat. She forced it back down. No one must know how much she was hurting, not Eleanor, and especially not Adam. He must not have that satisfaction.

With an enormous effort, she managed to pull herself together sufficiently to give the outward appearance of enjoyment. She even managed to laugh at some of Jonathan's jokes as he endeavoured, with Eleanor's encouragement, to outdo all in wit and charm. And then, at some time during the evening, she became aware that Adam was, with a few choice words, deliberately manipulating the conversation, and was listening to Jonathan's revealing contribution with too much focussed attention. More than once, she thought she detected a hint of scorn in his smile, and when, over the top of his glass, he turned baffled eyes to search her face, she knew he was wondering how she could ever have considered marriage with such a man. And well he might wonder, she told herself, and could not help but blush at her own foolishness.

Courses came and went. The evening passed slowly, but pass it did, until eventually coffee was served. By then, Maxine was ready to congratulate herself on a star performance, if a somewhat subdued one.

'Eleanor, which way is the ladies' room,' she eventually asked.

Eleanor placed her napkin on the table and pushed back her chair. 'I'll show you,' she smiled companionably, and led the way.

It was a little later, when Maxine was applying lipstick that Eleanor murmured, 'Your brooch is very interesting.'

Maxine continued to regard her mirrored image. 'It was a gift,' she muttered, feeling ashamed because this girl's lover had given it to her.

Eleanor hesitated as if trying to find the right words. 'It is from Shanghai . . . probably antique,' she said.

Maxine's focus slid down to the gift that had earlier brought her so much joy. Eleanor's knowledge was impressive. She wanted to know more, but the subject made her feel uncomfortable.

Eleanor waited for the questions to come. When they did not, she asked shyly, 'Eh . . . do you know what it says?'

'No, I've no idea,' Maxine replied, refusing to be drawn and wishing she had thought to remove the brooch from inquisitive attention. 'Something . . . nice, I imagine.'

Maxine was about to change the subject, but then she noticed that Eleanor looked uncomfortable with the information she wanted to disclose. She recalled the veiled curiosity of the waiters and the barman in the Captain's Bar, their poorly disguised smirks that had made her feel uneasy, and she frowned.

'What does it say?' she asked, curiosity finally getting the better of her.

Feigning embarrassment, Eleanor fastened her attention on repairing her already immaculate make-up. 'Maybe I shouldn't tell you,' she answered, becoming evasive. 'You may not thank me.'

This was beginning to sound ominous. 'Sounds suspiciously like there's something I ought to know,' said Maxine to Eleanor's reflection. She waited a moment, and then insisted, 'I think you'd better tell me.'

Now it was Eleanor's turn to refuse eye contact. 'It says . . . 'Bringer of clouds and rain.' She murmured, bashfully.

Maxine's frown deepened. 'Meaning?' she asked, completely baffled.

Slowly, thoughtfully, Eleanor returned her make-up to her bag. 'You must understand, in China these things are said with poetry.'

'What things?' Maxine pressed. She had no idea what Eleanor was talking about.

'Poetry doesn't always translate well . . . ' Eleanor warned, hesitantly. 'The meaning is sexual, a promise of . . . favours.' She paused, looked perplexed. Then, taking a deep breath, she turned to face Maxine, and explained. 'The brooch would have been worn by a Shanghai prostitute and would suggest that she specialised in . . . ' Eleanor shrugged noncommittally and would have left the sentence unfinished if Maxine had not raised her eyebrows in question.

Eleanor sighed and finished, 'It says the wearer specialises in . . . certain sexual favours.'

The silence that followed was eventually broken by Eleanor. 'And there . . . ' she said, turning to Maxine and drawing her attention to markings in one corner of the brooch. 'There is the original owner's grade. She was not even a *three/four*, only a *one/two*: the lowest of the low.' Eleanor was beginning to warm to her subject. 'That probably meant quickies in dark corners and cheap bordellos.' Remembering herself, she looked apologetic, and lowering her eyelashes continued with more delicacy, 'I would not accept such a present. I would not want a man to think so little of me.'

The intended insult was to Maxine like a slap in the face. Not in any way could Adam have dealt her a more humiliating blow. Blood suffused her cheeks and then as quickly drained away leaving her white and shaken.

And nor would I want to be thought so little of, she was thinking. How could she have been so wrong about a man? Easy, she had been wrong before and quite recently. Was she destined to always fall for the cheats and liars of this world? Would she never learn to be more discerning?

If Eleanor had not so quickly returned her attention to the mirror, she might have seen the devastating effect her words were having on Maxine. Instead, the white-knuckled grip on the vanity-unit went unnoticed, as did the eyes, bright with anger and unshed tears.

Maxine fought to steady a voice that did not seem to come from her. 'Tell me Eleanor,' she heard herself ask, 'what do the words *Tai Tai* mean?'

'*Tai Tai*,' repeated Eleanor. There followed a short silence. *Tai Tai* simply meant number one wife and Eleanor knew this only too well; but she was not going to say so and let an opportunity pass. Through the mirror, she looked meaningfully at the brooch.

'Did your generous lover call you *Tai Tai*?' she asked carelessly. Without waiting for a reply, she continued, 'I do not think I would like to be called by such a name. Loosely speaking, it means number one woman.' Eleanor did not mind distorting the truth, just a little. 'Since you are not his wife, and concubines are a thing of the past, he was probably referring to you as his mistress.'

Eleanor heard the gasp, but she felt no pangs of conscience. Her cause was a worthy one. She was protecting her brother.

She gave her reflection one last appraising look. Satisfied, she then turned to Maxine and was amused to see that the offending brooch was now nowhere in sight. Unable to resist temptation, she tipped her head to one side and commented in a voice full of innocent admiration, 'You're not at all the *old crow* I was led to believe. You're really very beautif . . . '

Her voice trailed away. Only now did Eleanor become aware of the ashen face and the shock-induced trembling of a hand that dashed away a falling tear. Only now did she fully realise the misery her words were causing.

'Is that what he called me?' Maxine whispered on a stifled sob.

Eleanor shifted uncomfortably. Niggling doubts now gnawed their way into her conscience. She had thought this girl hard, manipulative and uncaring. She had fully expected a show of resentment, temper even, but not this degree of sensitivity. Maxine looked as if her world was falling apart. Could it be possible that this English girl really did love her brother? Had she misjudged Maxine? If so, then she had done so with Jonathan West's help.

'He m . . . may have been joking,' Eleanor owned, her thoughts now thrown into panicked disarray.

Maxine did not hear the reply. With a shaking hand, she had wrenched open the door and disappeared into the corridor beyond.

Eleanor knew she had gone too far. Adam would not thank her for interfering in his affairs. In fact, Adam would be furious if he knew the half of what she had said and done. But then, Eleanor consoled herself, Adam was not likely to hear about it — not from Maxine anyway. She was so upset; she was unlikely to talk to him ever again.

★   ★   ★

Adam watched his sister return the napkin to her lap. Jonathan was coming to the end of a long-winded tale, but Adam was no longer listening. Maxine had not returned to the table and from the look on Eleanor's face, something was wrong.

Catching her eye, he looked at her searchingly with an eyebrow raised in question.

'Maxine's not feeling well,' she muttered, unable to meet her brother's gaze. 'She's gone back to the hotel.'

His eyes narrowed, and for a moment they remained upon his sister. Silently, he noted her distracted fiddling with the stem of her wineglass. Eleanor was keeping secrets. She'd been up to something. He knew . . . he always did.

'Probably too much wine,' chipped in

Jonathan, looking not in the least bit concerned. 'Doesn't always know when she's had enough. Happens sometimes,' he lied. 'Nothing to worry about, but just the same, I'd better go and check on her.' He drained the wine from his glass. 'Probably got her head down the loo by now,' he laughed, as if Maxine's imagined demise was some kind of joke. He came to slightly unsteady feet and headed for the door. 'Thanks for dinner Adam. See you around Eleanor,' he called over his shoulder.

Without a word, Adam let him go. By now, his dislike of Jonathan West was complete. During the evening, he had been treated to a fairly comprehensive insight into the character behind the thin veneer of charm. And then, during the absence of the women, with a little encouragement, Jonathan had progressed from the telling of jokes to the confessing of infidelities and seedy antics in the low-life bars of Hong Kong. He had been easy to draw out. He was a man who liked to brag.

No, Jonathan West was not a man to be trusted and he'd see him in hell before he'd let him loose again with his sister. As for Maxine, he now had some understanding of what she must have endured through loving such a shallow, self-indulgent man, one with neither scruple nor conscience. He pitied her, but with that pity came anger and a terrible sense of disappointment, because despite all this man's shortcomings, despite all the pain he had caused her, Maxine, was prepared to meekly take him back.

That was the power of love, Adam supposed unhappily; a power he was himself fast becoming on intimate terms with. No woman had ever affected him quite like Maxine affected him. He had not wanted to love her, and yet, somehow he had come under her spell . . . and from the beginning. Or why else had he moved heaven and earth to be with her, and at a time when Warwick International and Comp-Dynamics most needed his undivided attention?

He had tried to justify his uncharacteristic actions. He needed to be in Hong Kong: there was urgent business that needed his immediate attention. The location of the Mandarin Oriental Hotel was handy for his office, so why not hire a suite for two and cancel Maxine's reservation at the Excelsior and then he could keep an eye on her, and when possible, show her the sights. No harm in any of that . . . just so long as he did not complicate matters by sleeping with her.

Here, Adam almost laughed aloud. What-ever made him think he could resist that much temptation? She had far too much appeal. Of course, he was going to sleep with Maxine . . . eventually, if he could. He was no saint . . . and, as it turned out, neither was she.

No, Maxine was not the passing fancy he hoped she would be. She occupied his mind twenty-four hours a day, played havoc with his powers of concentration and even managed to insinuate herself into his nightly dreams. Somewhere along the way his feelings for her had grown. Love was added to the physical attraction, and a love so deep, it had him wondering if she was the woman he wanted to spend his life with.

But, tonight, his eyes had been opened to the unpalatable truth, to the realisation that he had been used: drawn into a cat-and-mouse game. Maxine had known all along that Jonathan West was in Hong Kong. Out for revenge, and apparently not caring who she hurt, she had used her body to repay her fiancé in kind for his faithlessness. Maxine, it would appear, was no better than the man she had promised to marry; they were two of a kind.

After this evening and all it had revealed, Adam felt he should despise her. Yet, strangely, he did not. He found he still loved Maxine, and as much as ever. Except now, all the wonderful emotions associated with being in love, had been replaced by the pain of loss.

* * *

Maxine had one objective in mind: to cover the short paved distance between the restaurant and the Mandarin Hotel, pack her case, and get on the first available flight out of Hong Kong.

This had to be the most miserable night of her life. Compared to Adam's betrayal, Jonathan's betrayal now paled into insignificance. But then, she had never before loved anyone so completely, so passionately, as she now realised she loved Adam. She had given to him her heart, body and soul and in return, he had passed her off as his mistress, treated her like a Shanghai whore and given her a gift which he must have known would eventually reveal exactly what he thought of her.

Maxine had almost gained the rear entrance to the hotel lobby when she became aware of footsteps hurrying after her and the familiar voice of Jonathan calling her name. She ignored him. She had nothing whatever to say to Jonathan.

Jonathan, however, had no intention of being ignored. She had played hard-to-get long enough, she'd had her fun and revenge, and now it was time to put an end to the play-acting. And besides, there were a few niggling doubts regarding Maxine's association with Adam Warwick that needed clearing away. He wanted answers, and he wanted them now.

Closing the gap between them, he reached out to detain her.

She shrugged off his touch and quickened her pace. 'What do you want?' she snapped, over her shoulder.

His face darkened into an angry scowl. 'Not so fast, darling. We need to talk,' Jonathan replied, deliberately using an assertive tone. Fresh air on too much wine was beginning to turn him nasty.

More than anything, it was his use of the word *darling* that caused Maxine's temper to flare. He had at last become an irritant beyond endurance. She halted, and rounding on him, gave vent to months of stored-up resentment. 'No Jonathan. We don't need to talk, not now, not ever again. You've done everything possible to ruin my life. But now I know you for the liar and cheat that you are, and I can't help wondering why I put up with you for so long.'

Jonathan recoiled as if he had been dealt a physical blow. Maxine had never spoken to him like this before and he was not quite sure how to handle the situation.

'What about all the good times?' he asked defensively. 'I suppose *they* don't count?'

'What good times?' she replied. 'If we had any, they were so long ago, I no longer remember them.'

Jonathan looked affronted. 'I didn't hear you doing much complaining,' he said, belligerently.

'Of course you didn't,' she agreed. 'You were rarely at home. And when you were, you were so busy making excuses; you weren't listening to anything I had to say.'

There was truth in her accusation. He tried a different tack. 'We could start again . . . ' he began to wheedle.

She had seen that look and heard that tone too many times before. 'We could not!' she exploded angrily, shocking him into silence.

Despite the lateness of the hour, there were still quite a few people out on the streets. Several curious glances came their way.

Maxine lowered her voice. 'I was going to break if off with you months ago. I suspected you were playing around . . . I just couldn't prove it,' she said. 'It took Annie . . . catching the pair of you at it, to give me the proof and that extra push needed.'

His eyes narrowed. He searched her face. 'I

don't believe you were going to finish it at all,' he said. 'You're just saying that to get back at me.'

He saw the contradiction in Maxine's eyes. But still he refused to believe her. 'Okay. So you've had your petty revenge,' he humoured her. 'Now, can we end this farce, go up to your room and make up in the way couples do after a disagreement?'

Maxine was dumbfounded. Surely no one, not even Jonathan, could be so crass?

'Look, if it makes you feel any better, I'll say it again,' he offered impatiently. 'I'm sorry. Okay?'

'Sorry for what?' she asked. 'For all the times you played away, or for finally getting caught?' She did not wait for a reply, but added, 'No, Jonathan. It's not okay. Sorry is simply not enough.'

'What more can I say?' he appealed, putting a touch of desperation into his voice. Pride would not allow him to give up and meekly go away. Being dumped was not an option; it would spoil his unbroken record. Beside, he had other reasons for not wanting to be cut loose. Maxine, passionate, in control, was suddenly far more interesting; far more exciting than the mouse she had become since those early days. This woman's love was not to be taken for granted, and that made her so much more desirable.

Again, Jonathan tried to wear down her resistance. 'Look, I've been a fool, I know I have. But it won't happen again, I promise,' he said. And then, he imprudently added, 'Now, are you satisfied?'

A scornful smile turned up her lips. 'No, Jonathan. I'm not satisfied,' she replied. 'As usual, the only one satisfied is you.' It took a moment for her meaning to register. Before he could respond, Maxine went on, slowly and clearly, as if talking to a dimwit, 'How could I ever have thought myself in love with anyone as selfish and pathetic as you? How could I have thought that marriage to you would offer anything more exciting than washing your dirty socks and playing second-fiddle to your colossal ego?' Taking advantage of his stunned silence, she assumed an air of wistful anticipation, and continued, 'I'm going to find myself a real man. Someone trustworthy and deserving . . . ' she paused to savour the thought, ' . . . a man who *really* knows how to please a woman.'

Maxine saw him flinch and took pleasure in knowing she had returned, in some small measure, the hurt he had inflicted on her.

With one last twist of the knife, she added, 'Now, will you please get it into your head that I'm just not interested in you any more?

You're a selfish rat and I don't want to see you ever again.'

Maxine turned on her heels, and without a backward glance, pushed her way through the swinging doors leaving Jonathan beaten and dejected on the pavement. The embers had been well and truly *doused with cold water.*

★ ★ ★

It was gone midnight by the time Adam returned to the hotel. He had waited for Ah Fong to collect a rather subdued Eleanor, and then he had gone on to a quiet late-night bar. He had not wanted to confront Maxine — not until he'd had time to think. His emotions were too raw; his temper too near the surface.

When had he ever been so angered by a woman, so bewildered — he who was always so in control of his life? He paused for a moment in the dimly-lit corridor, his forehead resting on the door. If she was still up, waiting for him, what would he say to her? He had no idea.

The suite was in darkness — no lamp thoughtfully left on to light his way, and not a sound to be heard from the adjoining rooms. He imagined Maxine in bed, her golden hair spread across the pillow, her long graceful limbs . . . entwined with those of her fiancé. A wave of despair washed over him. He closed his eyes, waited for the image and the pain to subside, and then he flicked on the masterlight. Maxine's door was slightly ajar and the room beyond in darkness. Instinct told him Maxine was not there. Even so, he crossed hurriedly to her room and pushed the door wide. Her bed had been turned back by the chambermaid, but it had not been slept in. There was nothing to suggest that Jonathan had ever been there and nothing remained of Maxine but the fragrance of her perfume. She had left him without a word of farewell. She had gone off with her fiancé.

A groan escaped his lips. 'Maxine . . . ' he murmured, as once again the anguish of loss swept over him.

Slowly, he turned his back on the room that had been hers. It was now an empty shell, and the sight of it hurt more than he could bear. He returned to the lounge, where, almost immediately, his gaze went to the dark-wood coffee table . . . to a white scroll tied with red ribbon, the one given to Maxine by Fu Chu Ming, and retrieved from its dark hiding place by a conscientious chambermaid. His attention moved to another familiar object . . . to Maxine's brooch. In her great haste to be gone, she must have overlooked it, and now it lay forlorn and forgotten, waiting to be noticed. He picked it up, ran his fingers over it, gently, lovingly, as if it was some great work of art and not the object he had regarded earlier with irreverence. He had noticed it and thought it far from beautiful, but now it was the most beautiful thing he had ever seen. It was Maxine's, and all he had left of her. He placed it in the palm of his hand, and as if afraid it would somehow disappear, closed his fingers tightly over it. For a moment he was motionless, feeling the sharp edges cut into his palm. He waited for the vice around his chest to loosen, and then he took a deep steadying breath.

His attention was claimed by other items discarded on the coffee table: an open jewellery box and torn gift-wrapping. He picked up the box and laid the brooch in its velvet bed. It nestled comfortably. The paper and ribbon suggested the brooch had been a gift: given to Maxine rather than bought by her, as he had assumed. But, a gift from whom? he wondered. Had it come from Jonathan? He picked up the card, and turning it over, stared at the message. A puzzled frown furrowed between his dark brows. The writing was very familiar . . .

Adam read the message over several times:

'*The measure of my esteem*'. But still it made no sense. Why would Eleanor send a present to Maxine whom she professed not to have met before this evening, and what was the significance of the message?

★   ★   ★

Adam let himself into the house. The door closing behind him brought Fong Quan hurrying from the kitchen. Her surprised gaze went to the case, placed in the hall.

'You're back,' she said in Cantonese. Her old eyes were reproachful and seemed to say, 'and about time too.' Instead, she asked in her direct way, 'How long will you be staying this time?'

He laughed. 'And hello to you too, Fong Quan,' he answered back in her own language.

She chuckled. Her well-worn face broke into a smile showing off the gold tooth of which she was so proud. Fong Quan could never be cross with him for long — not even during his mischievous childhood and turbulent teens.

On the black-lacquer telephone-table, in the early morning sun, a pile of mail awaited his attention. He scooped it up and leaving his case where it was, wandered into the lounge.

'I'm here for a couple of days,' he replied, 'and then I have to return to England.' He heard her tut-tut. 'I won't be gone long,' he soothed, 'and before you know it, I'll be back making lots of extra work for you.'

Fong Quan nodded her satisfaction. No home should be too long without a master, and certainly not a home that housed a child born in the year of the monkey. Missy Eleanor was up to no good, she was sure of it — positively sparkling with mischief one minute and moody the next.

Pleased to have Adam home, she took herself back to the kitchen to make a pot of his favourite Chinese tea. He had said 'no' to breakfast, but if she could get him to stay long enough, she would prepare something extra special for his lunch. Chinese of course: noodles, fish and vegetables, carefully selected by herself, fresh from the early morning market.

Ten minutes later, she returned to him in the lounge. The mail lay where he had put it, still unopened. She placed the tray on a table and poured the fragrant tea into a delicate porcelain cup. Holding the cup in both hands, she brought it across the room to where he stood by the light of the window silently studying an object, which he turned slowly, thoughtfully, between his fingers.

She stopped by his side, her eyes on the brooch and the tea for the moment quite forgotten. '*Aiyaaah!*' she muttered disdainfully. 'That obscenity again. I'm so pleased you have taken it away from Missy Eleanor.'

He turned inquiring eyes on the *amah*. 'You saw Eleanor with this?' he quizzed, raising the brooch between finger and thumb.

'Yes,' she replied. 'I told her to get rid of it or I would tell you.'

He was silent for a moment. A scowl played across his brow while he tried to fit together the pieces of a worrying puzzle. 'Exactly what does it say, Fong Quan?' he asked. Adam knew he was not going to like the answer and that somehow it would involve the two people he loved most in the world, but still, he had to know.

She hesitated, momentarily confused. Then, remembering the master had very little knowledge of calligraphy, she began to explain in the candid, no-nonsense way so typical of the Cantonese, 'It is a Shanghai brooch . . . a prostitute's brooch. It says: *Bringer of clouds and rain.*'

Fong Quan leaned in closer to read the smaller markings. 'Only a one/two . . . that's the lowest rank,' she said, scornfully, not mincing her words. After a moment, she raised her eyes to his, and asked, 'What was

Missy doing with such a thing?'

Into Adam's mind came the message written in his sister's handwriting: *The measure of my esteem*. His brow lowered ominously. 'That, Fong Quan,' he said, dryly, 'is something I intend to find out.'

With grim purpose, Adam moved in the direction of his sister's room. As he disappeared down the corridor, he bellowed angrily at the top of his voice, 'Eleanor!'

★ ★ ★

Adam could hear footsteps in the corridor and the opening and closing of office doors. The uniformed night-watchman was on one of his hourly rounds.

On his first tour of inspection, he had responded to the light showing under Adam's door. A quick look into the impressive, wood-panelled office had satisfied him that all was as it should be. A polite deferential greeting to the *taipan*, an apology for the interruption, and he had quickly withdrawn his head. The watchman had completed two more rounds since then, but had not interrupted his employer again.

Working steadily on, Adam had at last arrived at the bottom of his in-tray. He glanced at his watch and saw it was already approaching ten. Time flies when you're having fun, he thought grimly. He had let work pile up, something he never did. Well, he was on top of it now, and in a way it had proved therapeutic: it had helped to take his mind of Maxine, for a while.

He pulled back his shoulders, and rolled his head to ease the muscles in the back of his neck. He was stiff and tired from too many hours leant over a desk, but at least he now had the satisfaction of knowing there was nothing outstanding; nothing that could not wait a few days for his return. Tomorrow morning, with a clear conscience, he could board the dawn flight to England. He had urgent, unfinished business to attend to at Comp-Dynamics.

His thoughts turned to Eleanor. On hearing of his intended trip, she'd had the good sense to utter not one word of protest. In fact, after his verbal whip-lashing, she had, for once, been eager for his departure. He smiled indulgently. No doubt she hoped time away would sweeten his temper.

She had answered his questions, filled in the gaps, and then comically hung her head. If he had not been so angry, if her actions had not had such a devastating effect on his affairs, he might have found it in himself to laugh at her child-like antics. Only this time, he had not laughed. *The tiger may teach the monkey good manners,* Fu Chu Ming had said. The lesson, it would seem, was long overdue. Later, however, when his anger had abated, he had listened to her misguided reasons for jumping to the wrong conclusions. Jonathan West, he decided, had a lot to answer for.

Eleanor was fiercely protective of those she loved, and possessive of their time, especially his. He was the adored big brother who had come to her rescue when she had most needed him . . . who had carried her off from rags to riches and made all things possible. In her eyes, he could do no wrong.

When he thought of the secrets he had failed to share with Maxine, and the knock-on damage done to their private and working relationships, he had to smile at Eleanor's flattering, but misguided faith in him.

Had he also let Eleanor down? Had he become so remote, so inaccessible, that she had felt unable to bring her fears to him? True, since his return to Hong Kong, he had juggled most of his time between Maxine and his office, sparing little for her. Resentment, he supposed, had made her vulnerable to Jonathan West and his misleading stories.

This morning, he had intercepted a call

from Jonathan to Eleanor. Grudgingly, the man had confirmed Maxine's return to England. Since she had travelled alone, maybe Maxine had more sense than he had given her credit for. He hoped so. However, having Jonathan still in Hong Kong did continue to present a problem where his sister was concerned.

'It's Jonathan,' he had silently mouthed to Eleanor with a questioning raise of the brow.

With an emphatic shake of the head, Eleanor had adequately made her feelings felt. She did not want to talk to him.

'Eleanor's not in to your calls,' he had said into the phone in a cool emphatic voice. Adam had then called Patrick. Consequently, Jonathan was now without a roof over his head. He wished there was time and a way to add further to Jonathan's discomfort, but right now, there were other, more important, things to think about.

Adam looked at his watch. Ah Fong would by now be waiting for him in the car park. It was time to go home and pack. He reached across and pushed closed the filing cabinet drawer, and then he picked up a pile of prepared folders and his laptop, and slotted it all into the open briefcase. He paused — had he forgotten anything? He thought not.

He was on his feet, the briefcase in his

hand when the phone rang. A few seconds more and he would have been on his way. But someone was calling him on his private line and only family and closest friends had that number, plus a few, especially selected, who needed to be in the know. Reluctantly he turned back and raised the receiver.

'Adam,' said a familiar voice. 'This is Ian Wood.' Down the line came the background sounds of a busy police station. 'I tried you at home . . . might have known you'd still be in your office,' he laughed. 'Never did know when to call it a day.'

'You're lucky to catch me. I was just on my way out,' Adam replied. 'I'm going to be away for a few days. How about a game of squash when I get back?' he asked, assuming it was Ian's reason for calling.

'Yes . . . great, you're on. About time you let me get my own back.'

Like Adam, Ian came from a well-established ex-patriot family. They had attended the same junior school, and although they had parted company for the years that took them to different schools and universities in England, they had kept in touch, seeing each other during holidays and carrying the friendship into their adult lives. Squash was one of their many shared interests, they were closely matched and they enjoyed the challenge.

'Actually, this is an official call,' Ian continued, glancing at the police report in his hand. 'Thought you might like to know . . . there's a fellow just been brought into the Wanchai station for causing a public disturbance.' Ian gave a doubtful laugh. 'He insists he's a friend of yours.'

Ian was a Superintendent, and, as such, did not usually get involved with minor offenders. However, Adam's name had been brought to his attention along with the man's insistent claims to friendship.

'No wish to offend, Adam . . . but he doesn't look much like your type,' he laughed. 'But then, appearances can be deceptive, especially when you've just had a close encounter with a gutter.

'The silly bugger had a few too many and picked a fight with a bouncer built like a sumo wrestler. He came off worse, of course. Says you'll vouch for him. Gave his name as . . . ' a rustle of paper came down the line, ' . . . here it is . . . Jonathan West. Says he's a tourist, and booked to fly out tomorrow morning.'

Adam's fatigue vanished in an instant. The news that Jonathan West had been roughed up and was in police custody put a huge smile on his face. 'Yeeees!' he hissed, punching the air with all the enthusiasm of a footballer who has just scored the winning goal. Addressing the phone, making no attempt to mask his pleasure, he said, 'Ian, you've just made my day.'

There was a chuckle from Ian. 'Guess you won't be vouching for the fellow after all?' he said.

No, Adam would not be vouching for him. He would not lift one finger to help Jonathan West out of his present predicament. He did not want Jonathan West free to leave for England . . . not yet, anyway. But then, neither did he want the man on the loose in Hong Kong pestering Eleanor and attempting to freeload again off Patrick. He had a score to settle with the bastard for the lies he'd fed to Eleanor, for trying to mislead him where his relationship with Maxine was concerned, but most of all, for all the grief he had caused Maxine.

'You guessed right,' Adam confirmed. 'The man's a rat, and as far as I'm concerned, you can lock him up and throw away the key.' After a moment's pause, he added, 'Actually, you could do me a favour, Ian.'

'Sounds ominous,' the superintendent chuckled down the line, 'and I'm sure I'm going to regret this, but . . . go on, I'm listening.'

'Keep Jonathan West locked up as long as you can and then, when you turn him out, make sure he's on the next available flight.'

'Can do . . . but I'd like to know why?' Ian said. By now he was more than a little curious.

'I don't want him in England too soon . . . but then, neither do I want him here on the loose bothering my sister,' Adam replied. 'And believe me; you'll be doing the female population of Hong Kong a big favour if you keep him off the streets.'

The policeman laughed. 'Been bothering Eleanor, has he?' Ian knew Eleanor, and in his opinion, she was a feisty lady who was more capable than most of looking after herself.

'He's been bothering a lot of people . . . ' his thoughts turned to Maxine, 'and one in particular, for a long time. He has some very bad habits,' Adam said. 'No need to be too kind to him.'

He was remembering the words of Fu Chu Ming; *the tiger may banish the rabbit.* Guessing correctly that Jonathan had been born in the Chinese year of the rabbit, he added for good measure, 'And make sure he's on the airport immigration's list of undesirables.'

* * *

Fong Quan sat in the shade of the banyan tree. Her morning work was done and she was enjoying a quiet break. At the far end of the garden, young Winston, barefoot with trouserlegs rolled up, was hosing down one of the cars. His tuneless whistle carried on the warm breeze.

It was here, in this same spot that she used to sit with Lai Ho Mai when time allowed. And it was here, a few years after her re-employment by the old master, that Lai Ho Mai finally shared some ... but only *some* of her secrets.

Fong Quan had broached the subject of marriage. A nephew of Ah Fong had voiced an interest in Lai Ho Mai.

'I have no need of a husband, Fong Quan,' she had confided. 'Marriage cannot give me anything I don't already have.'

Fong Quan had supposed her to be referring to security: a roof over her head, a full rice bowl and a monthly wage. All those things she had, right here. She and Lai Ho Mai were luckier than most. Their gods had smiled on them at a time when the papers were full of reports of refugees pouring daily over the borders from China. Some were so desperate to reach the beckoning capitalistic lights of the then British colony, they were even prepared to risk swimming across the shark-infested waters of Myers Bay. Those that made it swelled the many over-populated shantytowns perched precariously on steep hillsides, and under the constant threat of rainy season mudslides. The less fortunate of the freedom swimmers turned up in bits — an uneaten limb here, a torso there, washed up on the beaches.

Another time, Lai Ho Mai said, 'I already have the greatest treasure life can give.'

Lai Ho Mai did not appear to have anything of value. Unlike Fong Quan, she had not even a gold tooth. 'And where is this treasure?' Fong Quan had asked, aware by now that she could only be referring to a child.

'My mother keeps her safe,' she had replied with a wistful smile.

12

Adam accepted the keys to the company car that was parked in the forecourt below and closed the door on the departing driver who had brought him from the airport. He had stayed in the Comp-Dynamic's company apartment on previous visits; it was familiar and beginning to feel more and more like home. Adam knew that he would be here a while and so, this time, he unpacked completely and stowed the contents of his case with a little more care than on those other occasions.

The apartment was airy and attractive, and not too far from the offices of Comp-Dynamics. Although an ideal base from which to come and go, Adam knew he was unlikely to spend much time in it. He would be spending his nights and most of his free time where he usually spent them when in England: in his mother's imposing Victorian house in Ealing Broadway, just a short ride along the M4. He had phoned ahead from Hong Kong, and was expected there in time for supper.

'Please, no company,' had been his earnest

request. 'I'll be thoroughly jet-lagged. Besides, I want you all to myself. We've a lot of catching up to do.'

'Not one of your fleeting visits, is it Adam?' his mother had asked suspiciously.

'No. I'll be around for quite awhile. Give me a day or two and I'll be ready for one of your dinner parties,' he had laughed.

His mother had a devoted friend who played host at her dinner parties, who spoilt her with gifts and attention, and accompanied her wherever she wanted to go. Edward Aubrey would have married her years ago and with Adam's blessing, if she had been free. But Helen Warwick had not filed for divorce. She had what she wanted: independent means, her faithless husband on the other side of the world, a host of sociable friends and a caring son, who, when in London, never failed to visit her. When the death of her husband did eventually set her free, although she loved Edward, she had refused to change the status quo. She was happy with life just the way it was, so why take a chance on upsetting the balance?

Adam checked his watch. He had gained seven hours on the flight. Here in England it was still that time of day when rush-hour traffic was at its worst. His mother did not dine early. There would be time for the congestion to ease before he need throw the handgrip into the back of the car and head along the motorway. He made himself a coffee in the well-stocked kitchen, and taking a file with him, wandered through to the open-plan lounge to sit in one of the soft leather armchairs.

Adam opened the file, but did not read for long. Talking to his mother never failed to stir up memories, and before he had even finished the coffee, his mind had turned the clock back six years, to those last days with his father.

Adam had gone into the family business straight from university and realised quite quickly that he had found his niche in life. He had a natural aptitude for the work; it interested him and was enormously challenging. That Adam was being groomed to eventually succeed his father went without saying, and it was universally accepted as his right. Warwick International was his future.

His father, he quickly discovered, was the powerhouse of the company. He had the vitality of a man half his age, had his finger well and truly on the pulse of all that concerned his company and appeared to be in the peak of good health. Under the circumstances, his retirement was never mentioned; to even think about it seemed almost blasphemous. There were years of work ahead of him, which was just as well, because it would be several years before Adam would be ready to take his place.

At that time, by choice, Adam did not live in the family house in Shek-O. Instead, he opted for a place of his own — an apartment in the more accessible Midlevels. Although he had an enormous amount of respect for the *taipan* of Warwick International, outside the workplace, he liked to keep him at arm's length. His father's selfish disregard for the feelings of others and his refusal to recognise and properly support Eleanor, his natural daughter, were just a few of the personal issues over which they eventually agreed to disagree. In business, James Warwick was ruthless; with women he was careless; and where both were concerned, he showed an unacceptable lack of conscience.

When his father had asked to meet with him at the Hong Kong Jockey Club, one of his favourite haunts, the request had taken Adam by surprise. He could easily have come up with an excuse, but he hadn't. There had been something unfamiliar in his father's voice, something vaguely disconcerting, and it triggered Adam's curiosity. What could he possibly have to say that could not be said during office hours?

In the work place, his father piped the tune, but not socially. Adam preferred to meet his father on his own territory. 'I'll be in the Yacht Club at eight,' he had responded.

'If Mohammed won't come to the mountain; then the mountain must come to Mohammed,' his father had greeted him on finding him waiting at the bar. There had been a forced joviality in the way he spoke, and again, Adam had sensed that something was not quite right.

With that polite wariness that had developed between them over the years, they had for a while talked shop, and then moved on to local politics. But, before long, it became apparent that his father's thoughts were preoccupied with other weightier matters.

'I've neglected your mother long enough,' he said, quite suddenly changing the subject. 'It's time to go home . . . I miss her.' Then, he paused for the reaction he knew would follow.

To his eternal shame, Adam remembered his cold, uncharitable reply, 'Are you sure she feels the same way about you?'

He had seen his father's pained expression, yet, even so, had felt no desire to tread softly. In his opinion his mother would be a fool to open her doors again to a man who had let her down too many times already. She deserved better.

Rattled, he had watched his father silently search for the right words to break the next piece of news. Not finding them, he simply dropped his bombshell. 'I'm going home permanently ... I'm talking about full retirement,' he said.

Adam stared at him over the rim of his glass waiting for the shock waves to pass. It would take time to grasp the full significance of his father's announcement, and to fully assess the knock-on effects his retirement would have, not only on himself, but also on everyone connected to Warwick International.

'And what's brought this on?' he asked with a hint of suspicion. If his father really did mean to retire, then there had to be a very good reason for it. He watched his father toy with his whisky tumbler, and for a moment, thought he was not going to answer.

'Heart,' he eventually replied. He raised the glass to his lips, and as if suddenly in need, downed a quarter of its contents in one. 'I've got heart trouble,' he said. 'I need a triple by-pass.'

Adam was shocked. His father had seemed invincible. He could not remember the last time he had been ill. There were so many other words he could have spoken, words of comfort and compassion, instead, in a cool, quiet voice, he said, 'And to help you through convalescence, you need a nurse maid.'

His father had blanched and looked away. 'I'll make it up to her,' he said quietly. Then, he seemed to brace himself for further bad news. His gaze returned to meet with Adam's own. 'There's more,' he said. 'We need to talk about *you* . . . *your* future in the company.'

Adam waited. He knew he was not reacting the way his father hoped he would . . . not saying the right things . . . not making it easy for him.

'I expected to go on another ten years at least,' he said. Again, it seemed he was carefully searching for the right words. 'But this has come out of the blue . . . and it's something over which I have no control.' He looked tired and dejected. 'Another ten years and you would have been ready to take over from me. But . . . ' He faltered and searched Adam's face for signs of understanding. 'I'm truly sorry.' He spread his hands in a gesture of defeat.

For once, there was no questioning his father's sincerity. There had never been any doubt in either of their minds that Adam would, on the day of his father's retirement, become the majority shareholder and, therefore, the new *taipan* of Warwick International.

His father was right, of course; he was not ready to shoulder the colossal responsibilities that came with so great a prize. The timing was awry and there was not a thing that either of them could do about it. This was, for them both, an unexpected and bitter blow.

'So . . . ' Adam asked in a quiet controlled voice, 'what now?'

'My deputy, Sam Farley will run the show, and continue to groom you until you're ready,' his father had said. He drained his glass and came tiredly to his feet. 'We'll discuss it in my office, tomorrow morning, with Sam.'

Those had been his last words to Adam. Within minutes of his leaving the club, an out-of-control car had mounted the pavement killing his father outright.

Perhaps, if his father's mind had not been on other things, he might have seen the car coming and moved in time. Six years later and Adam still wished he had taken a more tolerant view of his father and that they had parted company in a happier frame of mind, and on better terms.

Uneasy with his conscience, Adam stirred and took a deep breath. With an unsteady hand, he reached for the forgotten mug of coffee, but it had gone cold, and so he returned it to the coffee table.

There had been no time to grieve properly. Since none of his father's intentions had been put into writing, Adam had found himself catapulted overnight into the tough, cut-and-thrust business world of Hong Kong. No one was more aware than Adam that he could have done with a few more years of grace, but the fates had decreed it should be otherwise. As heir to his father's empire, the running of Warwick International had, after all, fallen squarely into his lap and not into the caretaker hands of Sam Farley, his father's trusted deputy.

His father was cremated, his ashes returned to his widow in England, and later, a requiem service was held on Hong Kong Island, in St John's Cathedral.

Having lost interest in the father, the newspapers had turned their intrusive attentions onto Adam, airing to the world his personal history, his youth and his inexperience. There was an abundance of speculation on his ability to successfully take over where his father had so unexpectedly left off.

At Warwick International uncertainty hung in the air like a dark cloud over all those with reason for concern. For Adam, there had initially been agonising months of selfdoubt. He had thought himself in over his head, but Adam was not one to go down without a fight. He was a fast learner and not too proud to listen to the advice of the astute Sam

Farley and other company stalwarts. Intuitively, he had known when to act on their advice and when to follow his own counsel. It had been an uphill struggle, but he had worked indefatigably, and gradually he had grown into the position of trust and power. To all, he had proved himself his father's son . . . to all but his father, who had not lived long enough to witness his son's success.

★ ★ ★

Maxine gazed out of the second floor window of her apartment. Autumn had arrived, and the early morning weather was about as miserable as it could get which was almost as miserable as she felt. The rain was falling as if in competition with the tears she had cried since her untimely departure from Hong Kong.

She had flown in the day before with a broken heart that she was sure would never be whole again. Due to a combination of misery and jetlag, she had hardly eaten and managed to get only a couple of hours sleep. She had dark shadows under her eyes and an incredible pain in her chest that sat there like a lump of lead.

Suddenly, feeling the urgent need to hear her mother's voice, she picked up the phone.

Just in time, she remembered the hour. She would think it odd to receive a call so early in the morning. And in any case, she had spoken to her parents the previous morning to report her safe return to England. Making a supreme effort to keep her voice cheerful, she had given a brief summary of the things they might expect to hear about a holiday that should have been a wonderful experience, not only at the beginning, but right up until the end.

Not once did she let slip the name of Adam Warwick, which was, in any case, a name unknown to her family. It was her intention that it should remain that way. By mutual unspoken agreement, Jonathan's name too had been kept out of the conversation. No need for them to know he had turned up unexpectedly in Hong Kong and been the cause of so much grief.

'Is everything alright?' her mother had asked at one point. She had a sixth sense where her children were concerned and her far-reaching antennae had just picked up on a slight catch in her daughter's voice followed by a barely audible sniff.

'Jetlag,' Maxine had replied, letting her mother draw her own conclusions from the inadequate answer. 'I'll take a few days to recover.'

Suddenly, she had felt overwhelmed by

loneliness and a desire to go home, and conscience too had kicked in to remind her that a visit was long overdue. 'Mum . . . is it alright if I come home for the weekend?' she had asked in a small voice.

'Of course, darling,' her mother had laughed, 'do you really need to ask?' Knowing where her daughter's main interest lay, her mother had shrewdly added for incentive, 'You can earn your keep by helping out with the horses.'

The minute Maxine hung up, she unplugged the telephone. No point in inflicting her unsociable company on anyone but herself. Besides, if Carrie and Janet had known she was back in town, they would have loaded up with wine and snacks and invited themselves round for a girlie evening and a sharing of confidences. One glance would have been enough to tell them that all was not as it should be, and then the questions and answers would have started. In no time at all, they would have wheedled the whole sorry Hong Kong saga out of her, along with another bucket of tears.

Maxine did not want that. Crying was something she liked to do in private and so she had spent the entire evening alone, prone on the sofa sniffing her way through an orgy of self-pity.

She returned to the window. The rain had eased, traffic was thickening and a few early bird commuters were scurrying, heads down, along the wet, windswept pavements.

Leaning close, she misted the window with her breath and wrote the name *Adam* in the condensation. His name put a lump in her throat. She swallowed and moved away. It was early for work, but far better for her to leave now and lose herself in activity, than for her to delay and lose herself in another bout of despair.

Maxine slipped on her raincoat and reached for her bag. She had survived the night, and now, somehow, she would face and get through her first day back at work.

★ ★ ★

The ringing of the telephone stopped Janet at the door of her cramped and rather cluttered studio-apartment. Quickly, she retraced her steps. It was Carrie, and by the sounds of it, she was driving in busy traffic and using her mobile.

'Did you manage to get through to her?' she asked hurriedly, after a perfunctory greeting.

'No, she's still not answering,' Janet replied. She glanced at her watch, 'and if I don't get a move on, I'll be late for work and have to go straight to the meeting.'

'It's okay. Do that if you have to, and I'll ... ' Carrie broke off and let loose a stream of invective. 'Where the hell did you learn to drive, you moron!' she yelled. Coming back to Janet, she continued in a perfectly calm voice, 'I'll run her to earth and make sure she's up-to-date with the latest. Talk to you later.'

The line went dead.

* * *

Boswell, the elderly night-watchman, peered at Maxine through the plate glass door. Recognising her he smiled, slipped the key into the lock and pulled the door open.

'You're early,' he scolded good-naturedly. 'Haven't you got anything better to do with your time?'

'I've been on holiday,' she replied, trying to keep her voice light, 'and I've probably got masses to catch up on. I thought I'd make an early start.'

He re-locked the door and walked with her across the polished stone reception area to the elevator shafts. Boswell had a lonely job; he liked a bit of company.

'Well, it's all been happening this past

week,' he said, as the lift opened to admit Maxine. He shook his head in wonderment. 'Who'd have believed it?'

After the week Maxine had just come through, she was prepared to believe anything. With a wry smile, she murmured, 'You can say that again.' She knew, of course, she and Boswell were referring to quite different happenings, but she did not ask for an explanation. She would soon catch up on news, and as for Boswell, he seemed happy enough with her reply. The door closed on further conversation, and she was whisked up to her floor.

The sales department yawned in front of her like a great empty cavern. Once more she was alone, and slipping back into despondency. The dream has gone . . . this is the reality. 'Welcome home Maxine,' she said with a long dramatic sigh.

'Oh, no you don't Maxine,' she told herself. 'That's quite enough of that.' Seeking a quick diversion, she crossed the room to click on the CD in the music-centre. *When a man loves a woman* filled the air with its mournful strains threatening to plunge her once more into overwhelming selfpity. Maxine clicked the music right back off again and retreated to her partitioned cubical. There, she ran a sceptical eye over her overflowing in-tray.

She ought to pull herself together and get on with some work, she supposed, though she had little appetite for it and zero concentration. God, how quickly work piles up. Had she been gone that long? Only nine days, she calculated, including the two weekends, and yet, it seemed a lifetime had passed since she had last sat at this desk, hurt and fuming over Jonathan's betrayal. Again, she wondered how she could ever have cared that much about him. He could now sleep with a dozen Annies and she wouldn't give a damn.

Well, Adam had done that much for her, at least. Her all-consuming love for him had ousted the last lingering remnants of her feelings for Jonathan. Gone were the resentments, nurtured over months of mistreatment. Gone even was the anger. For Jonathan, she felt nothing at all.

For nearly a week in Hong Kong, Adam had been her daily fix, and now he was on her mind night and day, like a craving for a drug without which she could no longer function properly. Knowing him, loving him, had kept her on a nerve-tingling high. Losing him . . . it was as if the sun had set and would never again light up her world

'Adam . . . ' she murmured in despair. His name was constantly on her lips; as if by saying it, by some miracle, it would bring him back into her life.

The ever-ready tears stung the back of her eyes. She placed her head in her hands. He, like Jonathan, had been a careless lover. She should hate him really, yet here she was, loving him more than ever and wondering how life could possibly go on without him.

Movement beyond the confines of her partitioned office brought her with a jolt to an awareness of the hour. Time had moved on, the early-bird enthusiasts were arriving and the department would soon be filled with noisy colleagues and even noisier office machinery.

* * *

Maxine answered her telephone.

'Just as I thought,' Carrie grumbled down the line. 'No one's told you about the meeting, or you wouldn't still be at your desk.'

'Meeting?' queried Maxine. 'What meeting?'

'The meeting for all staff, Junior Execs up; the meeting in the boardroom that started five minutes ago; the meeting you would have known about if your telephone hadn't been off the hook the whole weekend.' Carrie sounded peeved. 'Listen. I'm stuck in a traffic jam,' she complained. 'Wanted to speak to you urgently before the meeting, but now there's not a chance. Bloody traffic!' she fumed into her mobile phone. 'Janet will fill you in. Better get your butt into gear and I'll see you later.'

The line went dead, leaving Maxine to ponder over the melodramatic tones of Carrie's voice. She wondered if the meeting had something specifically to do with her department, and if she needed to take along any particular files. There was no time to make inquiries, she would just have to take herself and hope for the best. If the meeting had already started, she had better get a move on.

Quickly, but without enthusiasm, she wove her way between the desks towards the door leading to the stairwell and lifts. Some of her work-mates glanced up as she passed and smiled.

'Maxine,' one called after her. 'Have you heard . . . ?' He reached for the company's quarterly magazine and waved it at her.

'Can't stop Jimmy,' she responded quickly. 'I'm late for a meeting. Catch up with you later.'

He grinned at her retreating back. 'Have it your way,' he said, then murmured just loud enough for those nearest to hear, 'Don't say I didn't try to warn you.'

A couple of juniors giggled. 'What do you think you're going to tell her that she hasn't had a whole week to find out for herself?' one of the girls whispered to Jimmy, with a knowing grin.

Maxine did not pick up on the words, but the giggles followed her to the door.

Strange, she thought, merriment on a Monday morning? Whatever happened to office tradition?

★ ★ ★

Maxine was the last to enter the boardroom. The long polished mahogany table had been moved to one side so that the chairs could be placed theatre-style facing the other end of the room. All present were seated with eyes front on the door leading to the Directorate office. There was a low hum of conversation and the atmosphere was heavy with excitement and anticipation.

Maxine was relieved to find the meeting had not yet started. Quickly and as inconspicuously as possible, she moved across the plush burgundy carpet to a back row seat reserved for her by Janet with the aid of her well-placed bag and jacket.

'Maxine!' Janet whispered excitedly, pulling her belongings off the chair. 'At last. What kept you?'

'Just heard about the meeting,' Maxine whispered back. 'Carrie called, or I'd still be at my desk.'

'And not one of your dozy bunch of inmates thought to enlighten you,' Janet commented wryly. She glanced at Maxine, 'And I don't suppose any of them thought to tell you that . . . ' she broke off, and grinned. 'No, I guess there was no need. After a whole week away, you must be more in the know than we are.'

Maxine gave her the kind of blank look that says — I don't know what you're talking about.

Janet's grin turned into an uneasy frown. 'Been calling you all weekend,' she said, hesitantly, after a short pause. 'Something wrong with your phone?'

The room fell silent, and reluctantly, so did Janet. Question and answer time would have to wait. The all-important double doors, the focal point of everyone's attention, had swung open and Mr Hamilton was entering the room, along with one other: a man somewhere in his thirties, tall, handsome and smartly attired in dark suit.

Janet shot Maxine a look that was full of

curiosity. But Maxine was rummaging in her over-full bag, searching for the mobile phone she hoped she had already turned off.

Responding to the elbow Janet was digging urgently into her ribs, she looked up, and following the direction of her friend's gaze, saw the second man — Adam Warwick — the last person in the world she expected to see, on this dreary Monday morning, in the boardroom of Comp-Dynamics.

Her stomach did a sickening somersault. In shock, she watched the man she loved shake hands with a half dozen or so of the company's directors.

'Take a couple of deep breaths,' she heard Janet whisper in a worried voice. 'You've gone as white as a ghost.'

She took the advice and forced the blood back up into her head. The dizzy spell passed, but still her insides felt like mush.

What's *he* doing here? she wanted to ask. But, although her lips parted, the words would not form. She noted the comfortable rapport between Adam Warwick and Neil Hamilton, and her bafflement grew. Who *is* this man and why is he with our Chief Executive? These were just two out of the many unspoken questions that shot through her mind.

Maxine cast her memory back to their

evening in the Cajun restaurant, when she had quizzed Adam about his position within Comp-Dynamics. She remembered how he had neatly avoided answering her questions by turning the conversation around to her. Yet, somehow, despite the lack of co-operation, she had managed to conclude that he was the company's representative in Hong Kong . . . a salesman.

Had she guessed right, and could he be here because he had managed to land a lucrative Asian contract for the company? By the way he was being lauded by one and all it would have to be worth millions.

Maxine remembered asking Adam if they were likely to see much of him at Comp-Dynamics. 'Yes, quite a lot,' had been his reply. At the time, the thought of seeing him on home ground had thrilled her. Now, she found herself wishing him anywhere but here. She required more time — a long time — to prepare for the shock of their meeting again.

Her focus remained fixed unwaveringly on Adam until he took the upholstered carver chair that appeared to have been set aside for him, the chair ordinarily placed at the head of the boardroom table for the sole privileged use of the Chairman. Seated, he was hidden from Maxine's view by the backs of several rows of heads.

Mr Hamilton was now the only one still standing. He turned his golf-course weathered face towards his staff, cleared his throat, and looking over the top of his wireframed spectacles, said, 'As you will know from my letter to all departments, I am retiring from my position as Chief Executive Officer of Comp-Dynamics.'

This was surprising news to Maxine. Hamilton's retirement must have been a particularly well-kept secret, for not a hint of it had reached her ears, until now. She studied the broad familiar face and thought he looked quite pleased about his future prospects, or lack of them.

Mr Hamilton's next words came as even more of a surprise.

'As you also know, Comp-Dynamics has recently merged with a larger company; a company based in Asia. I am convinced that the timing for this merger is absolutely right and further convinced that the merger will escalate the growth and prosperity of our company.' He paused and smiled apologetically. 'Sorry about all the secrecy leading up to the merger,' he said, 'but you will appreciate, without me going into detail, that secrecy was absolutely essential until everything was legally signed and sealed.'

Maxine's mind was reeling. I'm away for

nine days and the place falls apart, she was thinking. Covertly, she glanced to left and right at the rows of worried faces and knew that, like her, everyone was wondering if their job would be affected by the changes, and if so, in what way. She couldn't afford to lose her job. She had rent to pay, a car to run, and no supportive partner to fall back on.

Mr Hamilton continued, 'Those who have been working on the account of Warwick International will know how important that account has been to this company.'

Maxine was suddenly unnaturally still. She felt as if she was caught in a sinister dream where she was trying desperately hard to assemble a particularly difficult jigsaw puzzle without the aid of the picture. Undoubtedly, Hamilton had just dropped a vital clue, and one that was sending loud messages to her brain.

'I want to put your minds at rest,' he was saying in a soothing voice, 'and assure you that nothing is going to change . . . except, of course, my retirement. Your jobs are safe and all will continue very much as before.

'After thirty-five years, the time has finally come for me to make way for a younger man, a man with modern innovative ideas who will take this company safely forward into the future of rapidly expanding technology. There are demanding times ahead, but I am sure my successor will be able to count on your full support and co-operation through this transitional period.

'This is a challenging and exciting time for you all, and I have to admit, I would like to be a part of the excitement.' He paused and smiled. 'However, the irresistible pull of the golf course goes a long way towards easing me painlessly into retirement.'

The golfing enthusiasts smiled and nodded enviously.

'But, rest assured,' went on Hamilton, 'the interests of Comp-Dynamics will be, as ever, close to my heart. I shall be here, continuing to serve on the board.'

There was a show of appreciation with a round of applause.

'It has been a pleasure and my great privilege to work with such a wonderful team of people . . . the very best,' continued Mr Hamilton. 'Thank you all for your hard work and tireless dedication.

'This is only meant to be a short informal meeting, but I look forward to seeing you all at my farewell party when I shall have the pleasure of boring you with a very much longer speech.'

There was a ripple of laughter and a number of humorous groans.

'And now it is my great pleasure to introduce to you the new owner of Comp-Dynamics; the Chairman of Warwick International, Hong Kong; your new boss, Mr Adam Warwick.'

As the speech unfolded, and more pieces of the puzzle slotted into place, Maxine had begun to suspect where the speech was leading. She had made the connection between Adam *Warwick* and *Warwick* International, and it had hit her like a nasty shock from a live wire. She wanted to believe she had misunderstood, but now she knew she had not.

For a whole week, she had shared a hotel suite with this man. In a romantic little guesthouse, they had shared a bed and made love . . . three times. She blushed at the memory. He had known all along about the merger, and that he was putting her into a compromising situation, and yet, he had said nothing, not one word of enlightenment to put her straight. He had let her fall in love with him, taken advantage of that love, and then, had tossed her aside. So much was now explained, but by her reckoning, not nearly enough. The puzzle was still not complete.

Seething with resentment, Maxine watched Adam Warwick come to his feet and confidently take the floor. In that deep compelling voice that had so charmed her, he eloquently thanked Hamilton for his glowing introduction. From there, he moved on to thank several members of the board and management for their co-operation and assistance in the months leading up to the merger.

He then addressed those who had not, until recently, been in the know. 'I've only been acquainted with Comp-Dynamics for a short time, but I have already had the opportunity to witness staff dedication to work . . . and for that matter, dedication to play also, since I was a guest at your company's annual ball.'

Remembering the lucky winners of the star prize, several pairs of inquisitive eyes sought and found Maxine, and it seemed to her that Adam's dark gaze, following their lead, momentarily picked her out of the crowd.

Maxine blushed to the roots of her hair, and sinking a little deeper into her seat, wished with all her heart she was anywhere but here in the boardroom. There was no doubt in her mind, that by lunch time, that dreaded super-efficient grapevine would have done a pretty thorough job of informing the entire staff of Comp-Dynamics that she was indulging in a steamy affair with the new boss. She would be the butt of everyone's smutty humour, perhaps not to her face, but certainly behind her back, and the envy of every singleton who fancied themselves in love with the new Chairman.

Adam's deep melodious voice brought her attention back to her immediate surroundings. 'No need to say how impressed I have been with the superior quality of your work,' he was saying, 'nor how impressed I have been with your dedicated loyalty to Comp-Dynamics. My enthusiastic pursuit of the merger says it all for me.

'It is a great honour for me to take over from Mr Hamilton, and reassuring to know he will continue on the board so that we can benefit from his vast knowledge and experience. I am confident that with his valuable assistance and your continued efforts, the merger will run smoothly.'

There was a natural pause, during which, it seemed to Maxine that Adam's focus again came to rest on her. 'I hope to meet *all* of you, *individually*, over the next few days,' he said. His gaze moved on, 'and I very much look forward to working with you.'

There were murmurs of approval and a round of applause from all but Maxine.

Not me, she was thinking, mutinously. You won't be meeting me over the next few days. I won't be here.

The meeting came to an end. Over the tops of heads, Maxine could see that the Company Secretary had moved in to claim Adam's attention. Hamilton also, came to stand at the side of his charismatic successor.

Taking their lead from the top, a low hum of conversation started up and increased in volume as the staff began to stir into life. Maxine waited for the camouflage of others before she too came unsteadily to her feet.

She was uncomfortably aware of covert glances in her direction, of whispers and knowing smiles. Janet was burning with curiosity, and would have come straight out with a stream of questions had she not been immediately side-tracked by her demanding and talkative department manager.

Maxine stole one last, lingering look at Adam Warwick. What was the name in Hong Kong for powerful people like you? She searched her memory for the elusive foreign word. *Taipan* . . . is that what he's called? A *taipan*? No wonder he was so comfortably at home in Hong Kong; no wonder money was no object; no wonder he was treated with deference by all who knew him, or knew *of* him.

As if drawn by the foreign name and the strange powers of telepathy, Adam's brow creased into a frown, and he glanced up. His sharp eyes found her and for a split second, locked with her own. Maxine was the first to look away. Turning her back on him and the assembly, she moved quickly across the carpet, and was the first to leave the room. Carrie was pulling into the parking lot when her mobile phone burst into tuneful life.

'You're never going to believe this,' said Janet's agitated voice, 'but, going on Maxine's reaction in the boardroom, she had absolutely no idea there had been a merger, no idea that Hamilton was retiring and no idea that the man she'd gone on holiday with was the new boss.'

'But she must have known,' Carrie said after a short pregnant pause. 'She's been with him a whole week. She would have been the first to find out.'

'No,' insisted Janet. 'The merger was news to her. And, what's more, she went as white as a ghost when Adam Warwick walked in and even whiter when she found out he was Hamilton's successor.'

For a moment, only the sound of static travelled between the phones. Then Carrie asked, 'So? What did she say about it all?'

'Nothing . . . nothing at all. As soon as the meeting was over, she was up and out the door without a word or a backward glance.'

'I've reached the lobby,' said Carrie with

some urgency. 'I'll be with you in two minutes.'

★ ★ ★

It was not long before Carrie breezed in through the department door, closely followed by Janet. Maxine groaned. She did not want to talk to anyone, not yet, and they were making straight for her cubical door.

'Welcome back, Max,' said Carrie, inviting herself in and plonking her tightly clad bottom down on the only available chair, leaving Janet to perch on the edge of Maxine's desk. She peered at Maxine. 'You look good,' she said without too much conviction. 'Lost weight, nice tan . . . ' she peered a little closer, ' . . . a bit heavy around the eyes. You okay, love?'

Maxine was not okay. She had just discovered a whole series of devastating facts, all of which she should have learned from Adam at least a week ago. No, of course she was not okay, and never likely to be again. But, right now, her problems were not something she wanted to discuss . . . not even with these two.

Her friends, however, had other ideas and they were waiting expectantly for her to confide.

What did they want to hear? Maxine wondered dully. That the man I went on holiday with has turned out to be our new wealthy and all-powerful boss? No need. They knew that already; had known long before she did. Did they want to hear how she had stupidly allowed herself to fall in love with him, that they had shared a room in a romantic retreat, and that, while a typhoon raged, they had indulged in a night of steamy lovemaking?

The word *lovemaking* jarred on her senses and for a moment, she puzzled over it. A cynical little smile came to play on her lips. It might have been lovemaking for her, but for Adam Warwick, that beautiful word was inappropriate. For him it had been just plain sex.

Maxine became aware that Carrie was watching her closely. 'Want to talk?' her friend asked quietly.

Maxine's eyes shifted evasively to the hands of the paperweight clock that jerked slowly around the dial.

Carrie turned to Janet, 'Go and get us some coffee, love,' she ordered, firmly.

Janet looked from one to the other. Maxine's friendship with Carrie went back a long way and ran deep. If she would talk to anyone, she would talk to her.

Always a team player and eager to please, Janet took the hint. She hitched her short rounded frame off the desk and on over-high heels, tottered back the way she had come. 'Okay. But first I've got to take some files down to Personnel.'

'Sure, take your time,' said Carrie.

'Save the juicy bits for when I get back,' Janet laughed over her shoulder. Unaware that her attempt to lighten the mood had hit a nerve, she left the office.

Turning her full attention to Maxine, Carrie asked, bluntly, 'Okay, let's have it, what's wrong?'

'Everything,' Maxine replied with considerable feeling. 'The man's a bastard.'

'Who? Our knock-down-dead-gorgeous Mr Warwick?' asked Carrie, wide-eyed with surprise and curiosity.

Maxine gave her a withering look. 'He's as bad as Jonathan . . . no, worse,' she fumed.

Carrie looked at her in disbelief. 'With a face and body like that . . . not possible,' she smiled wistfully. 'Besides, no one's as bad as Jonathan.'

Maxine didn't respond.

'Want to tell me about it?' Carrie asked, hoping for the whole, unabridged version.

Whether she wanted to or not, Maxine needed to talk. The floodgates opened and the story began to pour out. When she got to their romantic overnight stay on Lantau Island, Carrie stopped her.

'Eh . . . are you telling me . . . you slept with our new Chief?' she asked with a look of horror on her face.

'That's exactly what I'm telling you,' replied Maxine.

For a moment, Carrie was struck dumb. An unusual occurrence for a Cockney rarely lost for words. 'Whoops!' she eventually offered. 'You didn't ought to have done that.'

Maxine gave her a withering look. 'No,' she agreed, 'but then, I didn't know who he was, did I? He failed to tell me.' After an unhappy pause, she asked, 'When exactly did the merger take place?'

'Right after you left,' replied Carrie. 'Janet was the first to know when a memo, not strictly intended for her eyes, landed on her desk. Then there were letters to staff.' There was a short thoughtful pause, then Carrie continued, 'You were with the heir apparent . . . enjoying a merger of your own, it would seem, so how could you not have known? What did you two talk about when you were together, the weather?'

Maxine ignored the question. 'Why didn't you warn me . . . tell me who he was . . . what was happening back here?' she whispered in a shaky voice. 'There *is* such a thing as a telephone.'

'We did try. We emailed the Excelsior, but you weren't there.'

Maxine groaned. The blame lay with her. She had sent post cards but neglected to inform anyone of her change of hotel.

'And since we're on the subject, where the hell *were* you?'

'Booked into the Mandarin Oriental Hotel,' Maxine replied in a small, apologetic voice. 'He changed the reservation.'

Carrie reached into Maxine's untouched in-tray and pulled from the middle of the heap, a company magazine. She handed it to Maxine.

'This came out three days ago,' Carrie informed her.

Staring out at Maxine from the front cover were the striking features of Adam Warwick. Splashed across the top in bold print were the words 'Company Merger'. Maxine opened the magazine to a glowing account of Adam's achievements and more personal history than she had learned in the whole intimate week spent in his company.

There followed a moment of stunned silence while Maxine absorbed what she had read. This explained so many things. The daily early morning excursions in business suit with briefcase; the long absences; the late nights at the workstation in their shared lounge; the numerous emails and even more numerous telephone calls and messages.

'Rumour has it, he flew in last night and was driven to the company apartment,' Carrie informed her gently. She raised her eyes to the ceiling, as if it were possible to see through two floors. 'I expect, right now, he's moving into Hamilton's office . . . ex office,' she corrected herself. 'Better get used to having him around, at least until he appoints someone to take over from him.' Sympathetically, she added, 'Don't worry . . . he'll return to his Hong Kong office soon enough, and run the whole show from over there.'

'And I'll never know, from one day to the next, when he's going to fly in for some meeting or other,' Maxine pointed out. 'That makes me feel wonderful.'

Only now did it cross her mind that she might not be the only one disenchanted by the possibilities of a chance meeting. In fact, as the new Chairman, Adam would very likely find her presence an intolerable embarrassment. Might he want her out of his life? Might he fire her or find a way to ease her out of the company? Her fingers began to fidget nervously as if they had somehow developed a life of their own.

Suddenly, coming to a decision, Maxine pulled out a drawer and scrabbled for a sheet of paper. Frantically, she began to write.

Carrie leaned forward for a glimpse. 'What are you doing?' she asked, suspiciously.

'Writing my resignation, of course,' Maxine snapped. 'I'm getting it in before he can fire me.'

Carrie gaped. 'Fire you . . . why would he want to fire you?' she asked. 'You only slept with him. That's no great crime in this day and age.'

You don't understand! Maxine wanted to shout aloud. I love a man who's only an elevator ride away, and yet, no more accessible to me than the man in the moon. So close, but so far away . . . how will I ever be able to concentrate on my work? I'd spend my whole time searching for him, waiting for . . . longing for our paths to cross, in an office; a corridor; at a meeting . . . and yet, I'd live in constant dread of coming face-to-face with him.

And Eleanor . . . where will I find the strength to accept his eventual marriage to another woman?

With an enormous effort, Maxine calmed her thoughts. 'No, it's no great crime to have slept with him,' she said in an unhappy voice, 'but it's hard to call someone *Sir* when you've

346

seen him in the all-together.'

'Mmm . . . lucky you,' murmured Carrie, glancing admiringly at his picture and letting her imagination do the rest.

Impatiently, possessively, Maxine flicked the magazine out of Carrie's hand and slapped it face down on the desk. 'No, not lucky me,' she said angrily. 'He should have told me who he was, and then I would not have slept with him.'

'I guess that's why he didn't tell you,' laughed Carrie, refusing to take the threatened resignation seriously. 'Boys will be boys,' she added airily.

'It's no laughing matter,' Maxine flared, suddenly exasperated by Carrie's levity. And thinking once again about the brooch, she added, 'Anyway, you don't know the rest of the story. You don't know what he thinks of me.' She swallowed and blinked back the ever-ready tears that were threatening to spill onto her cheeks.

Carrie heard the catch in her voice. She frowned. 'Thinks of you? What does he think of you?' She asked. A more serious note had crept into her voice.

'Later,' promised Maxine. 'I'll tell you the rest later. Right now, I have my notice to hand in.'

With a flourish, she added her signature to

the bottom of the letter, stuffed it into an envelope, scribbled Adam Warwick's name and title across it and headed for the door.

★ ★ ★

Maxine stepped out of the elevator on the top floor, and for a moment hovered indecisively. There were two doors leading into the Chairman's office. One was via the board-room and the other via the office of the super-efficient Mrs Willimot. Which route should she take? She looked at the letter in her hand. Better do this officially, she told herself, and headed for the furthest door.

Mrs Willimot was a redheaded shrew, small and wiry, who was known to have a razor-sharp tongue. It was universally under-stood by all that one did not mess with the Chairman's Personal Assistant whose office guarded the inner sanctum. Well, not under normal circumstances, only these were not normal circumstances.

Maxine was on an unstoppable mission. Without pause, she straightened her shoul-ders, pushed opened the door and marched in.

Mrs Willimot was working at her desk. She identified Maxine at a glance and decided to keep her waiting. It was her way of demonstrating superiority.

Maxine was not having any of it. Addressing the top of Mrs Willimot's middle-aged and tightly permed head, she demanded in a clear and impatient voice, 'Is Mr Warwick in?'

The sharp tone momentarily took Mrs Willimot by surprise. She looked up, her supercilious eyebrows raised almost to her hairline. 'Do you have an appointment?' she asked imperiously. She knew very well that Maxine did not. Mr Warwick had specifically asked to be free of appointments during the hours leading up to the afternoon Board of Directors meeting.

Maxine did not give her the satisfaction of a reply and hesitated only long enough to note Mrs Willimot's lack of denial and furtive glance at the highly-polished door beyond. Reading the signs correctly, she pivoted on the plush carpet, and headed for the office occupied by Adam Warwick.

'Here,' flustered Mrs. Willimot coming hastily to her feet, 'you can't go in there.'

'Just watch me,' Maxine muttered, bursting angrily into the Executive Director's office, and thus into another world. In an instant, she took in the leather-upholstered chairs, a wall of box-files and impressive looking books, dramatic oil paintings and dark mahogany furniture. Her awed gaze moved quickly on and came to rest on the familiar face of Adam Warwick who, disturbed by the commotion caused mostly by Mrs Willimot, had transferred his attention from his PC to his unexpected visitors. Maxine had hardly crossed the threshold, when Adam's exulted position hit her full force, bringing her to an abrupt halt.

'I'm sorry Mr Warwick,' apologised his newly-adopted and noticeably nettled PA. 'I tried to stop her . . . '

Adam, immaculately attired, and looking every bit the wealthy and powerful business-man Maxine now knew him to be, came slowly to his feet. His focus was fixed on Maxine, and for a moment, he seemed unaware that there was anyone other than her in the room.

Maxine's throat went dry. All she could do was stare like some over-awed, tongue-tied adolescent at the man who, set against so lavish a backdrop, now appeared to her as little more than a stranger.

'Its all right Mrs Willimot, I'll see her,' Adam said politely but firmly, after a short pause.

Mrs Willimot hesitated, opened her mouth to protest and then changed her mind. Mr Warwick's tone had brooked no argument.

Reluctantly, and with a last scathing look at Maxine, she left the room pulling the door closed behind her.

'You're just the person I want to see,' Adam began warily.

Maxine was not going to be intimidated by the lavish surroundings, nor the lofty status of this man. Quickly, she found her tongue. 'You're too late,' she said, her eyes bright with defiance. With heart hammering so loudly that she felt sure he must be able to hear it, she crossed the room and tossed her letter onto the tooled leather surface of his desk. Then, she took a couple of steps back and crossed her arms to stop her hands from shaking.

Adam scowled suspiciously down at the letter. 'What's this?' he asked.

'My resignation, of course,' Maxine replied. Now that he couldn't fire her, she was not going to leave until she had off-loaded some of her resentments. 'You should have told me who you were,' she accused angrily. 'Then I wouldn't have gone on holiday with you . . . wouldn't have shared a suite.' Neither would I have shared a bed with you, she wanted to say, but didn't quite have the nerve.

As if reading her thoughts, he smiled knowingly. 'Think what we would have missed,' he murmured, sounding not in the least bit remorseful. As he spoke, he came around the desk to perch on its highly polished corner. His eyes had not left her face and he looked as if at any moment he would reach out for her.

Uncomfortably aware of his closeness, Maxine took another step back. Was he playing with her . . . after all he'd put her through? She searched his face, but couldn't be sure. Was that invitation she saw in his eyes? Did he think he could pick up with her and continue where he had left off?

As if reading her thoughts, he said, 'There are a few things that need explaining.'

Her chin went up. 'Your girlfriend already did all the explaining necessary,' she replied coolly.

She saw the white Chinese scroll that lay open beside him on the desk. And then, in an instant, she recognised the colourful and familiar object that lay in its open box on top the artistic black calligraphy. It was the offensive brooch that she had hoped never to see again, the brooch that had declared its wearer a *Bringer of Clouds and Rain* . . . a third class whore. What kind of a sick mind carried such a thing around the world and then took pleasure in its display?

'I thought you would have passed that on

to your next victim by now,' she said, acidly.

His gaze followed hers. 'Ah yes,' he smiled, appearing not in the least put out by her use of the word *victim*, ' . . . the infamous brooch.' He reached for the box in which it lay. 'I've been saving this for you,' he mused. 'When you hear what I have to say, you may want it as a keepsake.'

Maxine gave an audible gasp. 'A keepsake!' she exclaimed. She eyed the offensive offering with revulsion. 'I don't want it, it disgusts me.'

An impatient frown replaced the smile. There followed a short silence. 'You might . . . after we've talked things through. But not here, over lunch,' he suggested.

'I'm not having lunch with you,' she replied in a decisive tone.

'A pity,' Adam said. 'I've booked a table.'

'So . . . your guest cancelled,' she said, sarcastically. 'That's too bad. You'll just have to lunch alone, or find some other *old crow* to accompany you.'

Just for a moment, he looked baffled. And then remembering his humorous description of Maxine to Eleanor, he threw back his head and laughed. He did not take the trouble to explain, however. There would be time enough for that later.

Instead, he corrected, 'No . . . no guest. I

was just about to send for you.' He saw a flicker of interest in her blue eyes. Encouraged, he went on, 'You see, I have another present for you. One you might like more. One that will tell you more accurately what I think of you.'

Her eyes narrowed suspiciously. 'I don't much like your choice of presents,' she returned. On top of a filing cabinet, a silver frame was on display. She saw that it held a studio shot of Eleanor, and her heart lurched painfully. He had wasted no time finding a prominent position for his lover's picture. 'And I know what you think of me . . . Eleanor already told me, in some detail.'

He reached for the photograph; smiled fondly at it. 'Yes,' he said. 'I bet she did, the little monkey, and took pleasure in the telling.' He looked up; held her gaze with his own. 'Actually, the brooch didn't come from me. It came from Eleanor,' he said. 'And you know only what *she* thinks of you . . . which, I might add in her defence, was what Jonathan led her to believe.'

It took a moment for the full import of his words to sink in. Could this be true? Had the brooch really come from Eleanor? She thought back and remembered that the accompanying card had not been signed. She also remembered thinking the gift unworthy of Adam's more refined tastes. Yes, it was possible, she supposed. The brooch could have come from Eleanor. But, if that was indeed so, then Eleanor must have been fully aware of Adam's unfaithfulness. Sending the brooch must have been an act of revenge; a way to vent hurt feelings.

Guilt and remorse flooded Maxine's conscience. How could she have allowed herself to be the cause of another's grief, and in such a way?

'Eleanor sends her apologies,' Adam said, 'and hopes you will forgive her.'

Thoroughly confused, Maxine watched him return the picture to its former resting-place. Why, out of the three of them, she wondered, did Eleanor feel she should be the one to apologise and ask for forgiveness? Did Eleanor still not know about Lantau? Did she still believe that the *old crow* had been no more to Adam than a work colleague? And how could Adam speak so casually . . . so carelessly, as if his unfaithfulness to Eleanor amounted to little more than a harmless prank?

She watched him transfer his gaze to the letter of resignation that still lay unopened on the desk. A frown creased his brow. 'Do you want to take that back?' he asked, after a moment's thought.

Was he giving her a choice? Did it really not matter to him . . . to his position, whether she stayed or went? She searched his face, but could not tell what he was thinking.

'No,' she replied with certainty. Regardless of her deep love for Adam, Maxine recoiled from daily contact with a man who apparently thought nothing of playing one woman off against another. Besides, it was not only his position in Comp-Dynamics that had been compromised, but hers too. Soon, their names would be on everyone's lips and she would be the butt of everyone's smutty humour. Maybe he didn't care what people thought of him, but she cared too much to simply laugh it off and wait for some other hot topic to send their affair to the archives. Feeling the injustice of the situation, she said, 'I can't work for you. Not now, not after all that's happened, and certainly not after Lantau.'

She did not give him a chance to protest, but quickly accused, 'It should be you resigning not me. You should have told me who you were. It's your fault we went on holiday together.'

She saw the questioning raise of a brow and recalled the night of the ball. The sharing of the star prize had been her very own idea . . . helped along by too much tequila.

'It's your fault we . . . slept together,' she quickly amended.

'That's not the way I remember it,' he again contradicted.

Remembering that it was her who had, in sleep, put her arms around him, she blushed and looked away.

He waited for her to regain her composure, and then reasoned, patiently, 'I can't be expected to resign from my own company, now can I?'

'No, I suppose not,' she agreed, in a small deflated voice.

'Well then, since you're willing to resign — if you're sure it's what you want, then that's settled,' he said lightly. 'I accept.'

'You accept . . . just like that?' she returned sharply, astonished by his cavalier manner. Where was the apology she might reasonably have expected?

'It's a sensible solution to a tricky problem,' he said. 'And now . . . '

'It might be a sensible solution for you,' she interrupted, tartly, 'but I'm out of a job.'

Maxine was dangerously close to angry tears, but she was damned if she was going to shed them in front of the man who had already been the cause of too much grief. Abruptly, she turned her back on him and headed for the door.

There was movement behind her and a quick strong hand caught her wrist. 'Maxine, don't go,' Adam pleaded softly. 'There's so much I want to say to you.'

She swallowed the lump in her throat and looked down at the hand that held her fast. 'Let go of me,' she managed. 'I don't work for you, remember? I've resigned.'

'Yes, you've resigned,' he agreed. 'And now, don't you see, there's nothing to stand in our way. We can . . . '

'Continue where we left off?' she asked. 'Do you seriously think I . . . ?'

It was his turn to silence her. 'I have something for you.'

'I told you already, I don't want anything more from you.' Again, she looked at her wrist, willing him to let her go.

'That's a pity,' he said, 'Fu Chu Ming seemed to think you would.'

Her eyes followed his to the open scroll. For the first time, she was curious to know the meaning of the calligraphy. She waited.

Slowly, Adam repeated the translation as given to him by Fong Quan.

'*The fates are prophesying thus,*
There'll be two gifts for you.
The first should be avoided,
Accept when there are two.'

As he spoke, Adam took from his pocket a

small square box. 'I rather hoped you would accept this as . . . 'a measure of my esteem'. He flicked open the lid to display a large diamond solitaire engagement ring.

Wordlessly Maxine stared at it. It was the most beautiful thing she had ever seen.

'Will you marry me?' he asked.

Surely she was dreaming. Maxine refocused on the beautiful face smiling out of the picture frame. 'And what about Eleanor?' she asked.

'Ah yes . . . Eleanor,' he said. 'My sister sends her love and best wishes for our happiness and promises to behave impeccably at our wedding if only you will invite her to be your bridesmaid.'

Maxine stared at the photograph and then in a very small and incredulous voice, asked, 'Your sister . . . ? Eleanor is your sister?'

'My half sister, actually . . . ' he smiled.

Taking advantage of her stunned silence, he slipped the engagement ring onto her finger and pulled her into his arms.

We do hope that you have enjoyed reading this large print book.

Did you know that all of our titles are available for purchase?

We publish a wide range of high quality large print books including:
Romances, Mysteries, Classics
General Fiction
Non Fiction and Westerns

Special interest titles available in large print are:
The Little Oxford Dictionary
Music Book
Song Book
Hymn Book
Service Book

Also available from us courtesy of Oxford University Press:
Young Readers' Dictionary
(large print edition)
Young Readers' Thesaurus
(large print edition)

For further information or a free brochure, please contact us at:
Ulverscroft Large Print Books Ltd.,
The Green, Bradgate Road, Anstey,
Leicester, LE7 7FU, England.
Tel: (00 44) **0116 236 4325**
Fax: (00 44) **0116 234 0205**